The Cartwright Men Marry

Monique Desrosiers

A WOOD DRAGON BOOK

Cover design: Callum Jagger
Typeset by: Adin Nelson, Amaya Editing Inc.

Library and Archives Canada Cataloguing in Publication
Desrosiers, Monique, 1958
ISBN: 978-1-989078-40-2

Issued in print, audio and electronic formats.

Wood Dragon Books
PO Box 429, Mossbank, Saskatchewan Canada S0H3G0
www.WoodDragonBooks.com

For Kurt
&
for my parents
who lived with me
and endured patiently
while I wrote.

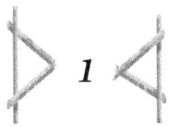

1

February 7, 1863

THE AIR WAS CRISP. THE HORSE'S HOOVES crunched on the snow. The exhale of breath from both man and beast could be seen. On an exceptionally warm February day, Ben Cartwright was heading home after a week in Sacramento. Because of the pleasant weather, he had chosen an alternate route through the mountains. He had never ventured this way before and thought it was high time he did so. Nothing like new scenery to tickle his curiosity. And what a sight it was to behold.

The snow on the tops of the surrounding mountains glistened in the shining sun. The valley below was heavy with fresh snow. Trees everywhere were peeking out of their white covers. He stopped the horse and inhaled deeply of the refreshing air. He had never seen such a peaceful place. He closed his eyes but even that didn't keep out the brightness warming his face.

He was not a man who traveled the mountains on a regular basis, especially in winter. He was aware of the dangers from mountain lions and wolves. Luckily, the bears would still be in hibernation—even though the sun was warming up the days to almost 45 degrees Fahrenheit. He thought he was prepared to face anything he might encounter. Besides, he should be in flatter territory in a day or so, where it would be easier to see approaching dangers.

He hadn't counted on an avalanche. His beloved

horse, Diamond, sensed the danger seconds before Ben did and reacted. The horse pulled against the bit, desperately fighting Ben's commands, but Ben was dominant and determined and held the animal to the path he had chosen.

"What's wrong, Diamond? There are no snakes up here. Do you smell a big cat? Don't worry, I'll protect us," and he reached for his rifle, scanning the terrain for danger.

Diamond jumped when he heard the pop of the mountain releasing its snow, triggering Ben to drop his rifle. Both man and animal could feel the ground trembling. Diamond could only do what came naturally, he tried to outrun it. Ben grabbed and hung onto the saddle-horn for dear life. He couldn't hear Diamond neighing and Diamond couldn't hear Ben's commands. The noise from the oncoming snow and uprooted trees was deafening.

The impending white blanket was quicker than Diamond could ever be. The horse tried to climb it, slide down with it, kick it, but eventually panicked. He was so wild that he bucked Ben right off.

Ben tried to get a hold of something, anything, but couldn't help falling and rolling. He tried to climb up and over the snow. When a tree branch caught him, ripped his sleeve right off and scratched his entire left arm, he winced at the pain and yelled out, but continued to try climbing, using the branch for leverage.

He couldn't see where he was going. Everything was a blur. Dark objects passed by, mixed with snow. Trees, he thought.

He fought to head upwards to the lighter side of the moving snow and debris. No time to pray, to panic, to think, to thank God, or for last thoughts of his sons.

Another branch came tumbling down and knocked him on the head. He fell for the last time, arms and legs flailing in the air—and lost consciousness.

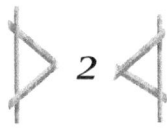

2

February 7, 1863

BARBARA WAS LATE GETTING STARTED ON A HUNT for meat and furs. She had put the kettle on the fire to boil but forgot to fill it with water, then she had reached for a clean garment to wear only to discover it was still wet, then she stepped on another garment that was, or rather had been, clean.

Then she stubbed a toe on her favorite possession. A tub. She had found it a couple of years ago in an abandoned farmhouse. It had a small hole on the bottom which she managed to plug with a mixture of horse hair and tree sap. She had to repeat that procedure every month or so, but she didn't mind.

She had rejoiced when she discovered it. She was now able to have much deserved baths inside her cave. Up until then, she had washed in the creek in the summer months and sponged down in the cave in winter. While at the creek, she was always aware of her surroundings and was sure that her horse would warn her if a person or animal was nearby, but the gift of a tub meant that she could bathe in the comfort of her enclosed space, any time, any day.

She sure put that tub to good use. She didn't have any family to object to her taking a bath a couple of times a week. When the summer hot days prevailed and she had been out hunting, she would bathe at least once a day. It also served as her tub for washing clothes. It was her one luxury.

Barbara's only regret was that she had yet to find

a new, used comb. The one she had was running out of teeth. Her hair looked unkempt most of the time. Even a bath could not rid her of all the knots. But there was no one here to mind how her hair looked and as long as she was clean, she was happy. So once again, she pulled her hair tight and tied it back at the nape and put her ratty hat on her head to keep her hair in place.

She scolded herself for her clumsiness that morning, but she did not let these small delays slow her day. She knew what three straight days of unusually warm weather preceded by several days of unending snowfall meant here high up in the mountains on the west-side of Nevada. A landslide or two or more. If not today, then tomorrow.

Several animals who didn't have the foresight to get out of the way of the avalanche would become hers for the taking. All she had to do was look closely for carcasses, dig a little, find treasure, skin them out of their furs and cut out the best of the animals' meat. This did not often happen so early in February—just when her supplies were starting to run low—so, to be sure, she was going to take advantage of it.

She got all of her gear ready, going back and forth several times as she forgot one thing or another—like rope and lots of it, the ax, a shovel, and her knife. Ah, no, that's on her belt loop already, she thought, her hand going to the hilt at her waist.

After all the annoying distractions and delays, she finally placed all the necessary items on the travois attached to her three-year-old horse, Vincent. The travois was an old Indian tool that was very effective for anyone who was by themselves and had heavy or many items to cart from one place to the next.

She was finally ready to head out of her home, a cave that she had found eleven years earlier. The cave was a better place to live in than the cabin she had resided in before it.

She rode away slowly. The past three days of warm weather had worked wonders at melting the snow that had fallen earlier on the path. Although riding the path was easy, it was difficult to see if you were in the way of an avalanche because the trees shielded any sightings of snow higher up. But Barbara knew this area very well. She was heading closer to where there might be an aftermath.

To the rhythm of the slow movements of her horse, she started thinking about what she often thought about. How long would she live? Was she meant to be here on the mountain alone? What was her purpose?

She had never found answers and hoped that one day she would. She had learned to live with her loneliness. At first, loneliness was like a friend. No one could harm her if there was no one else around. Often now, she wondered if she should be brave enough to let others know that she existed. No one who knew her when she was fifteen years old—twenty-three years ago—would recognize her. Probably no one cared.

Spring appeared to be coming early. It was her favorite season. It was also her least busy time so she could actually enjoy the wildflowers that were popping up everywhere instead of rushing to complete her chores. She would have to wait for late spring season for new vegetables that would grow in people's abandoned gardens—like asparagus, rhubarb, and fiddle heads. She would wait until full summer for a bigger variety of matured vegetables that grew wild or retook root in those same gardens like peas, green beans, shallots, and baby carrots—as well as for gathering and storing wild oats, barley and corn for her horse.

Fall was her busiest season. She gathered straw. She picked and stored her root vegetables like onions, carrots, beets and potatoes, to last her the winter. She prepared for the cold weather by chopping and stashing wood that had been drying for the past year. Winter was the season she would collect dead wood from fallen trees and hunt for small animals to enjoy as a fresh meal.

She snapped back to alertness with a sinking feeling in her gut. She had heard a loud bang, signaling a release of snow high up on her right side. Had she gone too far? Was she to be a victim of the avalanche? In a flash she knew that if she perished no one would ever know—but she couldn't dwell on that thought right now.

It was so loud! The earth was shaking! It was frightening!

The horse had been antsy and was now panicking. She managed to control him, quickly circling and moved back thirty yards to safety. She was facing west again and could hear nothing but the rumbling of the tumbling snow and rocks. Unbelievably, the sound was getting louder!

Even thunder had never been this loud—and here in the mountains she had heard some glorious thunder. She had never been this close to an avalanche's full fury. She could never have imagined such a noise. She could feel the earth moving and she could see the majestic trees ahead reluctantly giving up their grip on the thawing ground. Louder! Giant trees were being ripped off at their stumps and tossed down the slope as if they were twigs. Her ears overfilled with the noise and she covered them with both hands.

At the edge of the opening where the trees had once stood, she gawked at the sight of rolling snowballs racing down to the mess collected at the bottom. She released her ears and her head turned swiftly to follow a movement on her right in the last of the tumbling debris. She hoped it was a big animal like a deer but instead came to a sinking conclusion that it was the waving, gloved hand of a human being.

3

July 9, 2019

DOMINIQUE REMOVED THE PROTECTIVE HEAD gear from her ears and turned toward the motor hum coming from the east. Even from a quarter mile away, she could identify her cousin, Michael, on the quad. As usual, he wasn't wearing his helmet and his hair was all tangled up—which was typical for him but, oddly enough, added to his good looks.

He slowed down and came to a stop three feet away from her. She hadn't budged, she knew he was not the type to even pretend to hit her. He got off the machine and walked the few yards to the edge of the cleared section at the foot of the mountain.

"Did they just finish, Mick?" he asked, turning his five-foot-eleven-inch frame back toward her. Evidently, he was just making conversation because he knew the routine, having participated at the last site.

"Yes, they did. Joel sent the equipment operator home. Once we finish digging through what's left on this site, he'll call him to put it all back," she replied, referring to the twenty-foot-high pile of rotting trees and rocks that had been neatly moved. The government required them to return the mountain terrain to as close to what it had been before the excavation.

"Ah, another avalanche aftermath, another adventure. How many more do you think Joel will want to dig through if we don't find it this time?" asked Michael.

"Well, there are at least a couple more in this range lined up. We are waiting for the paperwork to come through from the Bureau of Land Management office in Winnemucca for those, so if we don't find what we're looking for at this site, we at least have two more to go through this summer."

"Do you really think he can dig through four in one summer?"

"Sure, why not? I'm helping. You're here. All eleven of us cousins are here!" she added, smiling.

Every Cartwright descendant had heard the stories of their great-great-great-great-grandfather Ben. They called him 4G Grandpa Ben and called his three sons—Adam, Hoss and Joe—their Triple-G-Grandpas. They had heard the histories of their ancestors as campfire and bedtime stories throughout their childhood. They knew the stories by heart and all the descendants had an interest in the findings from the excavations.

"Gabriel broke a leg—how can he help?"

"He can't dig wearing that cast, but he can sift through our findings. He found the locket and brooch at the first site, didn't he?" she explained, proving that things could be discovered.

"True, Gabriel has a gift for finding shiny things. But we are looking for something bigger, at least I think it will be bigger. And probably deteriorated and decomposed. Do you really think we can find it?"

"Well, Joel is the student of archaeology and he thinks finding the remains of a horse would lead us to find the metal from the remains of a bridle and whatever else may have been attached to the animal. And *he* thinks we can find it. So, yes. I think we can find it."

"Hey, you two ready to get going?" Joel asked, approaching his cousins with a shovel in each hand.

"Yeah, let's do this," Dominique and Michael

replied in unison. They each grabbed a shovel from Joel, put hats on to protect their heads from the sun and approached the freshly bared ground.

Philip, his sister Natalie, and Joel's sister Céleste were eager to begin picking away at the newly exposed soil. Each had devoted a week of their vacation leave to their brother and cousin's project.

Eriq was in between jobs and spent as much of his time with nature as possible. He had been the first one at the site that morning, as he had been each day he had worked on the digs. Joel had already put him to work earlier that morning, disassembling the tent and gathering the equipment from the last site, fourteen miles to the west. Now Eriq would set up the tent and organize the tools required for Gabriel to sift the dirt in shaded protection from the sun.

Joel took control of the site. He assigned everyone a four-foot-square space to dig through. The task wasn't easy work but divided like this, it was almost fun. The cousins, ranging in age from Michael's 21 to Natalie's 37, all got along famously.

At 12:30, Joel called lunch. A half hour later, they returned to work and by the time the sun was touching the mountain range to the west, they were picking up their gear and double riding the quads and trikes back to their temporary camp.

The Cartwright ranch had provided all the equipment and even a cook. A few of the ranch hands were volunteering part of their free time to assist in the dig and to watch out for the possible threat from mountain lions, coyotes or wolves. The diggers generally made enough noise to scare any wildlife away, but they welcomed the extra protection, nonetheless. The more workers, the better; the cousins were grateful for the extra hands, and no volunteer was turned away.

The young people were pleasantly surprised when their Great-Aunt Yvette showed up after their late supper. She was their oldest living relative.

"We weren't expecting you," said Camille.

"Well I had to see how you were all getting along," replied the seventy-eight-year-old woman.

"We have leftovers, if you're hungry," said Stephanie.

"I've eaten, thanks. But how's the food?" asked Aunt Yvette.

"It's really good. I was famished. Come, sit next to me," said Jacqueline, patting the cushion of the camp chair beside her.

"Okay, just for a moment."

"What? You're not camping out here with us tonight?" asked Camille.

"No way! My camping days are over. So are my trike days. I'm strictly a jeep kind of girl now. All the comforts of home for these old bones, you know," she chuckled.

All the physical activity of the day negated a late evening of conversation. Aunt Yvette left before nine and the exhausted group headed to their tents by ten o'clock.

The next morning, the rising sun warmed the tents and the heat drove the late risers to get up and start their day. As soon as bellies were full, the group made their way to the dig.

By day three, Joel's shovel hit something hard. Something that made a different noise than hitting a rock. He stopped digging with the shovel and took out his brush.

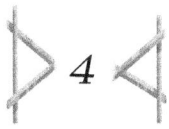

February 7, 1863

BARBARA'S REACTION WAS INSTANT. SHE UNTIED the shovel hanging from the side of her horse, jumped down and raced toward where she had seen the hand, never looking away from the approximate spot where she figured the person was buried.

Seconds were precious. She knew it. She didn't waste time. Underneath several tree branches, her efforts paid off. She couldn't believe it and yet, here he was. With great effort, she quickly removed the weight of snow off his chest. He was barely breathing. Still— she hoped. She whistled for her horse, but he would not be persuaded to set foot on the unsettled terrain.

She ignored her horse's reluctance and continued digging until the man's legs were free. She could safely leave him now to get the travois and pull him to her horse by herself. She was unsure of how to position him on the travois. She didn't want too much blood going to his head, so she placed his head on the elevated end.

All thoughts of hunting for furs and meat were forgotten. She had to see if she could save this man's life. In the last couple of decades, she had never seen a man who wasn't in a hurry to escape the posse chasing him! She hoped she would not have to fear this one.

The return trip to the cave was not as long as the initial half-hour ride it took her to encounter the avalanche. She quickened her pace considerably, worrying about the unconscious man.

She led the horse into the cave and dragged the

man to her bed. It wasn't very high off the floor and she managed to transfer him from the travois to her straw mattress. She gave him an overall check and surprisingly found no broken bones, not even on the exposed arm. What worried her most were the cuts and bumps on his head and that he was not waking, not even moaning, while she was checking him out.

Barbara decided to take advantage of his unconscious state to move his body enough to remove his boots and most of his wet clothing. She left the torn, long, white, soft garment that covered him from shoulders to ankles. She noted blood on several areas that indicated he had multiple cuts on his legs and other arm. A stained and torn area on his right side indicated that he may have at least one bruised rib. When she was satisfied that the only thing keeping him asleep was the trauma to his head, she went about nursing his wounds. The cut on his head would not stop bleeding, so she cleaned it and left it alone in the hopes that it would clot by itself.

She had no concept of how long the whole process had taken, but the somber lighting inside the cave suggested that the sun was setting when she finally relaxed and breathed a sigh of relief. She pulled her warmest blanket over him, tucking the end under his chin. She found she was hungry and she lit a lantern and proceeded to prepare her supper. She made extra and put some aside in case the man was hungry when he woke later. She also prepared herself another place to sleep for the night using straw and her two remaining blankets.

Barbara noticed her supply of straw was considerably low. She had traveled over thirty miles during the fall months the previous year to find a field of hay that had not belonged to anyone, or so she surmised had not, because no one had worked it. She was not a thief and would always go out of her way to make sure that she was not taking advantage of some other person's hard work for the things she managed to acquire for her personal use.

After cleaning up from her meager meal, she made tea from the dried leaves and herbs she had gathered the past summer. She poured herself a cup and finally approached the place where the man lay, the place where she had knelt a while back to tend to his wounds. The place that allowed her an up-close view of another human being.

She concentrated on his face now—his full head of gray hair, long eyelashes, his square forehead, his pointy chin, his clean-shaven face, his dry lips which she moistened with a wet cloth from the bowl near the bed. By the amount of space he covered on her bed, she correctly deduced that he was seven inches taller than her.

She looked at his clothing she had set aside to dry. They were of the best quality she had ever seen, and again she hoped that he was a man of means and not an outlaw.

She couldn't get enough of the sight of him, and knew she liked him even though he had yet to open his eyes or speak.

She turned and focused her attention on him once again. All of a sudden, she felt lightheaded and funny—different. Something she had never felt before. Her stomach felt like there was a butterfly or two fluttering inside. He opened his lips and she gave him water. She felt queasy and had a tightening in her stomach. She wondered if she was coming down with something.

She poured more water into his mouth, happy that he didn't choke on it, and studied his face. A kind face it was, it just had to be.

~

When she woke the next morning, she noted that he hadn't moved all night and hoped that he wouldn't be much longer in waking up. The bumps on his head didn't look too serious, but how could one really tell? The cut had dried somewhat, but fresh drops of blood occasionally would seep out. What would she do if he didn't wake?

She turned to stoke the fire. and jumped when the man woke suddenly. He struggled to get up and would have sprung sitting straight up if he could. He yelled out, "Diamond, NO! Hey! You! Where's my horse? Adam! Hoss! Joseph!"

He tried to move and ended up grabbing his ribs on the right side. He reached for his aching head and fell back just as Barbara was approaching to help him lay back down. He could see fresh blood on his fingers.

She had noted that he had not mentioned a woman's name. She had also wondered why he was yelling so loud. Couldn't he tell that she could hear him perfectly well without having to raise his voice? Then she wondered if the sound of the avalanche may have deafened him.

She handed him the warmed leftovers from last night, propped him up a bit and managed to say, "Eat first, talk after."

The aroma of stewed venison, chopped potatoes, onions and even carrots were soothing. He fed his hungry stomach.

He looked at his nurse now. She was average height, slender and yet very strong looking. Her face was almost void of any color except her tan and darkened freckles. It appeared that she didn't have any eyebrow hairs, making her look non-descriptive. The hair on her head was a bright red and any strand that had come loose from the knot at her nape was pale, almost blond. Her eyes were the color of the blue sky and seemed to be swimming in the white surrounding the pupils. She was really very plain.

He took a bite of the stew and tried to remember how he got here. But where was here? By the time he finished his food, the tea was ready. He rolled the brew in his mouth, trying to identify what it was made from. He felt stronger after food and drink, so he pushed himself up further off the low bed.

Once he realized that he was not seriously injured, he calmly asked, at a much more tolerable volume, "Where's my horse?"

Except for a few songs that she sang on a regular basis, she had not spoken much in the past two decades. It felt puzzling to hear someone speak. She spoke very slowly, missing verb conjugations, most adverbs, and a few adjectives.

"Avalanche, big snow fall off mountain. Take trees down."

He nodded, remembering the avalanche. He wondered if English was not her primary language but couldn't detect an accent.

"Horse—ah—under you, deep in snow. Not see horse. Sorry." She did hand and head motions as she spoke sympathetically and waited for more questions. She loved the opportunity to look into his light-brown eyes and hoped he would ask more questions right away.

"I hate to have lost that horse. He was my favorite. How did I get here? What's your name? Where is everybody else? What is this place?" Ben asked, indicating all around with his hand.

She decided to answer his questions in the order that they were asked. "Tra-vois, Vincent an' me pull you 'ere. Name Barbara. 'ere alone, twenty-tree year now. Dis cave," she nodded.

Her slow speech tested his patience. But she looked him straight in the eyes when she spoke almost challenging him to accept her as his equal. He sensed her determination and couldn't help but feel a pang of respect.

"Whad is name?" she asked, pointing to him in turn.

Before asking who Vincent was, he answered, "Ben Cartwright. I own a ranch about thirty miles north-east of here. I was on my way home and decided to enjoy the warm weather, so I took a different route through the mountains. I would never have lost Diamond if I hadn't taken an untried route home." He immediately regretted his decision of that leisure ride off the beaten path.

She missed understanding a few words, as he spoke so fast. But she was right. He was a man of means if his home was a ranch as he said. Wouldn't he have otherwise indicated he owned a farm? She wasn't sure. She could relax. He would mean her no harm if he was genuine.

"Dia-mond, y'ur horse?" she asked.

"Yes," feeling silly about his fondness for the horse, but he loved that bay.

"Horse name Vincent, after Pa," she said.

Ben smiled at her simple explanation of the name Vincent. She smiled back and realized that she had not smiled very much in a long while. She decided that would change starting right now.

He liked her smile. It lit up her face and gave it character. She could be attractive, he thought.

Ben had many other questions, but Barbara shook her head and told him to rest. He nodded and laid back on the straw mattress. As she moved, he watched her. She could sense it and was very uncomfortable. She had forgotten how it felt to be watched.

He, on the other hand, was trying to figure out her age. She was a strong woman, but her face did not give away her years. You could tell she spent a good measure of time outside and did a fair share of manual work because her hands were as tough as dried leather. She had a slender body, not girlish, but not old and bent over either. That was all he currently had to work with.

Halfway into the morning, Barbara asked him, "You be good alone? I need go for food." She didn't tell him she needed to get away from his staring too, wouldn't know the words for that anyway.

He nodded and she got her gear and left him with water nearby, food on a plate, and the necessities for his personal needs. He was still too weak to move around and got dizzy if he tried to get up.

As she was heading out, he noticed that the horse, Vincent, had been in the cave with them all this time. Now alone, he laid his head back and took a long, slow look around. There were tall, leafless branches leaning up against the walls of the cave and furs hanging on them. He couldn't tell if she was planning on making clothes or if these were the finished product. Or maybe these were providing insulation in the cave, he thought.

He noticed the chopped wood piled up on his left, a makeshift bed on the floor that he thought she must have made for herself after his arrival, a tub, followed by a shelf of sorts with a few mismatched dishes. The fire pit was in the middle of the cave. Other things were piled up on his right, but there was no other furniture to speak of. That was it.

He drifted off to sleep.

~

She came back with her travois holding deer and rabbit, both meat and furs. Several times while cutting up meat, she had caught herself wondering about Ben and would scold herself back into the moment. Then a little time would go by and she would be at it again. *What is wrong with me?* She thought, *Oh, but when he opened his eyes, they pierced right through me!* And back to daydreaming she went.

When she returned to the cave, Ben was astonished at her hunting ability.

She smiled at his false conclusion and explained, "Avalanche do work, me take."

He was happy to not see any horse hides in the pile. There may have been horse meat though—he couldn't be sure—and he didn't ask. At least, if she had found Diamond, she hadn't brought the hide back with her—and for that he was grateful!

While she busied herself with the meat and furs, he watched her and spoke of his family, his ranch and his home. She could tell he loved all those things. She remembered that folks rarely spoke about people and things they did not at least like.

She barely understood what he was saying but managed to make this much sense of it. Over twenty years ago, he had bought land and built a ranch on it. He had started small, bought and sold cattle, and as the good years and hard work proved lucrative, he bought more land and animals, and expanded. He told her that his prudent spending and paying attention to the cattle costs, land sales, and fluctuating markets, helped him amass his current holdings.

Later that evening, Ben no longer felt faint when he stood up. The cut on his head would still drip blood, but it didn't hurt, so he dismissed it.

Barbara, on the other hand, felt an increased, unfamiliar squeezing in her stomach—especially when Ben first put an arm around her as he needed a shoulder to support himself on. She had never, ever, been that close to a grown man before. Not even her own father. Her family had not been demonstrative and hugging, even a pat on the shoulder, was not habitual. She was blushing profusely and hoped the dim lighting in the cave prevented Ben from seeing his effect on her.

But she was wrong. Ben could see her girlish reaction and determined that she may be younger than he had at first thought. He then paid particular attention to his manners as he did not want to offend her.

The following day, she busied herself working the furs and storing the meat in her cache. She put on a roast of venison and also made a rabbit stew. She had very little vegetables left, which was not unusual in February. She was determined, even though she couldn't identify why, to show this man that she could cook and that she had means, albeit not monetary, even if she had to use the last of her stored goods.

Ben tried to pass the time asking questions, never expecting any answers. She was not very talkative. She, on the other hand, listened to his every word and tried to memorize what she thought they meant. She had forgotten so much. She felt too embarrassed to ask this man, Ben, to teach her to speak again. She thought that she could teach herself by listening to him. She would often give him a quizzical look in the hopes that he would reword his question or comment when she didn't understand. He didn't seem to get the meaning behind her pointed looks.

The next day, Ben said, "I'm feeling well enough to start traveling down the mountain if you'll help me get home. I'll pay you for your time."

Barbara never had need for money and would never have agreed to payment for rendering this sort of service. She wasn't sure traveling so soon was wise, but he was insistent, and she was curious enough to see his ranch and meet the family that he had talked so much about.

"Sure," she agreed. They would leave the next morning.

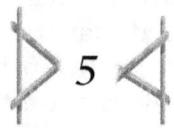

February 11, 1863

BARBARA WOKE BEFORE BEN AND LAY ON HER makeshift bed thinking. She eventually figured out what was wrong with her. She was attracted to the man she found. But she was mature enough to know that it was just what her mother would call an infatuation, that he was the first and only man she had ever spoken to—other than her father—and that she should give herself time to get to know other men before deciding on the certainty of her feelings.

Something else was bothering her. She finally had quiet time to think about her close call with the avalanche. It wasn't the first time she had been in a situation where she may have lost her life, but it was the first time that she thought being alone presented her with a disadvantage. With a sigh, she pushed her thoughts aside and started her morning.

They busied themselves—mostly Barbara was busy—with packing all the necessities for being out on the mountain for the following few days. The new meat supply was already going to be put to good use. The new furs would have to wait. Her old furs were packed high on the travois. She knew their function and didn't quite know how to explain it to Ben when he asked why they were packed, but he would soon see.

When Ben understood from Barbara that she would not get him off the mountain unless he was reclining in the travois on top of most of those furs, he started to argue. Even though Barbara was a woman with a limited vocabulary and couldn't argue with clarity, she was more stubborn than Ben. She was also the owner of all the equipment needed to get him home. He gave in, reluctantly, but respectfully.

With his head on the elevated side of the travois, Ben was buried so deep in the stack of furs that he couldn't see more than a foot or so down from the ceiling of the cave and the tops of the surrounding trees once outside. Occasionally, he would force himself up a little to see which direction they were headed, but he would soon feel the ache in his side and return to the prison of furs. He spent his time muttering to himself.

When they stopped a couple of hours later to rest the horse, Barbara didn't think Ben had clearly seen from whence they had come nor much of their surroundings from the angle he was lying. She was sure he could not find his way back to her cave, especially if the snow melted all trace of their tracks. She didn't think he would tell anyone where her cave was if she asked him to keep it to himself, but she didn't know him well enough to know that for certain.

She asked him, "Well, maybe you right. You good on horse bareback, you tink?" Had he asked her why she changed her mind, she would have pretended she was unable to answer.

He beamed the biggest smile he could muster. When she looked at his reaction, she couldn't help but smile back and acknowledge that pleasing him made her heart skip a beat.

With Barbara holding Vincent steady, Ben managed to mount by climbing on a rock, hanging onto the horse's mane and throwing a leg over. That little bit of strain caused the wound on his head to produce a few droplets of blood, but neither of them worried about it.

They traveled for another two and a half hours,

rested again, and traveled for another hour before Barbara decided that they had better set up camp for the night. As she had to do all the heavy work and setting up, Ben kept quiet on his mounting urgency to get home. He knew his sons would start to worry about him soon and organize themselves to go out looking. He couldn't help their worrying, so he decided it would not be fair to put any pressure on Barbara or upset her by expressing his desire to continue traveling. He didn't think she would quit on him and leave him on his own, but he didn't want the rest of the trek home to be an unpleasant one, either.

Little did he know Barbara. She would have brought him home no matter what he said or did and never spoken to him again if that was what he wished.

She cleared the ground between several mature, strong trees. Then she cut down a series of branches to the same length and leaned them against the trees in the clearing.

Eventually Ben could see the makings of a lean-to. He understood that the cold could come claim a man in the middle of the night if he didn't prepare himself. He thought the lean-to was too big and might lose some of its effectiveness to the cold, but he kept on watching her cover the branches with the pile of furs from the travois. Then she placed two pelts down on each of the sleeping places and the remainder on top of the first two layers and on the inside and outside walls of the lean-to.

"Why is it so spacious?" he asked. The quizzical look on her face made him reword his question, "Why so much room?"

She simply replied, "Vincent sleep 'ere, he 'ave no fur enough." And then it made sense to him. Vincent stayed with her inside the cave and didn't grow a thicker winter coat. Why didn't he think of that?

He could hear her muttering.

22

She wasn't speaking loudly enough for him to hear clearly, "Spa-ci-ous, spa-ci-ous ..."

~

After that long day Barbara relaxed near the fire, humming a tune he couldn't identify but knew he had heard before. *She is a good cook and reasonably well equipped and organized, but not much for company,* he thought.

She didn't have the words yet to tell him about her ending up on the mountain or living in the cave, so until she remembered and learned more words, she decided sharing her story would have to wait. Ben ended up doing most of the talking, but when he started getting blank looks from her after one of his questions or when she had provided only a couple of words in reply, he would surrender and cease talking.

Ben thought, *It sure is lonely talking to yourself. How did she do it for so long? I wonder if she really has been here twenty-three years, maybe she miscounted. Either way, it must be a long time. Some of her tools are certainly outdated. Definitely her garments are, even the handmade ones. Yet, even though her things are rugged, they're functional.*

Barbara enjoyed the silence when Ben stopped talking as she could think and process all that Ben had said. She thought, *I have learned so many words but I'm afraid I will forget more than I can remember. I cannot repeat and memorize them as quickly as I want when he keeps talking.*

But she was starting to form better sentences, conjugating more verbs and adding new words that had been missing from her vocabulary.

He would conclude exactly that when she mustered enough courage to ask a meaning of a word he used. Ben noticed that she was trying to speak better by forming more complete sentences. He encouraged her, spoke slowly and enunciated his words. He didn't want her to feel embarrassed for not knowing how to say or describe something. They were getting along very well and smiling a great deal at each other.

The first day proved to be strenuous for Ben. He grunted and had great difficulty bending to get down on the ground where his bed was. Barbara tried to help as best she could. Finally, she asked him to wait. She removed her footwear so as to not get the furs wet with her soiled shoes. Then she repositioned herself, standing on the furs closer to him to help.

She turned her back to him. He leaned heavily onto her and together they bent knees and descended. When his head finally touched the fur, he sighed with huge relief. Barbara was otherwise bothered. They were in a spoon position and remnants of her garments were stuck underneath his heavier and unmovable body.

He mumbled, "Good night," in her ear, unaware of her discomfort. He was fast asleep before she managed to pull her clothes free and stand. She led Vincent into the lean-to and settled herself next to Ben, facing him—but then quickly turned onto her other side.

She felt so many new emotions. She needed to examine these feelings to better understand them. She thought, *Why do I blush so when he is near me? Why am I tongue-tied beyond my ability to speak even with the words I do know? How come when he smiles, I can't help but smile back?* She fell asleep remembering the weight of him around her.

~

The morning brought on new stiffness in Ben's joints. Once again, Barbara backed up into him, moved in real close, and took the brunt of his weight while they struggled to rise. It was awkward but effective. As soon as Ben could move, he walked around and dislodged the aches.

Barbara was very efficient. Ben hardly noticed that while he was exercising, she had boiled water and poured it in a basin for a quick wash up, boiled more water and prepared a tea and warmed up food for breakfast.

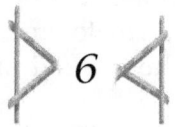 6

February 11, 1863

ON THE SECOND NIGHT, NEAR THE CAMPFIRE, Ben once again thought about Barbara's age. He decided that she may be in her early thirties or even late twenties. She may have had a family here on the mountain with her at one point and they may have died when she was very young, or they may have died just recently. He was getting more anxious to learn her story. He was almost sure she was young enough to be his daughter, very close to Adam's age, as a matter of fact.

He had learned if he repeated a question, he would only get a quizzical look, so he asked her instead, "Do you have any questions for me? I know I have been talking a lot about my sons and my ranch, but is there anything you would like to ask me?"

"Ah, sure," she said hesitantly. "I ask, wat you do wit all y'ur money?" She had never had any and couldn't imagine what a person would do with it.

He wasn't entirely sure he understood her question. He presumed she had never had any or much, so he said, "I will think about my answer for a minute before I tell you if that is all right with you."

She nodded.

He finally said, "The money I have made has provided me and my sons with a comfortable home. It has paid for an education that Adam wanted for himself. Oh, my two other sons would have been provided with the same if they wanted it. They didn't. I do not treasure money. I save it and spend it wisely. On a ranch, or

26

probably with any business I guess, there are many surprises and you sometimes are forced to spend more money just to get by."

She handed him a plate of food, a questioning look on her face at the last part of his comment. He noticed and thought of how to elaborate on his answer. He thanked her for the food and then answered her unspoken question, "For example, if we have a drought one summer, we might have to buy equipment to get water to the cattle, or buy more salt or even hay for them to survive the upcoming winter. Whatever the weather surprises us with, we have to be prepared for it."

She leaned in and he could see that she was wanting to ask more questions about the subject, so he continued, "Money is for a person's home and business, it's for buying clothes and supplies."

"My virtues, or rather the ones I teach my sons, are what I consider most valuable. I want them to live an honorable life. I want them to be proud of the good, decent men they will become one day. Oh, they each might think they are as good a man as they will ever be right now, but there is always something more for an individual to learn."

She was nodding her head and he was encouraged to continue. "I want to live my life using only my values and my virtues. I want to be the finest example for my sons. I want them to see me as decent and fair. But I can't just preach these values to them. I must live them every day. How else are they to learn and want to copy?"

She smiled. He knew she understood. There was so much more he could have said, but she yawned and he figured she must be exhausted. After all, she had done all the walking, leading of the horse, taking down the camp in the morning and setting it up again this afternoon, gathering firewood, feeding them both and everything else in between. He had only exercised his tongue.

Barbara reflected on what Ben had shared about his children. He had told her about his oldest son. Adam was the most serious of the three. He was very interested in his studies and in continuing to learn everything he could. He was as tall as Ben at five feet, eleven inches tall, had dark hair and very dark-brown eyes. Adam most often had his head buried in a book.

His middle son, Hoss, was the kindest of the three. He was also the giant among all men on the ranch and even in Virginia City, coming in at six feet, two inches tall. Hoss was fairest in hair color and had hazel colored eyes. He was very trusting and could therefore be gullible. His brother Joe had often played tricks on him, as children and even now that they were both men.

The youngest of the three, Joe, was the shortest in the family at five feet, nine inches tall. He always seemed to find something funny to laugh about. His lighthearted take on life occasionally annoyed his older brother Adam so much that Adam often left the room to get away from his younger brother's nonsense. Joe had brown eyes that matched his brown hair.

~

By the time they set up camp the third night on the mountain, Ben knew they were approaching his land and told Barbara that they only had a few hours left before they would reach his home the next day. He suggested that she ride with him on the horse as the ground would be more level and she wouldn't have to lead Vincent. It would also lessen the time spent out in the cold.

She didn't know what to say so she turned away to think. *We'll be approaching his home coupled like that, practically in an embrace!* She was apprehensive all of a sudden. Being alone with him on the mountain these past several days had made her seriously think of her future for the first time in over twenty years.

I know this is a sign, she thought. *This is my chance to get down off this mountain and stay off. I have met a kind man, maybe he can help me. I wonder how he would feel about that.*

She knew she felt fondness, or maybe more, for him. Was she attractive enough to fit in his world, to be considered deserving? She had never worried about what someone might think of her since she was a child. She reasoned with herself, *I can't change anything about my face, my history, my being.* She shook her head. She couldn't fully understand why she was thinking these things and decided it must be because of having met Ben.

As hard as her life had been up to now, she was going to meet more people the next day. How difficult was it going to be? She hoped she could face it with Ben by her side. She knew that she could always go back to live in her cave and never have to see people again if it proved to be too much of a negative experience.

She turned to face Ben and nodded. She agreed to double ride Vincent in the morning.

What she did know for certain was that she wanted to be near Ben. As a result, she had a very disturbing night thinking about double riding the horse. Ben would be near, too near. It would be different than helping him get into or out of bed. The nearness on the horse would last hours. Would he be able to sense her unease?

~

But the next morning, her worries of the night before were put aside when they discovered that they were practically prisoners in their makeshift abode. It had snowed overnight, and it was piled up as high as their

29

knees outside the lean-to. The rest of the way down the mountain would be very hard on Vincent so Barbara knew that they could not both ride him and add the extra stress on the horse.

She also seriously considered putting Ben back on the travois to help lessen the load on Vincent's back. This time Ben was the more stubborn one. He knew he could be of use up on the horse. He would recognize landmarks and help guide the way. He couldn't march through the snow like Barbara, but he could be useful. She gave in reluctantly. She hoped Vincent would be all right.

She shoveled the snow away from the lean-to so they could pack up with a bit more ease. She covered her body and Ben's with a couple of the furs as the temperature had dipped below freezing.

They ate leftover stew from the night before, not taking time to heat it thoroughly. They hurried through as much of what needed to be done so they could get on their way. Barbara even missed her morning ritual of washing her face.

The remaining four-hour walk to the ranch became six thanks to low lying pockets in the terrain where she had to shovel snow out of Vincent's way. Three hours into the trek, Barbara wanted to stop to eat again. Ben didn't want to waste another hour. He assured her they were very close to his home and that they could eat when they arrived. But later, she had to shovel more snow than anticipated and all on an empty stomach. They did not reach the ranch until late afternoon.

When the house finally came into view, Ben excitedly started to look for his sons. No one seemed to be outside, no wait, there was someone coming out of the barn. "Adam!" he cried out.

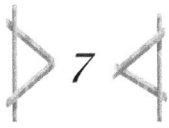

7

February 14, 1863

BEN'S SONS HAD JUST RETURNED FROM HAVING gone out in different directions asking the surrounding neighbors if anyone had seen their Pa. They were going to go back out the next day, working outwards from where they had left off.

Adam turned toward the familiar voice, gladly acknowledging his father by waving. He didn't recognize who was with him or why just the one horse and a travois. An Indian perhaps? He quickly ran toward the house, calling out, "Hoss, Joe! Come quick, Pa is home. He's okay. Come see for yourselves. Hurry!"

The three brothers ran towards their Pa and helped the fur-covered, exhausted Barbara lead the weary horse the rest of the way home while peppering their father with questions.

"Where were you? What happened to Diamond? Are you okay? You look cold even under that pile of furs. You two, ah, three," including the horse, "must be hungry! Do you realize that you have blood dripping down your face? Are you hurt much?"

Ben said, "I'm all right, well I have a few bumps on my head and sore ribs, there was an avalanche. Diamond is dead. It took days to get here, I didn't realize I was that far away from home and ..."

By now they had reached the front entrance. The boys helped him down and when his legs buckled from under him, they immediately fell silent and took action. They carried him the rest of the way into the house. Barbara tied up her horse, placed her fur over him but left the travois hooked up for now and followed the men.

Barbara walked in but stopped abruptly, in awe of what she saw. The entrance led into a great room with exquisite chairs and a sofa, upholstered with blue and red velvet, meticulously placed in front of the grand fireplace, warmly inviting conversation.

She was also witnessing a private moment. Ben's sons tenderly cared for the man they obviously cherished by gently laying him down on the sofa, removing his boots and outer garments, putting a blanket on him, giving him water, tending to the fresh drops of blood on his forehead, reaching for a pillow, and stoking the fire.

She turned away from the intimate scene deeply moved and deeply yearning. Barbara knew she had made the right decision to come down the mountain and at least meet Ben's family. She closed the front door to let the fire warm up the parts of the house that had cooled.

This wasn't just a house. It was huge! It was the biggest indoor place she had ever seen. The hutch to the left of the entrance currently held three hats and still had plenty of room for hers. The ceiling was taller than twice her height!

Once his sons were assured that Ben was only bruised and would fully recover, they turned toward Barbara to show her their genuine gratitude. She was still facing the entrance wall as she removed the knife and ax from her belt loop and placed them on the side hutch. Then she removed her scarf and hat.

When the three sons saw her long, red hair fall out of the old ratty hat, they were shocked to find that she was neither a man nor an Indian! They had even more questions now. Ben saw their stunned faces and guessed that they had just discovered his savior was a woman underneath all the fur and ill-fitting clothes.

8

February 14, 1863

BEN BECKONED HIS SONS, "WELL, DON'T JUST stand there. Offer Barbara something to drink, a chair to sit and a place to freshen up. She's been my legs and arms and must be exhausted. Go on."

Which they did, but she didn't need anything except, "Water, please." Joe handed her a glass, showed her a chair by gesturing with his hand. As she sat, she hoped the smile she placed on her face didn't show anything but sincerity. She said, "Thank you, Joe."

Joe wondered how she knew his name.

She thought that Ben could have told her how handsome his sons were. But then she wondered if he could see those things, even in his own sons. He hadn't described small details like Adam's square and determined jaw; Hoss' angelic face; and Joe's boyish good looks. Adam was a force to reckon with and one lucky woman would probably win him over one day. Hoss would make a woman feel special and loved, she was sure. Joe wore his heart on his sleeve, as indicated by the concentrated concern for his father's well-being. Some things she felt more than could see, even this soon after having just met them.

The longer she was in the room, the more out of place she felt. She feared they would judge her on her appearance and, deciding that she didn't fit into their cozy lives, would be anxious to send her on her way come a new day. She had yet to discover whether these people were arrogant folks.

She was distracted by the people and the items in the room. Were the sons as kind as their father? Were all the items functional or were some of them only for display like that statue of a horse on its hind legs? In all the excitement, she forgot her hunger.

Ben sensed her uneasiness and quickly excused his sons to her by dismissing their questions about Barbara, his accident and his trip home until later. "Boys, please. All in good time. After all, Barbara has done all the work getting me off the mountain and home safely. Surely our stories can wait until after a good rest and a hot meal."

Ben's dismissive tone of voice reminded them that they were staring, and they immediately stopped. In reflection of how well they were raised, they simply agreed with their father and apologized. Adam and Joe led Barbara to the guest bedroom.

The doors to the six rooms upstairs were left open during the day so the air could circulate. She slowed her pace and saw beds in the first four rooms they passed and assumed that they must each have a bedroom to themselves. She didn't know that people could have such luxuries. She remembered her growing up years—girls had one room and boys had another.

The fifth room they passed held a huge tub. The tub had to be big enough to accommodate Hoss, but she wouldn't think of that. She could only entertain the idea of having a bath in it real soon.

Pointing to the door of the last room, Joe said, "Over here." Barbara tore herself away from staring at the tub.

When she saw the prettiest room she could ever have envisioned, she stood in wonder—wide-eyed at the loveliness surrounding her. The curtains matched the dainty lacework on the bedspread. The colors were pastels—a word she would learn weeks later and never forget. There was a lovely chair in the corner with beautiful carvings on the wooden legs and arms. The four-poster bed held three plump pillows wrapped in delightful hand-made embroidered coverings.

She had never owned nor seen such riches in her youth. She didn't know some of these things even existed. She lightly touched the brush, comb and mirror set on the oak dresser and assumed correctly that she could put them to good use right away. But she didn't know what most of the other things around those were or their function. One was a short, colorful, round jar with a flat lid and the other was a pear-shaped glass bottle with liquid inside. But the lid on the bottle had a long thing coming out of it that ended in a round ball with a tassel hanging on the end. She understood about the water basin and the bed and for now that was all she needed.

She pulled her attention away from the items on the dressing table and looked back to the door. The three young men stood there awkwardly, each with their arms full.

Joe had brought hot water for her water basin. "Thank you, Joe."

Adam brought her towels and extra blankets for the bed. "Thank you, Adam."

Hoss had taken care of her horse and brought her things upstairs to her room not knowing if she would need them or not. She didn't indicate one way or another and he put them on the delicate chair in the corner.

"Thank you, Hoss," she said, and closed the door behind them.

She continued examining the room. When she saw a movement out of the corner of her eye, she turned. It was her.

She approached the full-length mirror with

childlike curiosity. She had not seen herself in so long. She was surprised to see her mother looking back at her. It brought her great joy to know that she looked like the only other woman she ever knew. Oh, how she missed her.

But when she looked more closely, she saw an older version of her mother. Her hair was unkempt, mostly because of wearing a tight hat for the past three days. Her clothes were unsuitable. She had not mastered making clothing with any material except deer hide. Even the furs she had cleaned were mostly kept in their original shape and just tossed over her shoulders for warmth.

Barbara realized then that she had been away from people too long. She did not know how to act or even speak for goodness sake. What would her parents have thought of her? A coward for hiding out so long? It may have been her new surroundings, or her decision to finally reveal herself to people, she didn't know, but she wept fresh tears thinking of her parents. She laid on the bed with the delicate lace trim and cried herself to sleep.

An hour later, there was a knock on her door. From the other side, Hoss said, "Ahm, Miss Barbara? A late supper will be ready to eat in fifteen minutes. Would you please join us?"

She couldn't believe she had slept at all. She guessed it was because she had no current responsibilities, not even in preparing a meal.

Looking in the mirror again, she remembered her freckles as a young girl and thought that they now just made her face look like it was dirty or stained especially on the cheeks and underneath her blue eyes. She didn't like her hair that hung down in knots. No, she didn't think she looked much like a proper woman. No wonder Ben's sons were staring. She decided that she would try to comb and brush her hair later before going to bed. For now, she gathered it as tightly as she could and tied it in a knot at her nape.

Seven minutes after Hoss' knock on the door, she was heading downstairs. She was not in the habit of changing her clothes before a meal and didn't even have a variety of her clothing with her. The dresses she salvaged all those years ago had long worn out and the odd item of clothing she had found since were better used as undergarments or for the warmer season. She only washed her hands and face in preparation for the meal.

The young men were surprised that she was still wearing her warm clothing made out of deer hide. Ben, however, knew that she had worn her cleanest attire because she had worn one upper garment every day for the past three days. He told himself he needed to address that issue. The younger men quickly forgot Barbara's clothing choices as they focused on the interesting dinner conversation about their father's adventure and Barbara's role in his safe return home.

Barbara tried to remember what it was like to eat at a family table. She studied the fancy cup and noticed the four men watching her. She smiled, put the cup down. When they started passing plates around, she served herself and started to eat with a deep hunger.

She asked, "Wat is dese?"

Hoss answered, "These are dumplings. They are the best tasting ones in all the county."

"How are dey made and who come up wit da idear dat dey be dis good?"

The men looked at each other and couldn't answer her questions. But she didn't sense that. Instead, she thought that her comments may be childish. The raised eyebrows and chuckles around the table caused her to stop talking and focus on the meal before her.

The men were actually delighted in her innocence and didn't know what they may have done to make her stop talking. Their cook, Lee, stayed busy in the kitchen during their meals. He had been employed by them for more than two decades but as the cook for the past fifteen years. Most guests of the Cartwrights enjoyed his food, but few would have wanted to know how he prepared it.

Ben discreetly redirected the conversation from the good food before them and proceeded to tell his sons about his trip southwest and how he, unfortunately, came to be on the mountain that slid down to a heap of rubble. He asked "Joseph, could you get me paper and pen after dinner?"

Joe nodded.

"I need to make a list of the items that were in the saddle bag," Ben continued. "I don't think I will have a problem getting another copy of my business documents, but I'm afraid I may have to disappoint Mr. Henry Devon though."

"How so, Pa?" asked Adam.

"About three weeks ago, I met Henry Devon in our lawyer's office. Mr. Devon was meeting with Fred Mason to make arrangements to change lawyers from the one he had in Sacramento. Mr. Devon sold his business there and retired to his new home just outside of Virginia City. When he found out I was going to Sacramento, he asked if I could pick up a package from his lawyer, Mr. Arthur Richardson, at Crow Law Offices. It was being engraved and it hadn't been ready yet when he moved away. I managed to retrieve it all right, but it is in the satchel."

"Oh Pa, it probably is too late anyway," said Hoss.

"What do you mean? Why would it be too late?"

"When we were out looking for you this morning, I was told by his neighbor, George Stevens, that Mr.

Devon died yesterday. I'm afraid he won't be able to do whatever he wanted to do with that package."

"Well, I'll be sure to ask Mr. Mason to contact Mr. Devon's lawyer with the news either way." He then muttered loud enough for the others to hear, "I wonder what it was. Just a small box, a family heirloom perhaps. It cost me a day's travel waiting for that thing to be engraved. I would have avoided the avalanche and would not have lost Diamond!"

9

July 11, 2019

WITH EXCITEMENT IN HIS VOICE, JOEL SAID, "I found something."

Everybody took the statement as an excuse to stop for a short break. They grabbed water bottles and headed towards Joel's squared-off section. By the time they were all there, he was pulling out a horseshoe from the rich soil.

They all cheered. It was not unusual to find bones from horses and deer, but it was unusual to find something from an animal that obviously was man-made. A horseshoe was undeniable proof that the horse had been domesticated.

Upon Joel's instruction, they expanded the square to eight feet by eight feet. They proceeded to dig and dump shovels of soil onto the trays and bring them to the tables under the canopy where Gabriel was already sifting through dirt from an earlier tray.

Gabriel put that tray aside and started working on the new one right away. Joel stayed behind to help him. Everyone else knew to dig two shovels of soil to a depth of four inches and deposit it in a tray. When eight square feet filled the trays, they would then help with the sifting.

"Why did we stretch out from four to eight feet? Why not six? Wouldn't that have been the correct span of a horse?" Michael's sister, Stephanie, asked.

Joel explained, "The horse would have been crushed by rocks and the weight of the trees. Eventually everything underneath that weight spreads out to a greater distance, especially if it is rotting flesh turning to dust. By the first summer after an avalanche, even more sinking and shifting occurs of the smaller debris that is beneath the aftermath from the first melt."

He tried not to be too specific. His cousins would tease him incessantly if he used too many big or technical words. But they did rely on him to be the expert—like knowing that finding a horseshoe did not automatically mean that you would find the head of the animal close by. That is, if you were lucky enough to be able to identify remnants of old bones as part of the muck.

Eriq came down with the last tray and said, "I think I have something that could be cloth."

"What makes you say that?" asked Joel.

"It just looks like dirt, but it's all tied together."

Joel, curious now, left the tray with the horseshoe and turned to Eriq's find.

"I agree. This looks like cloth, and I suspect it is leather from the satchel!"

Exhilarated now by the possible find, Joel and Eriq sifted through the tray together. But they found no further evidence of the possible satchel.

"Show me where you got this piece," Joel insisted. "Let's dig another four inches down from that space right away."

But nothing else was found in the first batch of trays or in the new tray of the earth dug immediately below the new find.

~

The following day, another four inches were dug up and brought to the tent for their collected efforts with the sifting. By ten that morning, Jackie yelled out, "I found a horseshoe!" and she did a little dance.

Five minutes later, Phil rhythmically started knocking on a rock with his pick until he had everyone's attention. Then he smiled and held up a third horseshoe. Smiles and thumbs-up acknowledged his finding.

Just fifteen minutes later, Camille almost recoiled, "This feels weird."

Eriq was standing next to her and looked over at what she was talking about. "That looks like cloth." He reached out to touch the item, running his finger lightly over the top. "It does feel weird though, right? Almost like it would have once covered an animal but more like skin than fur."

Joel came over and examined the piece. When it was laid out, he thought out loud, "This may have been the sheath for a rifle."

Gabriel said, "According to the story, the sheath had been empty because 4G Grandpa Ben had dropped his rifle."

They nodded, not sure whether to anticipate finding the rifle—or the metal parts of it—anywhere near the digs of the remains of the horse.

At two o'clock, Céleste called her brother over and he confirmed, "Yes, I believe these cloth-like findings are likely from a saddle."

Later that afternoon, when nothing else was found from the diggings of the fourth layer, Joel spread out the spaces to twelve-square feet. This proved to be a wise decision when Eriq called out, "I've found the fourth horseshoe."

Ten minutes later in the adjacent space, Michael was elated to report, "And, I've found pieces from the bridle and bit."

Although their discoveries were exciting, they could not prove that the findings at one time had belonged to their 4G Grandpa Ben. If there had been an insignia on the saddle or sheath or satchel at one time, the passing of years had erased it.

Joel soon called out, "Okay, let's go for supper."

They picked up tools and walked down toward the tent to gather Gabriel before heading out to camp. But they didn't need to go inside to find him. He was leaning on his cane, waiting for them to get closer, then waved something shiny in his free hand.

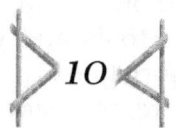

February 14, 1863

DURING THE MEAL WHILE BEN TALKED, BARBARA would steal glances at the pretty things around her. She thought, *What a beautiful cabinet and pretty dishes behind the glass. What a lovely table setting, oh my, why two forks and so many glasses?*

She glanced at her table mates. *I'll just do what everybody else does,* she thought.

She moved slowly and purposefully. She was enjoying every bite of the delicious food. She couldn't tell exactly what else she was eating, but it sure was good.

She tasted wine and didn't like it at first, but to be polite she decided that she would finish drinking the liquid in the small crystal glass. Halfway through the meal, she found she liked it very much. Her cheeks reddened quickly after a few sips and Joe commented on it. She smiled, not minding his teasing. She felt hot being around Ben in his own home and hoped that the wine would provide her with courage. She could at least blame her red cheeks on the wine if she blushed too much.

By the time tea was being served, Ben arrived at this part of his story, "I remember this feeling that Diamond was moving sideways and jumping plenty. His head was thrashing back and forth and his eyes were wide open with fear. He kicked me off him in an effort to run, I guess. That's when I bumped my head and he disappeared in a cloud of white, gray and black.

I tried to grab onto something but there was nothing there. That's the last thing I remember. Barbara will have to tell the rest." All eyes turned to her.

Ben smiled, patted her hand and said, "You'll do fine. Why don't you tell us all about yourself before the day we met. Take your time and tell us how is it that you are living up on that mountain and came to be the one who saved me that day?"

Ben motioned to Hoss to help him up to sit in the sofa chair by the fire. Joe stood to help Barbara up out of her chair. It took her a moment to realize that even though they all knew she did not need any help, it was just the gentlemanly thing to do. Adam went to get the brandy they would enjoy near the fire. Barbara thought correctly that they were readying themselves to hear a long story. She had nothing to lose, so she obliged. She also accepted a glass of brandy. One small sip warmed her throat on its way down. Its sweetness made her like it in spite of the burn.

Joe, suddenly remembering Ben's request, stood and walked to his father's desk. He retrieved pen and paper, brought it to Ben, then sat back down. Now they were all ready.

Barbara began, "I—ah—was first born—to Nettie an' Vincent Burke—'bout tirty-eight year ago." The men didn't think she needed to go that far back, but she didn't know any other way to begin to say how she arrived to be living on a mountain. She paused right away, but as she saw their encouraging nods and smiles, she continued in the best English she could muster.

Ben hardly registered that she was thirty-eight years old. She might be. She certainly acted younger than her age if she was indeed thirty-eight. Maybe she miscalculated. But she said she lived eleven years in the cave. Where was she before that?

"Dere's a sister after me den two broders. Deir

names was Agnes, Reid an' Felix. One day, when I jus' turned fifteen and helpin' Ma with chores, I was at de back of de house a-hangin' up bed sheets to dry when I hear horses comin' fast to our house. I hear some gun shots, people screamin' and horse screams too. I run to de secret room me Pa built, you know in case of Cheyenne or Paiute, where he tol' us to hide if dere was ever trouble of any kind," she explained, shaking her index finger, imitating her father.

She continued when they nodded in understanding, "But I was de only one who'd made it dere. It sure was surprisin' to know dat trouble come from white men!" Her tone of voice quickened and got louder, "I could hear 'em yellin' and cussin', laughin' and bein' 'xcited when dey found treasure like Pa's gun, dat dey'd add to what dey called 'loot from the bank'. Hours later, I heard 'em ride off. I stayed hid dere a whole day, you know, in case one of 'em stayed b'hind, but I guess dey'd all run off togeder."

"Next mornin' when I come out I found ..."

She paused and gulped, her eyes had opened wide and teared up. For the first time in her life, she would put into words for someone else to hear what she had seen. Almost in a whisper then, involuntary tears rolling down and off her face, she swallowed and whimpered, "When I come out, I walk to de front of de house and 'bout four feet in fron' of me lay me broder Reid. He had dried blood all on his head and it was," she stammered, "it was half missin'. Shot!" She paused, still incredulous about her findings.

"Just a little bit furder on, me little broder Felix was all twisted dere on de ground and his tongue was stickin' out. The flies were a-comin' out of his mout. So, I took de kerchief from around me neck, shooed away dem flies and put it over his face. I think he might like dat."

She swallowed several times, cleared her throat,

never noticing the tears freely dripping off her cheeks while looking into the fire. She didn't see the disbelief on the faces of the men stuck on her every word as she continued, "Me Pa was just a bit more farder off. He died quick from a bullet to de heart. He was de lucky one. Me Ma, oh me Ma," she sobbed freely, "was at de door to de house, she must' of fight wid 'em cause her clothes were torn right off. She must'of died from a bump on de head cause dere weren't no blood dat I could see anywhere. Inside de house was me sister Agnes who'd died from a bullet to de heart too. I guess dey didn't want to boder with her. She was almost 'leven and I remember she ain't ever stop talkin'. Maybe she save me life by dyin'. She would-a call'd out for me if dey let her live, den dey'd of come a lookin'." She thought, *God rest their souls.*

Ben thought, *Well I guess English is that poor child's primary language after all.*

She stopped, wiped her face with the back of her hand and then again after Joe handed her his handkerchief. She drank the rest of her brandy but declined a refill when Adam offered. Finally, she exhaled. Seeing the compassion in Ben's eyes, she felt able to continue. Ben noticed that the more she spoke, the more words she remembered.

She got up and began moving around the place absentmindedly admiring and examining objects on tables like the checkered game. *Oh look, a piano.* She brushed her fingers on the keys, "I fear'd somethin' fierce dey'd come back. I run to de barn but dey done took de horses. So I run back to de house and start puttin' tings on me blankets. I took tings I would'na ever use and throw'd away. I run to de woods and found a place I tought was well hid and safe to sleep for de night. I could'na stay at de house. De nex' day, I go back to our farm and got more tings like all de blankets and tools I can use. I put dem with de food an' clothes dat I already got and put back some kitchen tings and some stupid ones like a doll and a game. Shoot, when would I ever need dose tings?" she mocked. No one answered.

"I jus' move around de place like dere was no dead bodies. Dose tings was jus' bumps in me way. That was de only way I could do what I needs to."

"By de tird day I was tinkin' better and decided to move on. I ain't ever go back to dat farm, I jus' set off a-walkin' as far as I could go. Everyting I was carryin' got heavier. De idear of a tra-vois for me to pull come to me in de night and de next day I built me one to suit me. Pa always said I was good wid rope. Oder dan dat one time to built the tra-vois, I ain't stop walkin' for days—far away from people cause I didn' know who's I can trust. I walk 'til I get to an old empty cab'n."

She had made her way back to the sofa and sat again. She smiled then, "Me Pa'd taut me to fish an' hunt an' all kinds of tings cause for seven years he t'ought he weren't gonna be havin' any boys. He stopped learnin' me dose tings when Reid were five and I's twelve, but I knew'd how to do all dose tings by den anyhow. So at fifteen, it weren't hard livin' in the cab'n dat I fix up. Dere was good water in de well. I knew'd how to chop wood and fix a leaky roof, but I never know'd how hard it was to do tings until I had to do 'em all by me-self. But dere weren't no one 'round to rush me to do anytin' or tell me what I ought to do first. I wished lots of times dere'd been. Over de years, I b'come stronger and spend less time a doin' chores as dey got easier."

The men nodded in agreement that her youthful physical appearance would be unrecognizable from the frame of her now. She had muscular shoulders and arms, and a tiny waist that in contrast exaggerated the span of her shoulders. They immediately respected her strength inside and out and her ability to adapt to her environment and survive the unforgiving forest and mountains.

"Fur twelve years, I live in de cab'n. I found dat I weren't 'fraid s'long as I were 'lone. When I'd heard horses a racin' to me cab'n, I'd run out de back window and head for de woods. Two times I lost all me food to some bad men dat stopped in me cab'n. Some of 'em even took blankets. I watch 'em from de woods and when dey'd all left, I'd go back. Den I go look for an old empty farm and see if dose folks left anyting b'hind dat'd be good fur me to use. It only took me de first time of losin' everyting to built me a cache somewhere hid in de woods and keep me some o' me supplies dere."

Adam interrupted, "What did you hunt with?"

She replied, "Me Pa put a rifle an' bullets an' even a knife in his hidin' room. I could'na practice any, but over de years I got better at shootin' the rifle."

"Did you run out of bullets or find out that they were no good after so many years?" Ben asked knowingly.

"Yep, I run out of bullets two or tree times. But once I was lucky 'nd found 'alf a box of 'em behind a broken cabinet in an ole 'bandoned prospector's cabin and anoder time I find two boxes in a bag around de neck of a dead horse."

Adam asked anew, "How come the bad men didn't steal those things?"

She replied, "I's always had de rifle wit' me and grab me de bullets a'fore I run away."

"Ah, of course. I see," nodding his head.

Hoss asked, "Did you know how to butcher and tan pelts too?"

She replied, "Not 'xactly, I got better at dat over de years, but I ain't never got good at makin' proper clothes from de furs. Dey work, but don't fit good." Ben encouraged her to get back to the story and the two of them could talk furs later.

"Sure," she nodded, "years later when I were out a'huntin', de rain was a pourin' like dere were no t'morrow. I hunkered down an' hid under some big branch. I kept a'movin' back to de trunk of de tree but dere weren't one. I'd found a cave. I saw dat de openin' had space big, high, for me head. I mean tall 'nough. I look in it an' found a back way out on de oder side. It was a crooked way out, but a way out jus' de same. I also see a rock over me head dat was funny lookin'. It let light come in but not de rain. Later when it'd stopped a rainin', I climb up dere and seen dat dere were, I mean, I seen dat dere was a rock a hangin' over de hole. It caught de rain an' made it roll away from de openin'."

"It didn't take me long to move me tings in. I was sure dat no tief, I mean no thh-ief, would ever find me-my home now. I'd hardly found it me-myself! So I moved in and been livin' dere for eleven years dis-here summer." She thought that was enough information for them to learn how she had found the cave. She didn't want to tell them too much about her home and the surrounding terrain in case they wanted to go look for themselves.

That cave had been her most precious find ever. The cave was not apparent to the human eye. It just looked like a giant rock, all around. The front opening was actually a foot taller than her but when you looked back out toward the forest all you could see was bushy trees in front of the entrance.

The more she had learned about the cave, the safer she felt. The forest floor for at least five hundred square feet around was pure rock so she would no longer have to sweep away her footprints leading to and from her home because there weren't any. Leaving tracks in the winter snow never caused her concern of being detected because few people traveled that high up in the mountains in the cold months.

She could also enjoy the winters more because she could build fires as big as she needed and cook meat and not be mindful of the smoke and aromas coming out of her makeshift chimney.

There was a brook nearby that she used year-round. Even when it froze over in winter, she was able to chip away at it and melt the ice. It wasn't as convenient as the well back at the cabin as she now needed to haul water to drink and wash, but it was a minor setback that she easily looked past.

Adam remarked, "The outlaws knew better than to stop for too long. A posse might have been after them. Besides, they were probably heading to Mexico to spend their loot, as you say." Everyone nodded in agreement to Adam's observation.

Joe asked about her horse, "Where did Vincent come from?"

"Oh, 'bout tree years past, I saw stampedin' cattle surprise a herd of wild horses. De scar'd animals'd hurt a mare real bad, so I kill't her, took her hide an' meat. Her little one follow'd de smell of its ma. I name him Vincent, after me Pa. He is my friend. Vincent helps get goods to de cave, but I need to go a'lookin' for more hay or straw all de time jus' to feed 'im and care for 'im in winter," she said shaking her head back and forth.

"I give him all my 'tention," *and love*, she thought but didn't say it out loud.

"An' one day he let me ride him. I built a bigger tra-vois for Vincent cause he's bigger and stronger." She said with a smile that lit up her whole face and made the four men smile back.

Joe asked, "How do you know you were alone for almost twenty-three years?" Ben leaned in, anxious to hear her answer.

She thought, *I wasn't really alone, I had God to talk to every day.*

She stood up then and removed the belt from around her waist. She showed them the cuts in the leather and explained, "I take it from Pa a'figurin' he had no need fur it no more. And at de end of every spring or at de beginnin' of summer I cut anoder mark on it."

She had now explained her whole life. The men were impressed with her determination and courage—two virtues Ben respected very much. Other less strong people would have gone mad. She seemed to have grown because of the safety in being alone. Amazing, simply amazing!

Joe asked, "How did you get around to saving our Pa?"

"Well, 'bout a week and a half ago I seen that me supplies was gettin' low. I feeled the warm wedder come up fast and know'd dat thh-e mountains would let go of its snow after two or th-ree days of th-at. So I get my supplies ready to go take me some furs and meat that the avalanche would make. That's when I saw y'ur Pa's wavin' hand a'fore it got cover'd with snow. I worked as fast as I could to save 'im and I did. Well, you know that and the rest now," she smiled proudly as she pronounced her the's and that's correctly, standing to wander the room once again.

Ben gasped, "You mean to say you only saw my hand? That was it? What luck, pure luck that you happened to see it at all!" Indeed. She nodded, twice.

The boys let Ben's comment sink in and realized how close they had all been to losing their father. They sat in grateful silence still thinking about Barbara's lonely life and wondering how they might have fared in her place.

A beautiful sound suddenly filled the room. The men turned towards the sound and saw Barbara playing on the piano the tune she had hummed all those lonely years. She stopped abruptly and turned toward them. Seeing the amazement on their faces, she simply explained that she couldn't play any further because she couldn't remember the rest. Another wonder.

The tranquility that followed reminded Ben that

he was very tired. He asked Hoss to help him to his room and politely bid his other sons and Barbara goodnight. Barbara stood, wanting to tend to Ben as she had for the past few days—but relinquished the task to his capable son.

Adam asked Barbara if there was anything else he could get her. "Yes. Any chance I can have me-myself a bath a'for goin' to bed?"

While water was heated and hauled, she kept looking around the place. As she lifted up an item or turned her eyes to a painting, Joe quickly explained what the item was and where it had come from. Her questions about the objects fascinated Joe and he was stunned that she had never seen some of the things that he took for granted.

The tub was filled and Adam explained that she only needed to pull the plug for the water to drain. She pointed to a funny looking seat in the corner of the room and asked, "What's that?"

"Oh," exclaimed Joe, "that's a toilet. You do your business on that and pull this string when you're done. The best part is we don't have to haul it outside anymore. I think it's one of the greatest inventions that Adam made sure to build into the house. Don't you agree?"

She nodded, her eyes open as wide as they would go.

In her room later, after the long, soothing bath, she sat in front of the mirror and reached for the comb. She could remember her mother telling her to start from the bottom when untangling with a comb before brushing. After drying more tears from her tired and sad face, and for the first time in many, many years, she then picked up the brush. She brushed for an hour before braiding it and lying down to again sleep in a proper, soft bed. Tomorrow she would bathe and brush her hair again.

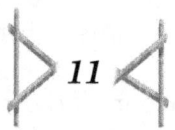

February 15, 1863

THE AROMA OF HOTCAKES AND BACON GOT Barbara out of bed. She had never slept-in a day in her life. She had always had too many things to do. She thought she could easily get used to such a soft bed, a luxurious bathtub, and a life without pressing responsibilities. She joyfully got herself up and ready for the day but when she opened her bedroom door, she discovered a boy's work pants and shirt neatly folded on the floor in front of her door. She smiled as she imagined that a younger Joe would have worn these, maybe not that long ago. She picked them up and quickly changed into them.

When she arrived downstairs, she was alone with Ben at the breakfast table. She wasn't disappointed with the lone company of the man she had grown very fond of, but she wondered if he had sent his sons away, and if so, for what reason.

Ben spent a moment looking at her attire and neat braids. He asked her to sit, pouring her a cup of coffee. She would have preferred her regular morning tea of dried dandelion leaves and wild herbs that she would have gathered and dried over the spring and summer months, but no matter. He offered her plates of food and she dished up her breakfast. Once she had satisfied her stomach, Ben leaned in and said, "I sent my sons to do their chores so we could talk."

She immediately felt disappointment. She was sure he was going to bid her farewell and thank her for everything she had done but that she would no longer be required now that he was home safe with the people he loved. She was at a loss as to how to express her desire to stay. How could she communicate it?

Ben smiled at her and she couldn't help but smile back.

He took her hand and said, "Barbara, I could never repay you for saving my life and for returning me here to my sons and home. I'm sure you know everything that means anything to me is right here. I don't have to explain that. But after having heard your story yesterday and having all night to think about how I could repay you, I've decided to ask you what you want and if I can give it, I will."

Barbara was a little surprised by what Ben said. It was almost as if he had read her mind. He couldn't, of course, he had just placed himself in her situation and assumed she may want such an opportunity. She concluded that Ben's virtuous gift was that of justice.

She said, "Don't know what ya mean, Ben. I don't know'd what I want, so how c'n I ask it?" She had to stop herself from reaching for the white bandage that covered the cut on his forehead.

Ben was a bit surprised by her answer but thought about it and said, "Well, if you want money, or a different life, new clothes—ah, meant for a woman, or lessons to relearn to read music and play the piano, or want to build a cabin on my ranch somewhere, or whatever it may be, I would see to getting you whatever it is, if I can provide it."

It was her turn to think. She ate a little bit, drank more coffee and said, "Ben, I been away from people fur a long, long time. Could I live here fur a bit to see if'in I c'n get alon' with people? I be no trouble. I c'n cook, chop wood, clean the barn, whatever ya say, I'll do. I jus' need to know if I like bein' round people ag'in a'fore decidin' if'in I want to live in a house or cab'n near here. I'm a gonna need new clothes, oh they don't have to be fancy or nothin', just more girly like. Can you help me with that?"

Ben was elated. He hit the table with an open hand and said, "I can most certainly do that. You will stay here at the house until you have decided if you like being around people. We'll buy you new clothes right away. Joe can help you with that. Then later on, we will bring you to town and introduce you to more people. If that is too much, too fast, we'll hold back and try again some other time. We can see what you need as we go along and help every way we can. How's that?"

She couldn't be more pleased. She smiled and said, "That suits me jus' fine. Yep, jus' fine."

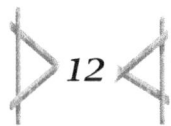

12

Early March 1863

FOLLOWING HER DECISION TO STAY ON THE ranch, Barbara made a point every day of spending time alone with each of the Cartwright men to see what she could learn from them. They each had different gifts that she wanted to draw from.

During the time she spent with Adam, he taught her how to read the musical notes on the limited music sheets he had and lent her books that he thought she could manage. He was surprised that she remembered how to write the alphabet and count numbers. She didn't think it was so astonishing. She spent her winter days counting to one thousand, and reciting and writing the alphabet in a sandy patch on the floor of her cave. How else did he think she passed time during the cold seasons?

Adam decided to also give her a book on etiquette. She appreciated that but after having read what it contained, she stubbornly decided to adapt only the teachings that suited her. She had been alone too long to mind what society said she should, could, shouldn't, and couldn't do. But she did benefit greatly, or rather her posture benefited, from the requirement that ladies walk with grace—as Adam had her practice daily, with a book balanced on top of her head.

Following her endless questions about what she had read, especially on etiquette, Adam would shake his head and often just walk away. His reactions would make her chuckle. Patience was obviously not his virtue.

Barbara's mother, Nettie, had a knack of discerning what other people's gifts were, and Barbara found herself trying to do the same thing.

When it came to Adam, she most appreciated him teaching her how to speak properly. In that aspect, he was very gifted and determined. He would correct her constantly until she ceased to use incorrectly conjugated verbs, mispronunciations and misplaced words in sentences.

She very much respected his knowledge when he tried to explain how he had built this house; that he had studied architecture and had become an architect through years of schooling. She disappointingly found that she had to stop him at almost every sentence to explain one word or another. She had so much to learn. To her delight, he eventually figured out that it was easier to explain the trade words as he went along.

She could tell he loved this house that he designed. Building it was a challenge and the final product had proven his idea that a high ceiling with a loft overlooking a grand room would hold if beams were placed in the appropriate locations. Not many houses had bedrooms upstairs in a loft, so his design was highly innovative.

Adam showed great interest in how she had devised her travois and the lean-to on the mountain and how her father had built his secret, hidden room. What started as conversations to test her spoken grammar became more as he truly was interested in the topics and her answers.

She liked Adam and knew he was a very sophisticated and educated man. She liked that he never made her feel small or a lesser person than he. She discerned that his virtues were diligence and determination—if not patience. He would never give up on something he knew he could teach her. He would find a way to explain it so she could eventually understand.

~

During the time she spent with Hoss, he taught her how to tend to the farm animals, to learn about the current equipment used to harness horses to buggies, and even how to drive one. Her father had never owned or driven anything but a wagon and she had never led a team of horses.

She was very shy whenever a ranch hand would be nearby, so Hoss took great care in protecting her. He treated her as a guest and the hired help knew better than to ask impolite questions as to the identity of visitors, even those who did not dress as expected.

He gave her tours of the ranch and showed her where the cattle grazed, where the lumberjacks cut down trees and where the best hunting and fishing were located. When they would pass by one of his favorite fishing holes or where he might have had a picnic had it been summertime, he would stop and explain what was there underneath the coating of snow.

She would tell him about the animals she had befriended over the years and the stories surrounding those encounters. There had been countless squirrels, several rabbits, a raccoon or three, a couple of foxes, a crow and even a lynx.

Her interests piqued when one day he introduced her to a Paiute woman. Of her tribe, the woman was the most skilled at tanning hides. In a few hours, Barbara had learned how to make herself a dress of tanned hide. She may not have use of the skill in the future, but she was grateful for learning. She truly loved Hoss' tender demeanor and his gentle touch with animals and how he had remembered her interest in working with furs.

It took time for her to learn to ride a horse using a saddle. Hoss was gifted at noticing what she was doing wrong and in helping her to get it right. But she mostly treasured how he taught her to fit her horse, Vincent, with shoes. Right from the beginning, she knew Hoss' greatest virtue was patience.

~

During the time she spent with Joe, he taught her to dance. He enjoyed the young ladies he met at social events and talked about them often. Barbara's curiosity was piqued on what the ladies wore, what music was played, and who would attend such a party.

Late in the second week of her stay at the house, on a supply run, Joe brought her into town and introduced her to the owner of the ladies' shop, Darlene, who fitted her into two new frocks, modest as they were. Barbara did not want anything expensive or elegant—she just wanted ordinary, everyday clothing. This was her first exposure to people in town.

Barbara insisted on bringing back Joe's old clothing she had worn before the purchase as she would use those for chopping wood and whatever other dirty chore there was to do around the house. But she loved the store-bought dresses and wouldn't wear anything else unless the chore demanded it.

She felt close to Joe—although he was young enough to be her son—he treated her as a sister and friend. She gradually drew up the nerve to approach him with something she was longing to ask. He was surprised to learn that she was questioning her femininity and that she wanted to learn how to be a proper lady. He couldn't see anything wrong with the person she was, and he asked her why she wanted to change who she was.

She thought about it for a moment and when she looked up at Joe, she had eyes full of tears. "I want to be the woman my parents would have raised, a woman they would be proud of. This is my chance to become that person. I'm not lookin', I mean, I'm not looking to change who I am, only to improve."

Joe couldn't agree more. "I see. I will help you with that as much as I can. But I think you are already doing it."

The next day, Joe showed her the ranch's herd of horses. He was proud of the fine line of horses they were developing at the ranch. He hoped one day that they would be the best line of domesticated Mustangs in the county. He, Adam, Hoss and the ranch hands spent great efforts and aching backs to tame and add good quality animals to the Cartwright stock.

Like all of the Cartwright men, Joe was kind. She decided that he was yet too young for her to determine his other virtues.

~

Barbara spent her time with Ben learning how to run a household and a ranch. She probably would never own such a large house or busy ranch, but the more she knew how to run one, the easier her future would be and the more likely she would avoid financial difficulties. Ben had gone so far as opening a bank account for her to manage. He paid her one dollar a week for the little bit of chores his sons left for her to do around the house and ranch. She was elated to finally understand the concept of money and spending.

Barbara asked Ben if she could take over the cooking and cleaning of the house. He answered, "Lee has been with us for twenty years. But about fifteen years ago he fell into a ravine and broke both his legs. Although he healed enough to stand and walk again, he has never been able to sit on a horse for more than an hour at a time. At first, we missed him on the trail, but then he volunteered to tag along in the cook's wagon. To stay busy and be useful, he learned to cook. He was good at it and we asked him to stay on as the house cook when the cattle drive was over. He eventually took on more housework when cooking didn't take up all of his time. This is his only way to earn a living. So, you see, I could not ask you to take over his jobs. You understand, don't you?"

"Of course, I understand. I didn't know." She thought for a moment and then suggested, "I need to learn those things. Do you think he would be willing to teach me what he knows?"

"I'm sure that can be arranged." Ben asked Lee to show Barbara how to do what he did so she could run her own place when she eventually would have one of her own.

Lee was all too happy to help and didn't feel threatened by Barbara's enthusiasm. Lee and Barbara quickly became good friends.

Wednesday of her third week's stay at the ranch, she accompanied Ben to town to run his few errands. They picked up the mail and then headed to the bank. She was relieved that the Banker was the lone occupant of the building at the time of their meeting. Her signature was required to complete the opening of her new account.

As Ben and Barbara exited the bank, they ran into the sheriff, Roy Coffee. When introductions were made and pleasantries were done, Barbara quickly excused herself and walked over to the buggy to wait for Ben. As Ben stayed to chat with the sheriff for a bit, passers-by mostly nodded at Ben, but some stopped and chatted while stealing glances at the stranger who everybody knew was staying at the Cartwright's ranch.

Ben—always gracious towards his house guests but knowing how shy Barbara was—cut conversation short and left. He normally tolerated idle chit chat, but he didn't want to encourage gossip, which he detested.

Ben was impressed with Barbara's capability to remember what he had taught her the week before and the week before that. He rarely had to repeat an instruction more than once. This was apparent when he had come upon her one day, cleaning her gun. He had shown her his great gun collection a day earlier and had taught her how to dismantle, clean and shoot with them. He was pleased when she used his materials to polish up her own weapon.

In all the things she learned, there was nothing she disliked and what she liked most was the time spent with Ben. Among others, like justice, he had the virtue of charity.

All four of her hosts were attentive and gentle. She felt very special and even loved.

13

July 11, 2019

GABRIEL WAS IMMEDIATELY SURROUNDED BY HIS ten cousins, curious about his finding.

Joel's eyes were sparkling as Gabriel said, "Open your hand." Then he placed an item in Joel's palm.

Joel's hand stayed open for the others to see the tiny gold bracelet. He then examined it more closely. "Is there an inscription, Gabriel?" he exclaimed excitedly.

"I believe so! But it is so worn, I can't tell what it says."

"What do we do now? How much do you think it is worth? Where exactly was it found? Should we look further?" Questions were being fired at Joel.

He held up a hand and said, "We'll get it cleaned professionally and see what it says. This might be exactly what we are looking for."

Gabriel said, "You know that if it is, we won't have to dig further."

Joel nodded and said, "The next thing we have to do is go to Virginia City and find the city's archived records."

Small details of Ben Cartwright's story had been lost over the decades, and the cousins needed to research the official records to combine with their findings. Only then would they have the entire picture of what happened all those years ago and possibly the answer to the mystery.

Joel continued, "We need to look up 4G Grandpa Ben's lawyers' files and the name of the man who asked him to bring back the package."

"Will you do that, Joel?" asked Camille.

"No, I have to stay here at the dig. We risk having the operation closed down by the Bureau of Land Management if the archaeologist responsible for the project is not present. Does anyone want to go in my place? I think two of you could handle the job. You may have to go to Carson City, too. It's possible that this search could end up nowhere, so be prepared to be disappointed."

Dominique and Michael suggested that they could go dig through the archives. After all, they were still in college and used to doing research. They pointed out that neither of them had to be anywhere special until late August. Neither did Eriq nor Gabriel, but they said they would rather continue working outside on the dig than sit in a stuffy file room in Carson City or Virginia City.

Joel said, "Yes. That's excellent. Now I think someone should find out if the leather remnants we found might have an insignia. Can anyone do that?"

"I have to go back to work," Phil said. "You too, Nat?"

His sister Natalie nodded. "Cel too," she said as she pointed to Joel's sister.

"But," Natalie continued, holding up her right hand's index finger, "I know someone who might be able to find something on the leather. I could bring the remnants with me."

"Excellent!" exclaimed Joel.

"I only have a day of my vacation left," said Stephanie. "I'll have to pack up at camp later and leave in the morning." She sounded very disappointed at the possibility of missing out on more discoveries.

Joel, Eriq, Gabriel, Camille and Jackie would stay at the dig. Jacqueline, who worked shift work hours, could stay for only another three days.

~

The members of the small groups parted ways the next morning, agreeing that they would text each other on any updates.

From Virginia City, Michael and Dominique were indeed sent to Carson City where the archives of the state's cities and towns, still existing or not, were held. They arrived late that afternoon and called to make arrangements to see someone the next day. They spent their evening watching sports on television in Michael's room and then Dominique retired to her adjoining room for sleep.

The next day, Saturday, they made their way to 100 North Stewart Street. They told the bedtime story of the piece of jewelry meant for a Mr. Devon. The attendant listened to their story and said, "I'm not sure you will find anything. But I am happy to say that about twelve years ago, we updated all our archives electronically. You can insert whatever name, person or town you want and read whatever information that has been captured."

He continued, "You can expand your search by inserting an underscore in between words you know should appear next to each other, like Virginia and City; otherwise, you will get all the articles that would have the first name Virginia in them and regretfully any item with the word city in it. You can also insert a hyphen in between words like Henry-Devon if you want only articles that would hold both his first and second name. Of course, that strategy doesn't promise you will find anything, but it might narrow it down from too many articles on Henry or Devon. And you should know, if the documents have the words in brackets, they might not show up as one of the hits. Good luck on your search."

He couldn't offer any other helpful search criteria. The attendant was not hired to search with or for them. He led them to an area where two computers were set up, side by side. The computers were strictly for use in searches of the archived items, so the responses were not cluttered with irrelevant google answers.

Michael and Dominique made a list of the names they wanted to look up and decided they would add to it if nothing was found on the first list. If too much information was provided on a name or their search was too vague, they might decide to call in more cousins for additional help.

They started with the name Devon. Neither knew Devon's lawyer's name in the Sacramento office, but they were not sure if that information would have shown up in the State of Nevada records anyways. The next name on the list was 4G Grandpa Ben's lawyer, Fred Mason.

They were pleased to see newspaper articles among the archived items. But as they couldn't insert dates into the search criteria, the matches for Mason numbered at 253,821. When they inserted the first name Fred, they were disappointed that the matches only decreased to 147,242.

Michael shook his head and returned to the search screen where he inserted a hyphen in between the first and second name. Dominique looked up Henry-Devon and Michael looked up Fred-Mason. Michael had 1,247 hits, but Dominique had 5,644. Those numbers were unmanageable and would possibly not even provide the desired results.

After the words Devon and Mason, they inserted an underscore followed by the name Cartwright in the hopes that if either man had dealings with 4G Grandpa Ben, the document would be singled out. Their searches were narrowed down to a mere 572 and 655 respectively. Almost manageable.

They tried anew with an underscore before Virginia. They decided that they need not add the word City. They thought the series of four words would suffice. The searches were narrowed down to 184 and 253. Very manageable. They started reading.

Hours later, Michael knew something important had been found when he heard the hum of the printer nearby. He looked up and saw a victorious grin on Dominique's face. It was not a competition between the two, but at this moment, it felt like one. She had found something first.

March 15, 1863

OF THE FOUR MEN, JOE WAS THE ONLY ONE WHO knew what Barbara learned from each of his family members. She didn't want the others to know what she was doing to better herself or how long it took her to advance to what she considered an acceptable level—a no-need to learn anything more level. She didn't want to be considered a failure or a slow learner, even if they had no one to compare her to.

Life on the ranch became easier for her to understand. She didn't have to go into town if she didn't want to and found that she could easily avoid it just by refusing an offer to tag along. No one would be offended. Smiles and laughter were always in abundance at the ranch and she never tired of them now that they were a part of her daily life again.

Around the supper table in the evenings, the men would talk about their day, issues that had come up, events in the near future, and the needs of the ranch. She felt very much a part of the family but never expressed it for fear that they would consider her an outsider, or worse, an intruder.

Joe often mentioned a special event that was to occur in less than a month that included dancing. Everyone else seemed to know all about it but her. She finally asked where it was being held and when.

Ben replied for Joe, "Why, it's here on the 17th next month. We have made it a tradition to welcome spring by inviting all of our neighbors and friends for a party and dance before the real heavy ranch work begins. You could meet a lot of people from town and around here. You already met the banker when we opened your bank account; our sheriff, Roy Coffee, who was walking by and I introduced you. Then we stopped in at the general store and you met the owner and his wife ..."

Joe added, "And, there is the woman at the ladies' shop where we bought your new clothes."

She remembered the trip to the ladies' shop well. She had marveled at the soft fabric. The woman, Darlene, was in awe at how Barbara did not have to wear a corset in order to fit them so well. There had been a disagreement as to what to wear underneath. Barbara indicated that she was most comfortable with little or nothing at all. She had come out of the change room wearing only the new dress. Almost scandalized, Darlene explained the various undergarments and Barbara finally agreed, to the owner's relief, on a full-bodied slip.

Even though Barbara thought the dresses she chose were fancy, Joe thought they were too plain and tried to convince her to make a different decision. He eventually agreed to buy them when Barbara insisted that they would be used for everyday. When they returned to the ranch, the other three men voiced that she looked fine and complimented her on choice of style. Secretly, Adam and Hoss did not really think that way about the dresses—to them the frocks were ordinary, but they kept their thoughts to themselves.

Ben continued, "Why a lot of the people you would deal with on a regular basis are going to be here. What do you say, do you want to come? Please, be our guest of honor." He felt a responsibility toward introducing her to more people, even possible suitors. He was already making a mental note to invite the two bachelors he knew who were in their late thirties, early forties.

She could feel her shoulders tensing up. She had not spent much time with other people. She was shy. She did not really know anyone other than the four men in the room and Lee. She was at a loss for words and excused herself from the table. In response to her panic, she fled. She ran outside toward the horses' meadow and stopped at the fence to look out at them.

Inside, the abandoned men at the table looked at each other questioningly and then Joe ran out after her, grabbing a couple of coats on his way out.

When he reached her, she said as she put on one of the coats Joe had brought, "I can't go to the dance. I'm not ready, Joe. I don't know how to act around people. I don't even know if I can dance well enough to not embarrass myself. I've been gone for so long. How can I be ready so soon?"

She couldn't tell Joe that what she really wanted to do was to impress his father. She had fallen in love with Ben in the past month. He never judged or reprimanded her. He had shown her great respect and she knew in her heart he was genuine. He didn't pretend when he treated her as deserving of all of the human kindnesses he directed her way. She couldn't bear to cause him any embarrassment. She was concluding that she would voluntarily leave the ranch with the pretense that she needed to go check on her things at the cave. But how could she do that when she had grown to like it here so much?

Joe said encouragingly, "You didn't know how to act around us at first but you do now."

That's true, she thought.

"Besides, we have more than one month to go before the dance. You know, those people are not as sophisticated as you might think and you have plenty of grace and skill when it comes to dancing, believe

71

me! You are a good student and even though I don't know everything the others are teaching you, I don't have anything more. You don't really have to worry about anything except for a new dress! What do you say, shall we go shopping? I'd love to help you buy a special dancing dress if you'll let me."

"Oh, Joe, do you mean it?" she beamed. He nodded and she asked, "Can we go tomorrow?"

He laughed now. "Tell you what," he said, nodding, "tomorrow we'll go look for a dress."

15

March 14, 1863

THE NEXT DAY, JOE AND BARBARA WENT SHOPPING and found two styles of party dresses that Barbara liked very much. Joe caved in and ended up buying both. One would be ready by Friday and the other would be ready the following Thursday.

She said excitedly, "Now I wish for another special occasion so I can wear them both."

Joe laughed knowingly and said, "How about planning a special supper at the International House Hotel across the street on Friday? We'll invite Pa, Adam and Hoss to join us so they can all see how you've surpassed your desire to better yourself and in such a short time too. It will be your coming-out dress."

"Yes, let's." Her eyes were wide open as she giggled and forgot all about her fears of facing Ben's peers the next month. She loved that she would be planning a surprise that might impress Ben as early as the following week. She loved that she would be the belle of the dance party. She loved that she didn't feel she would have to leave the ranch. But she also feared that Ben may never look at her any differently than he did now, like she was his ward or he her stepfather. Could he feel anything but protective toward her, she wondered. She sighed.

But excitement overtook the momentary glumness.

By the Friday, her first dress was ready. As planned by Joe, the evening for Barbara's special revealing supper had arrived. He had left her with a couple of his saloon female friends, Yolanda and Yvonne, who would fix her hair and apply creams and powder to her face.

During the time that Barbara had been at the shop trying on dresses the previous week, Joe had visited the saloon and met up with both women. He had told them about Barbara's lack of exposure to feminine rituals. He knew their curiosity would be piqued and challenged and that they would be eager to help out in any way possible.

By late morning on the Friday, Joe had introduced Barbara to the two women and left them to accomplish what they could. She was surprised to learn that saloon girls spent a great amount of time on their appearance. She was not reluctant to allow them to work on her. She actually looked forward to it when she could see how lovely they themselves looked.

The women studied her face and determined that added creams and blushes would make her eyes come alive and her high cheek bones pop out. Something also had to be done with the tied-back hair and her pale eyebrows.

Barbara was impressed with the creams that hid her overgrown freckles on her cheeks. They added powder to her eyelids that made her blue eyes come alive and demand being noticed and a dark shadow to her eyebrows that gave her a much-needed crowning to her new face.

She looked at herself in the handheld mirror and couldn't believe how a little bit of powder changed her from a plain old spinster to a lovely woman.

The two women then expressed their delight in the color of her hair. They started playing with it and convinced her that a certain style would be very flattering, if she would allow them to try it out. As Barbara was already impressed with the cream mixtures and powdered colors on her face, she enthusiastically agreed. She was overjoyed with the end result; that of shinier and healthier looking hair.

The hair above her ears all the way up to the top of her head was gathered, but not too tight. It was tied back and then curled to drape at the back. Wisps of hair had been drawn out to fall softly on both sides of her face. The rest of her hair had been curled as well but as it was not gathered, it easily covered her shoulders like a strawberry red shawl.

When she was finally ready, her heart was beating so hard in her chest that she felt sure people could hear it. The two girls convinced her that she was just imagining that. They told her to not forget to breathe and to remember what she had been taught with respect to good posture and etiquette. She didn't know if she could remember all the rules, but she hoped that she would remember the most important ones, the ones that she didn't mind obeying. The two women kept telling her she was going to be just fine and to rest assured that she did not have any bad habits to unlearn, to only put into practice what she had learned well.

Of all the hard things she had to do to survive on the mountains, this was harder. People didn't see or judge her on the mountain. Here, people had an opinion on everything. How could she be ready so soon to face society? But Joe had started her off slowly and convinced her that she only had to face the four of them this evening. That she would do just fine. That she had learned everything she needed to get through the meal.

He even gave her pointers on several topics of interest she could bring up if there was a lull in the conversation. If she could get through this evening like a lady, she would have absolutely no problem with the dance party next week or any other event, ever. He promised. But if there was a glitch, no one at the table would care and she still had some time to address it. She needed to know if she was ready. She needed a boost to her confidence.

The time had come. She exited the saloon girls' lodging by the side entrance and instinctively lifted her skirts to step up onto the wooden sidewalk. Not very many people walked the streets of Virginia City at the supper hour, but those who were there turned to watch the unaccompanied beautiful stranger make her way to the hotel's restaurant a few doors down.

The men seated at the table had been waiting for about ten minutes for their special guest. Adam even compared their wait for her to the first meal they had shared together. Hoss agreed and said she was becoming quite the lady indeed, making the men folk wait like this. Their father smiled at their jovial remarks.

Ben was facing the entrance and didn't recognize her when she entered the room. He mentioned to his sons that there was a lovely lady standing near the door—and he was right. Her hair, now reaching to her mid-back in shiny curls, her peaches and cream face, and the outstanding blue of the gorgeous dress that made her gentle blue eyes and red hair stand out, made her a stunner to be sure.

At Ben's comments, the boys looked back to the door and Joe was the only one to recognize Barbara's new dress. He quickly stood and offered his arm and looked her straight in the eyes and said, "You are the most beautiful woman in the room."

She sure felt that way. She gave him a warm smile, took his arm and let him lead her to the empty chair next to Ben's. The men had stood and waited for her to sit before sitting down themselves.

Ben was taken aback that he had not recognized her immediately. He couldn't take his eyes off the loveliness of the woman seated next to him. What grace. What charm she had. How could this woman possibly be Barbara? She was radiant, pleasantly different and yet the same wholesome person who had saved his life. How had he not noticed her perfectly chiseled nose before now or her eyes that held so much excitement?

As the evening progressed, there were eventual lulls in the conversation, just as Joe had anticipated.

At one point, she asked, "Adam, have you read about the difficulties and delays in the building of the Suez Canal?" Adam, giving Barbara a surprised and impressed smile, jumped in immediately to talk about one of his favorite new topics.

Later she said, "I heard that last week, one of your ranch hands caught a big fish in your favorite pond, Hoss." He was all too eager to retell the story.

She then mentioned, "I've come across an article about the financial scandal in Sacramento. It was fascinating how the men were caught embezzling!" and Ben added his comments and concerns to the story.

Joe and Barbara had given each other a knowing glance at each topic. At one point, she had managed to form the words "thank you" with her lips. He was just beaming with pride at her success. He couldn't take all the credit, but it sure was easy to be happy for her.

Prepared to be only an observer as Barbara impressed the other men, Joe was surprised when she pulled him into her circle of admirers. Turning her smile from the others, she looked at Joe and said, "I heard that someone in Utah bought a thoroughbred horse from England. I wonder how he got it here and how much he had to pay for such a prized horse." It was his turn to be totally engaged in a subject.

As the evening progressed, Ben found himself caught up in her transformation and almost forgot about the physically strong, rugged woman who had brought him down off that mountain. He forgot about her struggles with putting a sentence together. He forgot about her manly way of walking and her rough hands. That woman didn't seem to exist anymore.

He forgot about her ponytail and bland face because tonight her hair was loosely curled around her clear, soft face. Her hair wasn't tied tightly back behind her head or left free to get all tangled up. Her hair looked as lovely as it smelled, draping her bare, inviting, shoulders. Its style was quite effective in bringing out her lovely eyes. Her skin looked invitingly soft, but he only allowed himself the occasional patting of her hand.

Her outer appearance may have improved tenfold, but when she spoke, she was the same honest, innocent Barbara. She was not superficial. She probably couldn't become a fake, not now after all her years away from people and opportunities for developing bad habits from poor examples. She knew that her speech had improved one hundred percent. She was grateful that they were too polite to point out how bad her English had been just a few weeks ago.

After the fine meal and stimulating conversations, Joe managed to get Adam and Hoss to leave with him with the excuse of a poker game calling out to them somewhere in town. They thanked their special guest and said they enjoyed the lovely evening. They apologized for abandoning her to their father who would be kind enough to bring her back to the ranch, they were sure.

She felt just a little panic in her stomach, but that quickly disappeared. She smiled and turned to Ben and was locked into his eyes. His own eyes had hardly left her face all evening. The boys noticed and liked what they saw happening between the two. Barbara had worked hard to be acceptable at the social level she imagined Ben would expect from a potential wife. There, she had finally said it to herself. She wanted to be his wife! The boys knew too. It wasn't hard to guess.

But the rest of the evening was, disappointingly for Barbara, uneventful! Ben took them back to the ranch and then he excused himself to focus on his paperwork. She played the piano for a while, then retired for the night. Ben was distracted and couldn't get any work done, even after Barbara stopped playing the piano and bid him goodnight.

He slammed his journal shut and pushed himself away from his desk, poured himself a whiskey and began to wonder about his newly developed attraction to Barbara. When he had first met her, he admired her genuine innocence; her refreshing honesty and mature decision to step back into society. But his attraction to her this evening was on a physical level. He had thought of her as plain, but tonight he saw her for what she was—a beautiful woman. Wouldn't everyone be able to see that? He hadn't really seen it until this evening. He hadn't seen her feminine potential until tonight.

In spite of his attraction to the new beautiful Barbara, Ben decided that it was probably better if he continued to treat her like his ward. That was the decent thing to do. He didn't want to be a man who would be thought of having manipulated her in any way. She was a woman in her late thirties and not a young impressionable girl looking to settle down and start a family. She may be looking for companionship or love or even happiness, but she could still easily have the wool pulled over her eyes. He didn't have the right to expect that she should settle for him. Even though they were only eleven years apart in age, she needed to experience the attentions of men her age. Didn't she?

He knew she was infatuated with him. He wasn't blind to her signals. But she was naive and innocent. She should be more like a younger sister to him, shouldn't she?

April 11, 1863

THE NEXT EVENING, BEN EXCITEDLY BROUGHT a couple of papers with him to the supper table. He took Barbara's hand, noticed her blushing at the gesture and he was again reminded of a younger woman's reaction. Her youthful behavior made him more determined to treat her accordingly.

He told her and his sons that he had wired most of the towns down south and west on the other side of the mountains about Barbara's family and had finally received the answers. He proceeded to tell her where she came from and what happened to the farm where she lived, in that it had been sold to a group of miners who thought there were valuable minerals on the land. Then he began to tell her about her family's fate. Her neighbors found her family, but never found her body. Because of her age and gender, they surmised she had likely been kidnapped by the murderers for their use and abuse.

He asked, "Barbara, why did you not wait for relatives to come claim you?"

She looked at him in disbelief, "Other relatives? I don't think I had any. My mother told me once that they were all as good as dead."

He had details on how each member had been killed and with pity began to share the information, but stopped when he noted Barbara sitting in silence, staring at her plate. He immediately sensed how insensitive he had just been and tried to apologize.

He hadn't truly realized how the news was not all that good. He thought knowing exactly where she came from and what had happened to her family was of the most importance. Barbara excused herself, got up and quickly went to her room.

For the first time since she met him, she thought him inconsiderate. Could she ever be anything more to him than that hermit who became a woman? Crying in her pillow, she wondered if she would ever breathe normally again. How could she let herself fall in love with him? But she knew falling in love hadn't been something she could control. She loved him and that was that. He didn't love her and there was nothing she could do about it.

No one followed her to her room and for that she was grateful. She wouldn't have been able to put into words what she was feeling or explain the true reason as to why she was crying.

Downstairs, the men looked at each other grimly. No one followed her as none of the men could even begin to know how to console her or understand how she was feeling.

Upstairs, Barbara resigned herself to the new reality that she loved Ben and he would not be reciprocating. She would go to town on Thursday and get the final fitting for the dancing dress. Thanks to Yvonne and Yolanda, she knew how to apply the creams and to fashion her hair. All this would keep her busy.

After the party, she would move away and try to meet someone who would love her. She knew she could no longer live alone on the mountain, but more importantly, she knew she couldn't live here at the ranch house anymore either.

That evening, she spent over an hour in the clawfoot tub. She spent time crying and soaking. The crying didn't solve anything. It only made her feel a little bit better.

The bath worked its usual soothing magic. She ran her hands along the rim, remembering her beaten up tub at home. She wouldn't return to her cave retreat, but neither could she see herself staying here any longer.

April 17, 1863

FRIDAY THE 17TH WAS A BEAUTIFUL SUNNY, WARM day. Even though Barbara appreciated each new day given to her, she did not feel especially joyful today. She had taken special steps in her care of Vincent that morning, telling him about the two of them moving on again, but not back to the mountains. She would ask Ben for that cabin he had promised.

It would need to be far enough away that she wouldn't be able to see Ben from her house. She didn't want to be within yelling, whistling, singing or even a gunshot's hearing distance from Ben's home. She had to remove herself and the sooner she did, the sooner she could and would move on to find someone else to spend the rest of her life with. Making up her mind about her future helped her to cope through the rest of the day.

~

The temperature determined the set up for the evening of the dance. A favorable warm one meant the party would be held outside, the dancing on a floor made of rough wood planks. Inclement weather would move the festivities inside the ranch house. The ladies had full use of the toilet upstairs. The gentlemen were expected to use the outhouse at the back. Everyone was free to use the grand room for comfortable seating and as a quieter venue for conversations. Tonight, folks would begin their evening outdoors.

Barbara began to feel nervous as she watched people arrive within minutes of the specified seven o'clock. Shortly, she would meet so many people. Her hair was styled, her powder applied. She smoothed down the skirt of her new dress. On the outside, she was prepared to join the party, but emotionally, she wasn't near ready.

From the upstairs bedroom window, she watched the neighbors greeting each other. Folks were enjoying the cool evening and the refreshments while waiting for the music to begin. But there was also the anticipation of meeting the woman—the subject of gossip—who had been staying with the Cartwrights for the past couple of months. Why folks even knew her horse's name.

Adam, Hoss and Joe would never have left her to face all these strangers by herself—and they shortly knocked on her door to escort her from her room to the crowd outside. She noticed everyone looking in her direction but she calmed right down when she saw the smile on Ben's face. He approved.

Her smile faded. Ironically, Ben's approval didn't matter anymore because she didn't care to impress anyone now. She was leaving soon. Nothing about succeeding this evening was important anymore.

From the smiling faces in the crowd, everyone approved of her appearance. Well, not everyone. Not the widow Martha Cochran, who, according to most of Virginia City society, was the epitome of class and good manners. She believed herself to be the one everyone would look up to for guidance on how to better themselves and she certainly didn't think that the Cartwrights sheltering this strange woman was in good taste or sound judgment.

Barbara had not yet met Martha, or hardly

anyone else present, for that matter. She certainly didn't seek any stranger's approval or advice.

Ben beamed a huge smile, excused himself to the guests he had been talking to and, as promised, danced the first dance with Barbara. After the delightful dance, which made him wonder how she had learned it so well, he began to introduce her around to his other guests. But as one by one, his fellow ranchers began talking business with him, he left his sons to do the honors.

The widow Cochran had noticed how Ben and Barbara had looked at each other while they danced, and she needed to know the extent of the attraction. Would it lead to scandal? Was this brazen hermit after Ben's money, just because she saved his life? Was he going to be naively swayed or coerced by this cave dweller and have his reputation ruined?

The widow narrowed her eyes in determination. She was going to save her misguided friend, Ben, from this wrongdoing by calling out this deceitful little wench. She would confront her alone at first and if that didn't rectify the situation, she would publicly humiliate her in front of Ben's guests. In the end, Ben would thank her. Certainly, this Barbara was only manipulating Ben to get whatever it was that she wanted.

After Ben and Barbara's dance ended and the other guests had stopped staring at Barbara, Martha gracefully and purposefully walked up to Ben, fondly and almost intimately caressed his arm and gave the impression that she wanted to dance. He got the hint and of course, politely asked. They made their way to the dance floor, arm in arm.

The couple swayed to Barbara's favorite waltz— well her former favorite one now, she told herself. *What a handsome couple they make*, Barbara thought ruefully.

Martha, a beautiful and sophisticated woman, stayed close to Ben and monopolized his time. She continually made her presence known to him by caressing his arm or hand. His sons saw what she was doing, but felt helpless. They couldn't determine how to pry her away from Ben's polite attentions and they feared he was blind to the claws of this nasty widow.

After the music died down between pieces, Martha spoke to Ben loud enough for everyone within ten feet to hear. "Ben, you must come over to my estate on the thirtieth. Bring your wallet," she giggled. "I'm holding a fund raising event for the orphans in our region. We are endeavoring to sponsor one child a year by paying for their much-needed advanced education."

She leaned in towards Ben, as if they were co-conspirators, lowering her voice only slightly, "I am only inviting those whose contribution would be significant enough to make a difference, of course. There are so few who belong to that elite class such as ourselves."

She continued, louder now, "It will greatly add to the building of your reputation as being a leader in society and help you repair it from the unfortunate events of these past months," referring to the scandal of meeting a woman who chose to live alone and kill animals for food—and whatever else she did that was not civilized.

Ben was shocked at her comments. He knew that the remark was targeted directly at the woman who had saved his life and that if he were Barbara, he would have been insulted. But he was uncertain how to proceed—he knew that Martha had few boundaries when it came to what she considered protecting matters of society and reputation, yet he certainly felt insulted that Martha thought his reputation was somehow sullied by his relationship with Barbara. He excused himself, stumbling on his own words as he told the widow that he would think about it.

Folks who had overheard the entire conversation, pretended they had not caught the innuendo as they looked away.

Ben was distracted by Martha's comments and found it difficult to enjoy the rest of the evening. His sons instantly knew that Martha and her overt affection was testing their father's good manners. But Barbara did not know that. She just became more convinced that leaving this place was the right thing to do. She had already decided that the handsome couple deserved each other.

There had been one or two occasions in the past when the widow Cochran had been so pleasant that Ben had considered courting the well-mannered, good-intentioned, leader of society. But with her words this evening bouncing around in his head, he couldn't help but detect weaknesses she possessed. Weaknesses he could not tolerate—pride and arrogance.

The widow Cochran believed that she was superior to others in the county and that she was respected for her attributes of sophistication and community work. However, she was completely self-serving. She never showed recognition or gratitude to others who deserved it more than she did. She cared so much about her own reputation and with whom she associated that she behaved despicably to those who did not matter in society. Ben was disappointed to discover that about her and was relieved about the timely discovery before making a fool of himself.

After Martha's demeaning comments, Ben's sons were even more determined to make the evening truly memorable for Barbara. They introduced her around, took turns dancing with her and bringing her food and punch. Eventually, other men asked her to dance, some out of politeness and others out of curiosity. It didn't matter that Ben wasn't near her. She laughed at silly things people said and truly enjoyed herself.

With mixed feelings, Ben couldn't help but notice that even the older bachelors were talking and dancing with Barbara.

Mrs. Cochran was patiently waiting for the musicians to take a break. When they did, she made her way over to where Barbara was standing and visiting with a couple of the guests. The widow interrupted the small group and said, "I have been waiting all evening for an opportunity to talk to you, Miss Vincent. Shall we go find a more private place for a chat?"

Barbara took notice that she had named her after her horse! She had only met one other person in her whole life to whom she had taken an immediate dislike. That had been the school bully. But bullies were all the same, different genders and looks, but all the same underneath. Cowards! Barbara suddenly remembered her father had said that honesty and straight-forwardness often disarmed bullies.

With a smile, Barbara politely corrected the other woman but avoided the actual intent of the reference to her horse, "Vincent is my father's first name. I am Barbara Burke."

The widow took Barbara by the arm and led her to an unoccupied room near the study on the main floor. Barbara noted that the widow knew her way around Ben's house but was distracted from her thoughts as the widow continued, "Oh, I'm terribly sorry. How rude of me Miss Burke," Martha lied. She had fully intended on implying the horse by name. "I do believe I have never met any Burkes in all my travels. Oh, and there have been many."

Barbara thought, *Lucky Burkes for missing out.* She was too naive to have caught the inference that Martha was making—not only was *she* well-traveled and educated, but that the Burkes were *not* the rich kind of people who would be welcome in her circle of friends and acquaintances.

Martha was so determined to diminish this woman and put her in her place, she did not notice that Ben was in the study adjacent to the room where she had chosen to crush Barbara.

Ben was retrieving a book he had just finished reading, intending to return it to its rightful owner—a fellow rancher, who was in attendance at the party. He was about to rejoin his guests when he began to overhear a conversation. Although he hadn't seen who was in the other room speaking, he thought he would leave as it may be confidential or a private affair. But when he heard Barbara's name, he stayed.

Martha started, "I can tell that you are a jealous woman, my dear Barbara. Oh, I'm sure you can't help it. You've never had anything. Why even now, all of this belongs to the Cartwrights," she said, waving at Barbara's new dress.

Martha arrogantly continued, a crooked smirk of enjoyment on her face, "At some point this evening, you may have compared your sun-stained face to my soft, fair skin." Barbara unconsciously touch her cream-covered cheek.

Barbara's involuntary movement couldn't have pleased the widow more. She gleefully went on, "I will have you know that I have never spent a full hour out in the sun at any one time. You poor dear. You have probably compared our dresses and thought how we both look so elegant. But your dress was bought as a motion of charity by Ben Cartwright. That was kind of him, but you are not a woman worthy and deserving of Cartwright comforts."

"Now, I mean you no harm when I say these things my dear. Personally, I think you should distance yourself from the Cartwrights and make a proper life for yourself somewhere appropriate."

"You may know that I am known for my generous nature. I could arrange for you to go east to further your education—now that you have returned to the civilized world. You could become a more socially acceptable woman; one some man might consider as a wife one day. I have family out east whom I'm sure would accommodate you if I asked them. Why, I believe they even have an empty room in the maid's quarters! Now, please think on it and let me know. I'd like to help any way I can," she finished smugly, her hands finally resting after having waved around at almost every syllable.

She was sure she had pegged Barbara correctly and that the woman would not refuse her generous offer if she wanted to amount to anything in this life. Having fully enjoyed herself, Martha turned to leave the room.

April 17, 1863

BARBARA WAS STEWING BENEATH HER CALM composure. She might have considered such an offer to further her education from anyone else, but certainly not from this distasteful woman. She would never give the widow Cochran the satisfaction of having helped her in any way.

In the room next door, Ben was incensed. But before he had the chance to storm into the adjacent room and come to Barbara's defense, she spat back at the black widow in her sweetest voice, "Why, you are wrong Martha. I am not jealous of you or your things."

Martha turned back at the door, surprised that any words had come from the quiet woman.

"I have everything I could ever want. You see, when I wake up in the mornings, I am provided with fresh air and aromatic flowers to smell. I am surrounded by nature and animals that appreciate their freedom as much as I do. I go to bed at night with a sky full of stars that rock me to sleep with their stories. How could I possibly want what you have when I'm already the richest person in this room? With respect to my skin, I have never been vain enough for it to matter to me." She fully meant the innuendo.

Martha was surprised by Barbara's words. For someone with very little education, she certainly expressed herself very well.

Barbara went on, "As for Ben Cartwright, you do not know much about your host this evening if you think he notices the expensive lace wrapped around your skinny neck and wrists, or even cares. You cannot pretend to decide for him what he could and could not afford. You can think what you want of me. I, on the other hand, do not think of you at all. You're not important to me. Now, if you will excuse me, I have a dance to go back to."

And she dismissively left Martha. The widow's eyes and mouth had opened in disbelief that someone had the nerve to speak to her in such a way! The leader of society. How dare she!

Oh, that Barbara will pay for that rhetoric now, she thought. *You just wait! She really has no idea with whom she is up against.*

As she left the room, eager to go outside and put Barbara in her place, a hand on her shoulder held her in place and a stern "Martha!" made her catch her breath.

She wondered how long Ben had been there—and more importantly, how much he had heard!

"Oh Ben. I'm so glad to see you. I have discovered something very unnerving about your house guest." She was already working on her plan to oust Barbara from Ben's life.

But he wouldn't give her the chance. "I want you to know that I wouldn't be caught dead at your party on the thirtieth. If I have ever done anything to harm my reputation, it would have been because of something dishonest. But that is not a trait I practice so my reputation, the reputation I worked hard for, is, in fact, intact."

"I will also have you know that I will support poor, unfortunate orphans any way I please," he continued. "I do not need *your* parties to help me spend my money or build my reputation as one of *your* kind. I do not care about the elite snobs of the world. People know that about me and I am not about to change because of something *you* might think is good for me. I do not care about what *you* may *think*!"

"And another thing!" he continued, "Somebody needed to put you in your place and you should consider yourself lucky that it was Barbara. She did so as kindly as she could but she managed to put a punch in her message, didn't she?"

The widow Cochran had no doubt now that Ben had heard the entire conversation. She blushed with embarrassment. He added, "What would someone with a lot of good manners do right now? Apologize?"

She choked out, "I'm truly sorry for what I said to Barbara. Ben, I'm sorry I thought untrue things about her, but I ..."

She didn't have a chance to finish. He did not want her to save face. He just said instead, "Now, I will thank you to leave my house and take your inconsiderate and impolite manners with you. Allow me to show you out!"

Several minutes later, the dancers outside were surprised to see Ben escorting the widow Cochran toward her buggy, a firm hand around her upper arm. She was blushing profusely and stunned into utter silence.

Martha dared not look toward Barbara, but left abruptly without bidding anyone, who were all staring by now, a good evening.

Being the perfect gentleman, Ben did not provide anyone with an explanation of what had just transpired, and the guests minded their own business, politely. The invisible tension that had risen with the widow's earlier conversation with Ben—that had been loud enough to be overheard by the group—lifted and the party continued, almost as if it had just begun.

Ben's thoughts were no longer distracted. In fact, he was sure of himself. He realized that his initial thoughts of Barbara—being much younger than she actually was—was due to her innocence. It was this innocence that motivated him to protect her, always.

Eventually, Ben had the good fortune of enjoying two more dances with Barbara. He was no longer busy with the arrival of guests and everyone seemed to want to enjoy themselves as much as possible.

He very much relished the few dances he had with her. He couldn't get over how graceful she was. *Joe must have taught her*, he thought. She simply amazed him with all her talents.

She couldn't help herself. She felt enchanted by the nearness of him and the romantic movements of the dances. She sighed many times, yearning for something she couldn't explain. He was attentive, he looked into her eyes and made her feel as if they were the only two people at the dance. He would smile and she would smile back. He loved when she smiled; her face took on a whole new beauty when she did.

After the last of the party guests had left, Ben joined his sons and Barbara gathered in the grand room—not really wanting the evening to be over.

Ben started pacing, his earlier emotions over Martha's words to Barbara resurfacing. Finally, he stopped, sat, and let them all know of the conversation he had overheard between Martha and Barbara. Barbara was shocked to learn he had overheard and wondered what negative impact that may have on the friendship she had with Ben and his sons.

"Ben, I ah, I have decided to take you up on your offer to move ..." but Barbara was interrupted.

Adam, Hoss and Joe looked back and forth at each other in disbelief. They knew what Ben had offered her a couple of months ago. Did Barbara want to leave?

Ben appeared not to have heard what she said. Instead, he excitedly repeated almost word for word what was said by Martha. His sons were angered and disappointed that Ben had not kicked her expensive frock off the ranch at that point. But when he told them of Barbara's response, they all burst into laughter and remarked on how much the widow deserved the verbal spanking. The boys looked at her with gleeful pride. Barbara breathed a sigh of relief and was amused by their reactions. She shouldn't feel shame for having put Mrs. Good Manners in her place.

Then Ben told them of his one-sided conversation when he had caught up to the misguided widow before she had a chance to rejoin the rest of the guests.

Turning towards Barbara now, he said, "And then I told her, 'There is something else you need to know. For the past two months, I have been supporting an orphan. But this orphan is different, she is not a child anymore. She is a grown woman. She is the strongest, most pleasant and honest person I know. Never any pretense. She has worked very hard at bettering herself, something you could never recognize as a need in *your* own self.' I was ready to throw her out right then!" The boys laughed at that truth.

"Just before I did show her the door, I said, 'Barbara has become more than the woman she once was, if that is possible. She is a lady through and through. She is gracious, can play the piano like any famous pianist, or tenderly care for a sick animal and if you were a man you would have discovered this evening that she dances like a graceful swan. She has a multitude of talents and doesn't boast about any of them. She is humble and kind; always willing to learn from the smallest of people around her. I have seen her rise above her goal to learn what she considered she had lost in her many years alone. She amazes me. She would have made her parents proud.' and then I booted her off the ranch!"

Barbara actually started crying when he said that about her parents. How could he have known her most desired wish?

Ben stopped and looked at his sons now. "It's true, I said all of that. Well, you can imagine," he chuckled, "it didn't take her long to want to leave so I escorted her off our land." Joe was laughing so hard he fell to the floor while holding onto his sides.

Barbara was both surprised and pleased by what Ben had said and told him so. "Ben, you make me blush. No one has ever said such nice things about me. Well, I guess no one had a chance, they didn't know me," she chuckled.

He said, "Well they are all true, Barbara. I meant every word. I wouldn't lie about someone's character." He signaled his laughing sons to leave the room, which they did awkwardly. He walked to where Barbara was sitting. He leaned over and took both her hands in his. She rose to meet him, trembling with the nearness of him.

He looked directly into her eyes and said, "I owe you an explanation on my behavior earlier. I should have defended you in front of our guests when Martha extended that disgusting invitation. I'm sorry that I didn't decline right then and there but I was stunned. Truly! I was so surprised that she said those things that I was dazed and couldn't react in time before the music started up again."

He paused, tilted his head back as if he needed to think about what he next wanted to say. He immediately looked back down to her eyes and said, "I have been haunted by the knowledge that I am the first man you met. I feel like I have a responsibility to make the best impression, one that should be representative of all decent men. But in fact, I only have to be myself. Other people have to make their own impressions. I can't be responsible for them all. Thinking that I had to was stupidity on my part. Barbara, I have come to realize that I am very fond of you. But, not as you might think."

She didn't know which way to think about the fondness he felt. Fatherly or as a man? So, she let him go on, daring to hope. Although there was something different in how he spoke, she couldn't figure out exactly what it was.

"I—when I saw you this evening, I was pleasantly reminded of how lovely you are. I have been awestruck by your beauty since our special supper last Friday evening. I didn't, no, let me reword that more accurately—I *couldn't* tell you how I felt then because I was afraid that you might think I was taking advantage of you in some way. I know now that you couldn't think that. You would have probably just left here instead."

"I wanted to spend last Friday evening getting to know you better, but I stopped myself. I know that you are a woman of few words and that you don't want me beating around the bush and that you are as honest as the day is long ..."

She interrupted, "Ben!" She repeated more urgently, "Ben."

When he stopped long enough to listen, she said, "Please just say what you want to say. I need to take these shoes off. They pinch!"

He looked down at her feet, laughed at her genuine, refreshing honesty and told her to kick them off—which she did. She now came up to his chin in height. He moved closer to her yet again, put a serious look on his face and said, "I am in love with you."

She held her breath. *Could it be so?*

"I was reluctant to tell you for fear that you would reject me."

She didn't know how to respond. Should she tell him she had the same fear?

"I love you very much, and I want to tell you that every day for the rest of my life. Barbara Burke, I'm sorry your father is not with us for me to seek his blessing but at our age, we don't need it anyway, so will you marry me?" Ben asked, and he stood even closer.

"I want nothing more than to be your wife, Ben. I love you, too," she said with pure joy.

He bent his head down to meet hers and kissed her virgin lips. She held her breath and welcomed back the butterflies to her stomach.

When it dawned on him that this must be her first kiss, he wrapped her in his arms to kiss her again, more slowly, more passionately. She kissed him back; he had no further questions. She couldn't get over how well they fit into each other's arms and never wanted the kissing to end.

He felt there was something else he needed to explain to her, "I never met anyone that I thought I would want to marry again until you. I was always aware of the lack of companionship in my life since Joe's mother died when he was three. Oh sure, three sons can be half of your life, but they can't be everything. They are great company but theirs would never compare to a woman's love. I admire you for the woman you are and am honored to know you. You are one amazing woman."

Later, in her bed, she would replay his kind and loving words as well as relive the feeling of his lips on hers. It was the softest and most powerful feeling she had ever experienced. His lips were tender on hers and yet had the ability to send shivers down her entire body. She had no idea that kissing could infiltrate her senses. She also marveled at the feeling of his arms wrapped around her. She had never felt so safe. Many men had put their arms around her this evening in dance, but none made her feel what she felt when in Ben's arms.

The next morning Ben and a blushing Barbara told the boys. Adam was the first to congratulate the bride and groom to be and said, "I couldn't be happier for you both."

Hoss, always so shy and clumsy when it came to romantic or personal emotions, just repeated what Adam said.

Joe, on the other hand, said, "Yippee! I knew you were meant for each other. I am overjoyed to have you as my stepmother, Barbara." And he gave her a kiss on the cheek and hugged her long and hard. Joe was so young when he lost his mother that he had often yearned for a woman to become a mother figure in his life and fill his motherly needs, even now.

She couldn't help but shed a tear. She remembered crying from having hurt herself physically and for the loss of her family. She cried when she thought Ben didn't love her. She didn't know that happy emotions could also bring on tears.

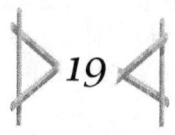

April 28, 1863

WEDDING PLANS WERE NEW TO BARBARA, SO once again her new friends, Yolanda, Yvonne and Darlene, helped her. They guided her from colors and style to sexual activities and marital advice.

Yolanda and Yvonne had not stopped talking while they were helping Barbara. They knew her situation and determined that as she would not be having that mother to daughter talk with another woman before her wedding night, they would step in. They nonchalantly spoke of some things she should be aware of, like what to expect on her wedding night, what to do if she and Ben had a disagreement, and so on. She just smiled and wondered if there was any truth in anything they said. She looked forward to finding out.

Ben and Barbara were married by the end of the month and not surprisingly, they did not invite the widow Cochran to the wedding. As a matter of fact, they never thought about her again.

On her wedding night, Barbara came to Ben wearing a very flimsy garment. It was the finest material to ever touch her skin. Ben wasn't sure he could control himself seeing her like that. The years she spent working to survive on the mountain sculpted her the body of a goddess. She had wide sinewy shoulders, an extremely small waist that rippled in muscle, and long shapely legs. Her hair had been combed down to cover one side of her chest.

Ben inhaled, felt his pulse quicken, and couldn't help but let out a deep moan of anticipation and delight. He would strive to be gentle, but the sight of her like this blinded him. He was surprised that he felt apprehension about making love to his bride. But the feeling quickly passed. Everything came naturally.

That first night with Ben was more than she had ever imagined. She had observed many animals in the mating season and often wondered if it was like that for humans. She need not wonder anymore. It was nowhere near that impersonal. Animals did not kiss and caress. They didn't whisper sweet words of affection to each other. They didn't care about their partner or sleep in a spoon position. She did not ever want to sleep alone again.

~

They left for San Francisco later that week. The distance by coach was difficult for Barbara because she had never traveled by buggy farther than to Virginia City. Many times she wanted to get out and walk alongside the horses for much needed exercise. But Ben engaged her in conversation and pointed out landmarks as they went along. With him by her side, she felt that she could face anything.

She liked the city of San Francisco. The height of the buildings amazed her and even made her feel dizzy. She was enthralled at its variety of shops, even though she had never had any need for many of the things those shops offered. Had Ben not visited them with her, she might never have purchased anything at all.

He insisted she buy herself a new mirror, brush and comb set. She argued that the one from the guest room would suit her needs just fine. But he told her that those were to stay in the guest room and that she deserved a new set that she had personally chosen. Only then did she accept that new ones be purchased.

Ben was not extravagant as he knew she would think many things unnecessary. Eventually, he convinced her to have her picture taken. She agreed provided he would have one taken of himself separately as well, and another taken together.

Weeks later they received the developed pictures. Barbara thought it odd that they were delivered in a box that was more than a flat envelope holding just the three pictures.

Ben had requested that one copy of the individual pictures be cut to fit inside a locket that he had purchased while in San Francisco, as a wedding gift. The box contained the locket, with his picture and hers coming together as if in a kiss when the locket was closed. She treasured it until her last day.

20

July 15, 2019

DOMINIQUE AND MICHAEL WERE TOO EXCITED to wait for an online meeting to communicate to the group what they had found. So, they scanned the document and shared it in a text instead.

It was a letter from Ben Cartwright's lawyer, Fred Mason, to Henry Devon's lawyer, Arthur Richardson, in Sacramento. After the salutation and introduction, it read:

> *Mr. Devon communicated to me that*
> *he had entrusted Mr. Ben Cartwright to*
> *pick up a package from your office that*
> *you would have received from an engraver*
> *in Sacramento last Tuesday, February 3,*
> *1863. Regrettably, Mr. Cartwright was a*
> *victim of an avalanche on his return to his*
> *home. He survived the disaster, but his*
> *horse and the satchel that contained the*
> *said package were lost.*
>
> *Most unfortunately, and as you*
> *may know by now, Mr. Devon passed*
> *away on February 11, the morning before*
> *Mr. Cartwright's arrival back home. As*
> *we are not aware of what the package*
> *contained, Mr. Cartwright and I wish to*
> *convey our services and assistance if you*
> *have need of them in any way to now*
> *enact the desires of Mr. Devon's last will*

and testament. I understand that Mr.
Devon was in the process of changing or
updating his will and of relocating the
documents to my office.
  Please convey my sincerest
condolences to Mr. Devon's family.

Not all cousins read the attachment at the same time. Messages of hurrahs and yippees kept coming in all afternoon.

Dominique and Michael headed out to Sacramento the next day. After finding a hotel, their first stop would be the Sacramento History Museum on Sequoia Pacific Boulevard.

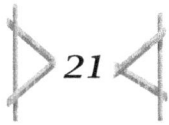

Late March 1865

SPRING CAME SUDDENLY IN NEVADA. EVERYONE knew that there would be no more days off until the round up and branding of the new Hereford calves was finished. This year promised to be more fruitful than any other year in the ranch's history so, to be sure, there was a lot of work to be done.

Even though every head of cattle counted, they were bound to lose some valuable stock. There were always some mishaps, but the day Hoss came across a calf with its back leg caught in a fox trap, he was beside himself. Ben and he had come upon the calf together.

"Who would be setting their traps on our land, Pa?"

Ben replied, "I'm sure I don't know son, but we're going to find out." They worked together on getting the animal free. Hoss was sick to his stomach when he discovered how badly the calf's leg had been marred. He was sure his father would insist they put it down.

Before Ben could even say anything, Hoss began to argue on behalf of the poor thing, "Pa, let me take this little fellow back to the barn, and try to nurse it back to health. The bone may have enough meat left on it and if I could have a chance to give it a try maybe we could add another animal to the herd after all. What do you say?"

Ben carefully thought about his response. Although there was the risk of time spent needlessly on injured animals that would need to be put down anyways, he wanted to give Hoss a chance to bring the calf back to health. Also, he knew Barbara, who loved all animals, would want him to give the calf as much of a chance as possible. Ben agreed, surprising Hoss.

When Hoss carried the calf to the wagon, its mother followed.

Later that day, Joe and Adam brought him another animal that was found with a front leg caught in a trap. When Ben and Barbara arrived just before supper time with yet a third calf in the same predicament to a front leg, the family knew they had a serious problem on their hands.

The discussion at the supper table involved the traps and the hopes of finding the trespassers. Hoss had wrapped the mauled legs as best he could but did not think he could nurse all three animals back to health if he wanted to sleep and eat too. With his head down, slightly discouraged, Hoss asked "Pa, could we get Doc Swenson over here to help?"

Ben didn't want to invest too much money nor allow Hoss to use valuable time nursing the calves when it looked like there might be no alternative but to eventually put them down. But he didn't like to see his son so distraught and he feared any other response might upset his wife, so he consented. "Yes, sure. Why not? As long as it is not going to keep you away from branding for more than one day. Send one of the hands to go get him in the morning. In the meantime, Barbara and I will go out to the barn and you can come relieve us later."

Both Joe and Adam offered to watch for a couple of hours too.

Hoss was quite grateful for their offers but declined, "No use all of us going without some much-needed sleep. I'll do the watching and stay in the barn tonight." He knew how physically exhausted he was at the end of each branding day and how relief was found in sleep. It made no sense that the rest of his family should be worn out too.

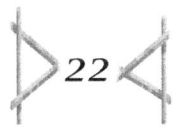

Late March 1865

IT WAS AN EXCEPTIONALLY LONG NIGHT FOR Hoss. The poor animals did not get any rest and didn't quiet down for longer than about an hour. Hoss slept very little. By the time morning arrived, he was dog-tired but still declined to leave the animals when Ben offered one of the hands to stay back.

"No, but thanks, Pa. I'll wait for the vet and then I'll do what he says needs to be done."

So, Ben and the rest went back to the tasks at hand of herding the cattle and branding the new calves.

At around 8:30 that morning, Hoss was relieved to finally hear someone riding up to the barn. He went out to greet the vet but instead he saw a tall skinny boy. When the rider dismounted and turned to face him to shake his hand, Hoss found himself face to face with a very attractive, auburn-haired woman. He was embarrassed to think that he at first thought the person was a boy when he could definitely see that she in no way filled the pair of pants and shirt the same way a boy would. He clearly was in need of more sleep. He abruptly asked her, "Who are you?"

"You sent for a vet, Mr. Cartwright?" she replied smiling.

"Yes, we sure did. Are you here to tell me Doc Swenson can't make it?"

Noting his curtness and rejection of her extended hand, her smile disappeared.

THE CARTWRIGHT MEN MARRY

"Oh, he's on a farm about forty miles north of here. They discovered bad water up there and many of the animals got sick, some even died. I'm his daughter, Evelyn," she said, extending her hand again but he didn't see it nor shake it.

Everybody knew on some level the family structure of each neighbor. Hoss, like his father and brothers, certainly knew that their vet had five daughters, but didn't specifically know them by name. Hoss wouldn't have necessarily known that Evelyn was the oldest of five siblings, all girls; she being eighteen. It was the same the other way around. Everybody knew the Cartwrights but had not necessarily met them or knew one when they met him.

"Dat-burn-it! Oh, pardon me, ma'am. I mean to say, gosh-darn-it! We need a vet and we needed one since last night," he said, his fatigue thinning his patience.

"My father taught me everything he knows. He said I am just as good a vet as he is," she said again to a surprised Hoss, excited by the possibility of practicing her skills.

"Well, why didn't you say that when you arrived?" he asked, anxiously.

"Didn't I?" she asked, getting lost in his boyishly good looks.

"I don't care if you are a monkey. If you can treat those calves in there, I'd be truly beholden. Please, come this way. And, I'm Hoss." he replied hurriedly as he turned toward the barn. She grabbed her medicine bag and quickly followed him.

Evelyn was truly happy to be given this opportunity to apply her veterinary skills. She wanted very badly to be of assistance in any way she could. But when she entered the first stall where he indicated what she presumed was the most wounded of the three Hereford calves, Hoss removed the bandage and she felt deflated. Torn flesh? But she couldn't stop her own compassionate nature and immediately knelt and caressed the suffering little one. She reached into her bag and found the medicated salve that would diminish the calf's pain. It would soon settle down and stop bawling long enough for her to examine him in peace.

Hoss said, "That ointment sure made him stop bawling. Could you give the others some of it now before you treat this one? I can't stand much more of their hurting cries."

While doing so, she noticed the two other calves, both females, had ripped flesh down to the bone on their front legs. She was appalled to learn about the fox traps. How cruel.

She started working on the worst of the three, explaining, "If this poor little guy had one of his front legs caught in the trap like the other two instead of the back leg, it would not be as bad. But because it was the hind leg, he had more weight to manage when he tried to pull it out, causing the muscle to tear like that. It will be a lot harder for him to heal."

Seeing the genuine disappointment on Hoss' face, she added, "But you found him early enough. I might just be able to … could you hold him? No, like this," and she showed him how and went back to work, not taking time to look up or around or wipe her brow. But she did notice the strong arms gingerly holding the fragile animal in place.

While she diligently worked on the leg, Hoss stole looks at her. He admired her caring hands and how tender they were with each touch. He studied her face and wondered how he just now discovered her loveliness. Her hair was neatly tied back in braids. Her mouth appeared stuck in a permanent smile that was likely caused by her high cheek bones. He could have sworn that little fairies were circling his head with heart-shaped arrows.

Hoss watched Evelyn place a splint on the leg and asked, "Is it broken?"

"It seems to be. The calf isn't putting any weight on it, so I'll just add one for extra strength. Do you have a swing or the material needed to build one?"

Hoss gathered what she needed and together they placed the animal in it and off the floor.

He placed himself in the same position as for the previous treatment, but as she now had to tend a front leg injury, he was wrong. He laughed at his mistake and she joined in on the laughter. He was more than lightheaded in her presence—he couldn't think straight.

Shortly after noon, all three animals had been treated as best as possible and had bandages covering the ripped flesh.

Hoss asked her into the house for lunch, which she accepted. After they had both washed up, Hoss relaxed and became his usual amiable self.

"I'm sorry for my bad manners earlier. I didn't mean to be rude, but I haven't slept in more than a day." And almost in the same breath, "I sure am pleased with your knowledge and your expert care of the little fellows."

She smiled and couldn't help herself by saying, "You are too kind," and thought, *what beautiful hazel colored eyes I'm seeing*. If she remembered correctly, what she'd heard of the three brothers, he was the only blond one. She had always liked men with lighter colored hair and she couldn't help but like this one.

She had, of course, heard how handsome and serious Adam was, but she was of the impression that he was moody. She had also heard about Little Joe's good looks and how all the available girls wanted to date him, but she didn't think she could ever attract his interest. If anyone asked her, she would say she was too mature a girl for Little Joe.

She had always wanted someone who was kind, considerate and serious about his future. When she heard that Hoss was a gentle giant, she had already started feeling an attraction toward him even though she had yet to meet him. And now, here they were.

Hoss was elated when she said, "I would recommend that all three of these animals be given a chance to recover. I'd like to come back every day, examine their legs and change their bandages as needed for at least a couple of weeks. Then if I don't see any improvement, I would suggest they be put down. There would be no point in continuing if there were no positive results. What do you say, Mr. Cartwright?"

"Hoss, Miss Evelyn."

"Yes, Hoss. And, I'm just plain Evelyn," she replied shyly.

"No, you're too pretty to be just plain anything," he said, quickly grinning when he realized he had said that out loud. They then both smiled at each other. She was truly impressed with his genuine soft nature.

He was sure happy to be giving the calves a chance. As they finished their lunch of bread and cold meats, Hoss and Evelyn made arrangements for her return.

"Come back tomorrow before supper to meet Pa. Then come after supper for the next two weeks, 'cause I sure want to be there, Miss Evelyn, when you treat the calves."

Hoss knew he would be needed in the pastures during the daytime and wanted to be in the barn when she would be so he could see firsthand if the animals were recovering.

"That suits me fine."

Evelyn didn't have a problem with that as long as the bandages were changed as needed, and that was something she would do when she came around, no matter the hour.

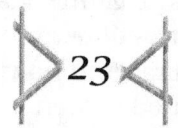

Late March 1865

THE NEXT DAY EVELYN ARRIVED BEFORE SUPPER to tend to the animals. She came to the house first to let Hoss know that she was heading to the stables. There was no one in the house, so she veered towards the barn.

The five adults turned when she said jokingly, "Good evening everyone. Exactly how many nurses are here to help me tonight?"

They immediately liked her soft bantering and greeted her by shaking hands, even Hoss—as that had been overlooked on their first meeting.

Evelyn's eyes softened when they met Barbara's. Everyone had heard her story—almost two years ago now—and Evelyn was in awe of the courage it must have taken for Barbara to live alone all those years. In turn, Barbara had looked forward to meeting this young woman who, according to Hoss was exceptionally good at veterinary work. Both women nodded in respectful salutation.

Ben smiled at Evelyn and asked, "How is your father? On demand as usual this time of year?"

Looking away from Hoss, she replied, "Oh, he is very well, thank you. And yes, so incredibly busy."

"Hoss told me about the tainted water up north. That is really too bad. Tell him I said hello."

"I certainly will, Mr. Cartwright. Now, what do we have here, Hoss?"

Both Adam and Joe were immaturely poking each other in the ribs with their elbows. Evelyn was sure paying Hoss a lot of attention.

But before she had an opportunity to start her examinations, Ben motioned toward the house and invited her in for supper. "We'll be more comfortable discussing matters at the table, and I don't know about you, but the rest of us sure are hungry."

She would appreciate some nourishment right about now too and accepted.

Ben gave his two dark-haired sons a discreet disapproving look aimed at their obvious childishness. They were both immediately sorry to have been caught behaving that way.

Hoss was just shy. He thanked his father under his breath for extending the supper invitation then followed Barbara and Evelyn inside.

At the table, Barbara showed great interest in what Evelyn and Hoss were discussing. She loved animals as much as they did. Hoss knew that and told Barbara everything that Evelyn had done. In the telling, he portrayed her as quite a heroine—which was embarrassing to Evelyn.

Hoss, Ben and Barbara accompanied Evelyn to the barn after supper. Barbara observed that Evelyn was indeed very thorough and gentle. There was no one the Cartwrights liked more than someone who loved animals and treated them well. Miss Swenson was certainly one of those people. Barbara also noticed the similarities between Hoss and Evelyn. *They would make a great couple,* she thought. Other than the obvious knowledge of medicine, Evelyn's gift was kindness.

Ben said as he motioned toward the house, "Please excuse me, I have paperwork to do and less time during the day to do it now that we are in calving season. Come back to the house before you leave." Evelyn nodded and moved on to change the bandage on the second calf.

When Evelyn finished her examination of all three animals, she rose and said, "I believe I might actually see a positive change on those two tomorrow, next day for sure. This one though will need more time," she said, indicating the calf in the swing. "But," she continued, "I would understand if you put him down right away."

Hoss said, "What? No. You said to give it two weeks before deciding and there are a dozen more days to go, Miss Evelyn. But please don't mention to Pa about that little one, not yet. Give it the chance. That goes for you too, Barbara."

"Oh, you don't have to worry about me, Hoss. I'm also rooting for this little one," replied Barbara.

Evelyn agreed and reported the improvement on the two calves to Ben when she came back to the house before leaving. He was sure happy to hear that they would probably be saved.

Evelyn then said, "I would like to look at your herd Mr. Cartwright." When she noticed a raised eyebrow, she quickly added, "Oh, I'm not looking for an excuse to treat them and charge you, or anything like that. I just need to practice some things I learned from Pa. We don't have a lot of animals ourselves and you can imagine that not many ranchers around here have allowed me to look after their sick animals either, especially if Pa is handy."

Ben sighed with relief, looked at Barbara who was obviously siding with Evelyn and said, "Sure. That would be acceptable." He liked her and her eagerness. "We leave for the branding fields tomorrow morning at six. Head out with us or meet us in the north west section when you can."

"Oh, I'll be here," she said excitedly.

Barbara walked with Evelyn to her horse and mentioned, "Consider wearing your grubbiest clothing for tomorrow as the field is muddy in some places and surprisingly dusty in others."

Evelyn appreciated her advice.

Late March 1865

THE FOLLOWING DAY, HOSS MADE IT HIS PERSONAL duty to introduce Evelyn around as the very capable and thorough junior vet that she was. Every time another hand approached Hoss to report on the number of animals he had herded back to the corral or about his findings from the search for more traps, Hoss would go through the whole speech again.

Evelyn became embarrassed. She felt a bit more pressure at each introduction. The calves had better live now before the word of her successes got out prematurely!

Adam and Joe distanced themselves to avoid laughing at Hoss' attempts at wooing Miss Evelyn. Or at least that was their take on his behavior.

Evelyn did prove to be an asset to Ben's herd of cattle after all; not that she had an opportunity to treat his vast herd, just the animals who were at the branding corral that morning. Besides treating more than a dozen steers and cows for eye infections, Evelyn had also noted a lump on the upper part of the leg of a two-year old steer that probably would benefit from its removal.

Later in the morning, Evelyn called out, "Mr. Cartwright, could you come here please?"

When Ben approached, she asked, "Can you smell that?"

"I don't smell ... oh, yes. I smell something rotting, like flesh. What is it?"

"It is rotting flesh and it's coming from this cow's mouth. I've noticed that she has great difficulty chewing her cud." They examined her together and noticed that she had a fractured jaw.

Upon further examination, Evelyn pointed out that the cow was scarred from her right eye to underneath the jaw. "She must have been mauled by a mountain lion during the winter months for such an injury. It's surprising that she survived at all from the attack."

Ben agreed and said, "Something like a bullet or the presence of a human might have distracted the cat from its prey." Everyone wondered how come the cat didn't finish the job. As there was nothing to be done for the cow and as she was not nursing a calf this summer, Ben marked her for slaughter.

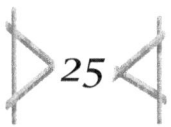

25

April 1865

BY THE END OF THE FIRST WEEK, IT WAS determined that the two front-legged injured calves were going to make a full recovery. The back-legged injured calf had hardly made any progress. Evelyn promised to keep coming back every couple of days to care for that one and then her job would be done.

Evelyn and Hoss were enjoying each other's company very much. Time passed so quickly when they were together that one evening she had stayed at the barn longer than usual. Hoss offered to escort her home.

"I don't see why that would be necessary. I am just about a half hour later than ..."

Hoss interrupted, "Miss Evelyn, those trespassing trappers are still out there. I would feel terrible if something were to happen to you. No, I insist."

She didn't argue. They would have an extra fifteen minutes or so to spend together. They got on their horses and took off toward the northwest. Evidently, Hoss wasn't too worried as he only carried his holstered gun and left his rifle behind. She smiled to herself, wondering if he was only looking for a reason to spend more time with her or if the rustlers were a real concern.

When her family's home came into view, Hoss tilted his hat, bade her goodnight and said, "See you tomorrow Miss Evelyn, same time."

"Goodnight, Hoss. Thank you for looking after me. See you tomorrow," and she quickened her pace toward the barn.

Hoss turned his horse after a long last look at her retreating figure.

Five minutes later, he was still deep in his thoughts of Evelyn when he heard a calf bawling on his right.

"Whoa," he ordered his horse and dismounted. He tethered him to a bush and stood still. There was no denying that noise. It was either a hurt calf hiding here in the bushes or one that had become separated from the herd. He stepped forward carefully, wishing he had a lantern. The bushy area grew into a forest the further west you went towards the mountain.

When he came upon the calf, he was disappointed to find that no matter how frightened it was of him it could not run away because its hind leg was caught in a trap. "Dat-burn-it," he said as he crouched down to release it.

WHOMP!

Hoss may not have heard the butt of the rifle coming down hard, but he felt it on the back of his head. He dropped to the ground unconscious.

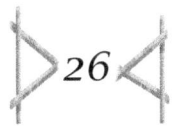

26

April 1865

"HOW ARE THE CALVES?" ASKED HER MOTHER, Mary-Lynn, as Evelyn entered the small four-room house. Her fourteen-year-old sister was helping out with supper, while the twelve-year-old was looking after the four-year-old, and the nine-year-old was playing quietly by herself.

"Two of them are doing great. Still not much change in the other one though."

"Where is your medicine bag?" a surprised Mary-Lynn asked.

"Oh, I guess I left it ... no. I didn't leave it in the barn. Hoss has it. He insisted on carrying it. Don't worry, I'll get it tomorrow. Why?"

"You'd better go after him and get it now. You have to go see Mr. Norton about his horse first thing in the morning," smiled a very proud Mary-Lynn. Another neighbor who had learned about Evelyn's success with the Cartwrights' cattle had decided to have her tend to his sick animal in her father's absence.

"Really? Mr. Norton asked that I come take care of his horse?" she was pleased even though she knew that if her Pa was home, she wouldn't be called on. "I'm leaving now. He's five minutes ahead of me already. I'll hurry Ma."

April 1865

"I CAN'T MOVE HIM. HE'S TOO HEAVY, DANNY. HE ain't seen our faces. Can't we jus' leave him and go?" asked the younger man. He had disarmed Hoss and had been ordered to drag the big guy back to their camp a hundred yards further into the bush.

"Naw. Can't do that Al," said Danny, wiping Hoss' blood off the butt of his rifle. "Billy-Bob ain't gonna like it. Me neither. Naw, we either drag him back to camp or wake him up and force him to walk there by hisself."

"All right. I'll git a bucket of water," said Al.

Moments later a wet Hoss, roused and at gun point, got up and walked in the direction the men told him to. Danny was by then leading Hoss' horse with the calf strapped on the saddle.

Billy-Bob was expecting them. Al had told him when he came to fetch the bucket of water.

"Well, well. Who do we have here? You trying to steal my calf?"

Hoss didn't say anything.

"What's a matter? Cat git yu'r tongue?" Billy-Bob poked Hoss in the ribs.

"That's a Cartwright calf 'cause you're on Cartwright land." Hoss replied.

"Is that so? Well, it don't bother us any. You know Mister, those Cartwrights could make they-selves a lot of money. Don't they know those Chinese men down in 'Frisco pay a lot of money for veal? I kinda have a likin' for it meself, but I like money better. I'll eat the meat from the mothers that chose not to abandon their youngen'."

Thus, the reason for stealing calves. Hoss didn't like it. Not one bit. He had to get himself out of this predicament and bring these men to justice. He didn't know how, yet. He hoped he would have the chance to figure it out.

Every few minutes the men would look his way and then talk among themselves. Hoss thought, *They sure are agitated at being discovered by me. I figure the odds of me being left behind alive are pretty slim.*

He was still dazed when they tied him to a tree and went about their business of muzzling and caging the calf. He knew his time was running out; he tried to ignore his growing headache and think on freeing his hands.

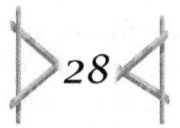

April 1865

EVELYN RACED BACK TO THE CARTWRIGHT RANCH but never caught up to Hoss. She guessed that he must have sped up too. But when she arrived at the ranch and made inquiries, everyone replied that Hoss had not yet returned.

A worried father and brothers saddled up, gathered their pistols and rifles, and a couple of lanterns and followed Evelyn. It didn't take them long to find the spot where horse tracks showed that Hoss had tethered his horse to the bush and they dismounted. They soon noticed something was wrong with the tracks they were following. The set of footprints that led the horse into the forest didn't belong to Hoss.

They cautiously entered the bush and stopped at the site of the fox trap. They continued to follow the trail farther into the bush. The footprints now indicated that Hoss was leading and being followed by two other sets of human footprints along with the horse. Not a good sign.

Ben turned to Evelyn and said, "Evelyn, I think you should stay here with the horses." He gave her one lantern and kept the other.

"Mr. Cartwright, I can't. I feel responsible. I ..." argued Evelyn.

But Ben wouldn't hear any of it. She watched the men huddle together and devise a plan. Ben motioned for Adam and Joe to follow him into the area thick with trees, where they would probably find Hoss. She waited about one minute after they proceeded again, turned out her lantern and followed as quietly as she could.

The Cartwrights came upon the camp quickly. Their guns already drawn. Hoss was to their right tied to a tree, struggling to escape.

"That's far enough," beckoned Billy-Bob. "Danny there ain't afraid of killing a man even if he is tied up like an animal."

Danny was standing guard with a rifle to Hoss' head. A younger man was standing to the right of the man who appeared to be the leader. The leader and the younger man each had a rifle pointing toward the Cartwrights.

Even though the light from the campfire could be seen from a distance, Ben had purposely continued to use his lantern to find Hoss. He had intended on removing the element of surprise. He didn't want to make any move that might get Hoss killed. As well, if all three Cartwrights were armed, then likely the trespassers would not relish a gun fight.

"Let him go," Ben said sternly, motioning toward Hoss. "You can keep the calf and leave Cartwright land—alive."

"And who might you be?" asked Billy-Bob.

"I'm Ben Cartwright. You're trespassing on my land and killing my calves. This has been going on long enough and it's going to stop today."

"Well, ain't you funny. As I sees it, Cartwright, you ain't got the upper hand here. I does. You will do as I say or you're all gonna die, startin' with him," pointing to Hoss.

Al was getting antsy and interrupted, "Maybe we should do as he says, Billy-Bob."

Billy-Bob didn't even twitch.

He said, "You don't scare me Cartwright. You

and your two guys there don't look mean enough to outsmart me and Danny here. Maybe this young'en behind me here is scared, but he ain't seen enough gun fights I reckon'. No sir, you don't scare me one bit."

Evelyn's heart was beating loudly in her ears. She started sweating but didn't stop her slow advance toward Hoss. She veered wide past the camp site and circled back to where he was sitting, tied up to the tree. She removed the knife from her belt and gently placed a hand on his forearm. He jerked at her touch.

Danny looked down at the movement, "What're you up to?"

"Nothing," replied Hoss, "just shooing away a pesky fly, that's all."

Billy-Bob had stopped to listen and now continued, "As I sees it Cartwright, I don't believe you either. You will get the law to come after us. No sir. You won't let us git away with nothing. We'll have to kill you all or you'll have to kill us all."

"That can be arranged," said a miffed Joe. He would do anything for Hoss.

"Now, let's not get hasty," Ben said, still holding onto the one lantern and tightening his grip on his gun in the other hand while trying to think quickly on his next move.

He didn't have to wait long. Hoss' hands had come free when Evelyn cut through the rope. Hoss reached up for Danny's rifle and yanked it out of his hands. Before Danny had the chance to look down at their hostage, Hoss extended his right hand, grabbed and pulled down on Danny's arm that had held the weapon. The momentum of Danny falling forward made it easy to strike the thief in the mouth—hard— with his left fist. Even from a sitting position, Hoss could deliver a powerful punch. Danny fell to the ground.

While heads turned toward Danny and Hoss, Joe fired a shot at Al's gun, disarming him and wounding him in the upper arm. Billy-Bob spun towards Joe, but before he could take a shot, Joe threw himself on the ground and circled back up to his feet, dodging any gunfire that would be coming from Billy-Bob and mesmerizing the rustler with his fast footwork.

Adam took advantage of the rustlers' diverted attention and grabbed Billy-Bob's rifle, threw it to the ground, disarmed him of the gun on his belt and stuck his own gun hard into the leader's side.

Ben hadn't moved. His sons were his swiftness, his actions, and his pride. The thieves were defeated, defenseless and disbelieving. It was over in seconds.

"I thought I told you to stay with the horses, Evelyn." Ben said.

"I know. I told you I couldn't. I ..." she replied as she emerged from behind the tree, anticipating the scolding.

Hoss opened an arm towards her, and she walked into the safety of his side. "Are you all right?" he asked.

She nodded but kept silent, her heart still beating too fast.

Ben smiled at her. She wondered then if he knew all along that she would disobey him. After all, the Cartwrights' lantern had provided her with the shadows she needed and their conversation had covered her noises.

"How did you know I would sneak in behind you?"

"Just a hunch," replied a very happy Ben. He was grateful for her actions. He wasn't sure that she would follow them into the woods. Adam and Joe had questioned Ben when they had left Evelyn behind, and he had replied, "Never doubt the determination and strength of a woman who feels responsible for something and wants to help correct it."

Adam and Joe chuckled. Hoss couldn't figure out why they were doing so.

"Thank you, Evelyn," Hoss said, his chin resting on the top of her head. "You saved my life."

"Ah, Hoss, I didn't do it alone," she replied, snuggling closer in his embrace.

"Well, I was afraid for my life until you freed my hands. I think Little Joe might not have come out of it unharmed if I hadn't been able to knock that Danny out cold."

Evelyn thought, *Afraid? This man was afraid? He is a much bigger man than what I thought at first. He didn't hesitate to admit he was scared. I admire him for that.*

The more she thought about it, the more Evelyn sensed that Ben Cartwright knew she was going to follow them and do something to help Hoss.

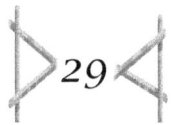

Late April 1865

IN THE END, THE MALE CALF NEVER MANAGED to walk and carry his own weight. He was put down. Hoss and Evelyn did that sad part of the job together to which they both exclaimed "Dat-burn-it". Evelyn had taken up Hoss' manner of speech.

Hoss had developed quite a fondness for Evelyn. Now that the calves had been dealt with, he saw an empty life ahead without her in it. He couldn't wait for a time in the future when they might need a vet and the Doc was not available.

So, he asked, "Would you be interested in allowing me to court you, Miss Evelyn?"

She was elated that he had finally asked. She quickly accepted and invited Hoss over to ask her father for permission.

Evelyn informed her parents when she got home and the following day when Hoss came by, he did not encounter any difficulty getting the vet's permission to court his oldest daughter.

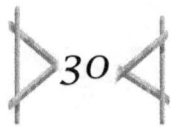

May 1865

THE VERY NEXT SUNDAY AFTER A PICNIC ON HOSS' favorite part of the Cartwright land—that being the river-fed pond—Hoss laid back and closed his eyes, happy to be with Evelyn and having a full stomach. She finished clearing the food and dishes and then sat down next to him. She leaned over, looked at his peaceful face and kissed his puckered lips.

He opened his eyes, quite surprised that she had made the first move. He put an arm up and said, "Come here, Miss Evelyn," and pulled her closer to him.

They kissed again. This time it was more than a pucker. Evelyn swooned over how gently Hoss kissed. It was like his lips invited hers to touch his, dared hers to respond and, in turn, his would receive them and give back again. She did not have any experience in kissing, but she knew that she didn't want to kiss anyone else ever. No one could make her feel that way, she surmised. She felt so special.

She gazed into his eyes then and was reminded of a field of wildflowers. In the sunlight, the hazel in his eyes appeared to change color as he looked deeply into hers. His eyes, like flowers, were in full bloom and sharing their beauty. She had never seen such beautiful eyes. They embraced and spent the balance of the afternoon there on the blanket in each other's arms, content.

Hoss was not unmoved by the experience and even hours later, he could still feel the warmth of her body on his side.

~

The following day Evelyn had a lengthy discussion with her parents. "Yes, I like him. Very much, as a matter of fact."

"Then you have to tell him the truth, Evy," said her mother. Her father nodded in agreement in the background.

"Honesty is the only way to go. Especially with the Cartwrights. I promise Evy, that's the truth," said Karl Swenson.

"But what if he won't want to see me anymore?" she argued.

"Better to find that out now than later when you've fallen hard for each other and have to deal with a broken heart," her mother exclaimed.

"But he may never find out. Then I would have told him without ever needing to!" she said, knowing full well that she had already fallen hard for Hoss.

"Ah, but what if you get married or are about to and the truth comes out?" her mother insisted. "Then the whole town will know. What then? Think about that. He will have to break it off just because you weren't the one to tell him ... that you kept him in the dark over the matter."

"I guess. All right. I'll tell him. I don't want to. I don't want anybody to know."

"It will be all right. The Cartwrights are good, decent people. They will be kind. I promise," said an uncertain Mary-Lynn, hoping her fears didn't show.

Evelyn was ridden with doubt and regret. On her way to the Cartwright ranch she scolded herself and thought, *How could I have been so brazen yesterday? What must he think of me?*

She hadn't told her parents that she and Hoss had kissed already. She certainly did not want to repeat history. She had a confession to make to Hoss and the sooner, the better.

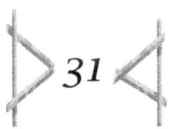

31

May 1865

WHEN EVELYN ARRIVED, SHE DIDN'T KNOW IF SHE should be relieved or not to find Hoss there, alone. She faced the man who held her future in his hands.

She had such a grave look on her face that Hoss felt an inexplicable panic churn in his stomach. She wasn't expected at the house and she was not acting like her usual self. Not that he knew her that well. She was just acting like a nervous cat. He sensed something was wrong, very wrong.

"Evelyn, please tell me what's up so we can try to fix it, whatever it is. The suspense is killing me!"

She smiled weakly at him and hoped for the best. As she started speaking, she noticed Ben and Barbara had come into the house from the back door. She motioned for them, "No, please, don't leave. I'm happy you're here. This way I won't have to repeat what I need to say."

She sounded very serious. Ben's heart suddenly ached for Hoss. He knew for a while how this young couple felt about each other. What could possibly be in the way?

She motioned for them to sit at the dining room table while she paced.

"You might know my mother, Mary-Lynn," Evelyn started.

"Not at all. We'd like to meet her," they practically said in unison.

She bent her head. Then she looked up at them

131

and continued, "Well, my life started in a little town, Carlston, Utah, with our neighbors believing my grandmother, Gertrude Singet, was my mother and that Mary-Lynn was my sister." She let the news sink in.

They looked at each other and back at Evelyn, expecting further explanations. Her eyes tried to take in their reactions and couldn't find any.

She inhaled deeply and continued, "She was sixteen when I was born in 1847. She was engaged to be married to a man who worked in the silver mines. There was an accident and he died when a load of rocks fell on him. Then my mother realized that she was pregnant with me. She had me with only my grandmother present to help with the birth. From then on I was a lie. It was easier for these two women to pretend that Mary-Lynn and I were sisters than to live with the scandal and shame."

"At a very young age, I could feel an undercurrent. I couldn't explain why I was different, only that there was something about me that other children didn't experience. When I got older and started to learn arithmetic and the way of nature, I realized that my parents were married three years after I was born."

Evelyn still couldn't observe any reaction from the three faces, so she hoped and dared to go on.

"I learned that my grandfather had died about three years before I was born and that after I was born, my mother and grandmother moved from town to town to avoid judgment and shunning. Then one day, in Pillon, a small town east of here, Grandma Gertrude's health started to fail. Mary-Lynn and Karl Swenson were courting at the time and grandmother blessed the courtship and convinced Karl to marry Mary-Lynn sooner than later."

"When Ma and Pa were first married, the four of us lived together. Soon after, grandma felt good enough to travel and she moved back to Utah because she said she belonged there. That's when we moved here and Ma took on the title of mother."

"Karl is a fair and kind man. He wanted me to accept him as my father. He didn't know how to do that until he saw my love of animals. That is when he started taking me to our barn to work with him. He didn't want me to go with him when he went to other people's ranches because he didn't want me in the way, but if anyone brought an animal to our place, I could watch everything he did." She smiled and sighed.

"Eventually, I forgot about the stares and shame that had followed us from town to town. People don't know that the years of marriage between my parents isn't more than my age because they don't ask. Ma and Pa wouldn't be telling anyone. I was part of a growing family and by the time I was old enough to start my schooling, things were going to be as normal as they could ever be."

"I just wanted you all to know that about me before Hoss and I do any more courting." She hung her head down, wondering if they would throw her out of their home and lives for bringing possible scandal to their reputations. She felt renewed shame for having been the one to kiss Hoss first.

"I didn't want to keep something secret that might come out one day and have you regret knowing me," she added. "But if you don't want to risk bringing shame to your family, I will leave now. I won't blame any of you."

Evelyn exhaled and sat down, not daring to look any of them in the eye. She was embarrassed now, suspecting that Hoss would probably think of her as incapable of earning his or anyone's respect.

The three looked at each other.

Ben put a hand up toward Hoss and was the

first to speak, "Evelyn, we will not judge you nor your mother. We will never shun you or them. We will feel toward you what we feel based on who you are and your actions. You must know that we would stand by you if you and Hoss ever got more serious. We will never feel ashamed of knowing you. Even if you and Hoss were to stop seeing each other. We also will never gossip about you nor point fingers."

Barbara was nodding and smiling in agreement. "I may not be able to put into words what I think as well as Ben has. I like you, Evelyn. You are a wonderful young woman."

The younger woman finally looked up. She was in disbelief.

"Really?" asked an incredulous Evelyn.

Hoss' breathing calmed down to normal and he said with a smile, "I couldn't be more proud to know you right now. What you just did took a lot of courage. I admire you for deciding to tell us your story. If anything, it just made me want to get to know you even better."

Evelyn was grinning and crying at the same time. He said she had courage. He was so wrong. That was the most frightening thing she had ever done—even scarier than sneaking into the woods to untie him. But she liked that he thought she was brave, so she never mentioned otherwise. She got up and walked into Hoss' arms. Then she gave Ben and Barbara a hug. She couldn't believe her good luck.

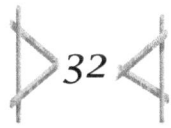

32

June 24, 1865

HOSS AND EVELYN WENT FISHING, SOMETHING they both enjoyed doing. The lazy afternoon was quiet, but there was chaos going on in Hoss' mind. He was in love with Evelyn. He had known it for a long time. Today, he would tell her how he felt.

But he wouldn't just tell her and leave it at that. No, he had come prepared. A month ago, he had ridden into town and ordered and paid for an engagement ring. It was a square-shaped emerald, set in silver. When he received it a couple of days ago, he thought it was the prettiest ring he had ever seen. He hoped she would like it and accept his proposal.

While they sat at the edge of the pond, he rose to one knee and asked, "Miss Evelyn, will you marry me?"

But he lost his balance while reaching for the ring still in his pant pocket and fell backwards into the pond.

Evelyn laughed and laughed. When he re-emerged and realized how funny he must look, he grinned from ear to ear and heartily laughed at himself. He climbed out of the water and she jumped into his arms, exclaiming, "Yes." Her embrace and momentum knocked him back down the bank and sent them both in the drink.

Emerging while still embracing, Hoss said, "I love you, Evelyn. I always will. Of that you can be sure. I will make you a great husband. I promise."

"I know you will, Hoss. I have no doubt. I want you to know that I love you very much, too. I started having feelings for you when you held that first sick calf. Remember?"

He nodded.

She continued, "You are gentle and kind. Those were always the qualities I wanted in a husband. But I am blessed with a whole lot more. Why, just the fact that you love me would be enough. I can hardly wait to be your wife."

"Evelyn, please believe that you deserve to be loved. You deserve all the happiness in the world."

She nodded, unable to speak.

He lifted both hands off her waist to her cheeks and bowed his head to kiss her. She lifted her arms to his shoulders and he lowered his to lift her to his height, all the while kissing. Finally, they released their embrace and he helped her out of the water before climbing the bank himself. For a moment neither spoke, focusing on wringing water out of their clothes and calming their emotions. They couldn't ignore the feeling of passion that had overtaken them when they were clinging onto each other while wet—there was just something erotic about it.

Hours later, still slightly damp and laughing about it, they headed out to tell their parents about their engagement.

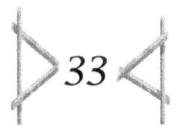

June 24, 1865

KARL, MARY-LYNN AND THEIR FIVE DAUGHTERS arrived around five o'clock the next Sunday, ready to meet the Cartwright family after being told the good news and being invited for dinner. Introductions were made and folks settled in to get to know each other better. After the delicious meal, Adam and Joe agreed to entertain the younger daughters with pony rides.

"Have you set a date?" asked Barbara, turning her eyes away from the giggling girls as they skipped out the front door accompanied by the two attentive brothers.

"Yes. We have," replied an excited Evelyn. She and Hoss looked at each other and in unison said, "July 7th."

"But that's two weeks from now!" gasped Mary-Lynn.

"Why, that's wonderful," replied Barbara.

Both women looked at each other and started laughing.

Mary-Lynn said, "I guess there is no point in waiting. You two belong together."

Barbara said, "What can we do to help?"

Evelyn and Hoss wanted a simple wedding. Only immediate family would be in attendance. They wanted the pastor to marry them in the church, followed by a celebration meal at the Cartwrights' house.

July 7, 1865

WHILE GETTING DRESSED FOR THE CEREMONY, Hoss reflected on his being the first of the brothers to wed. He always thought that Adam would be first until he had announced that his studies were his priorities. Then possibly Joe, with his good looks and talent at attracting the fairer sex, would be the first to marry—until Hoss witnessed a trail of bruised hearts as Little Joe moved on to the next pretty girl he met.

He was just so happy to be marrying a girl like Miss Evelyn. She was beautiful and he couldn't believe his good luck that she thought enough of him to want to marry. But she did. Many times, he didn't feel deserving. But he knew he loved her and would let her know it every day for the rest of his life.

~

Mary-Lynn cried at the ceremony and Barbara wondered why. Ben tried to explain it but emphasized that he really wasn't sure why women often cried at weddings.

He deduced, "Women cry both happy and sad tears. But at weddings, I think the crying also has something to do with the future of the young bride. You see, she usually has to leave the comfort of her home and family. She may experience some very lonely times in the future of her married life, especially if her husband has to work someplace where she can't join him, like a mining camp."

He continued, "The tears may even represent the mother's own difficulties she had in raising her children if the husband was more absent than supportive. No woman wants hard times to fall upon her daughter especially if she is not nearby to help."

Barbara thought for a moment about how her own mother would have worried about her if she had known her daughter would have been all alone at such a young age.

Ben added, "Hoss is not likely to move away from the ranch; and the Swensons are probably going to stay put too as long as a good veterinarian like Karl is needed this side of Virginia City. Even though Mary-Lynn knows all this and that the couple is very much in love, she likely couldn't prevent the tears from coming anyway. We both know the family situation— it may likely be she is crying happy tears knowing that Evelyn is marrying the man she loves and that her marriage is starting off without any difficulty or scandal."

Barbara was nodding her head up and down in understanding.

He leaned over and said, "Your mother would have cried at ours."

She gave him her best smile now. Oh, how she loved this thoughtful man.

35

July 7, 1865

THE NEWLYWED COUPLE WAS FINALLY ALONE. They chose to spend their wedding night in Hoss' bedroom—at least his was private—Evelyn shared hers with four sisters. Evelyn didn't have any money as she always gave any wage she received for veterinary work to her parents. They decided they would save Hoss' current and future funds towards a house instead of spending needlessly on a hotel or a trip away.

Because they had to put clothing on to go out into the hallway, they had to set their modesty aside while changing inside the bedroom. They were inexperienced and awkward. But their shyness did not diminish their passion for each other.

They started by kissing while trying to disrobe each other. Delicate buttons on Evelyn's dress proved to be too challenging for Hoss' big and clumsy fingers. When he pulled one off instead, Evelyn took a hold of his hands and told him to not bother. She would undo the rest.

This break gave them both time to step back from the rush of the building hunger for each other. When Evelyn had removed all her clothing with buttons, they resumed kissing. Their passion quickly heightened once more.

Evelyn had always prided herself with her meticulous planning. But her wedding night did not go as she thought it might. It was better. How could she have planned for the unknown? She would have missed out on the giggles they shared when she realized that she had forgotten to pack a housecoat and had to wear Hoss' over-sized one when she needed to go down the hallway? Or the return of the erotic feeling they experienced when they were both drenched at the pond. Or when Hoss had removed a strand of hair from her face when he thought she was already asleep.

What the two shared in these most intimate first moments of their marriage would forever bring on smiles to their lips.

August 16, 1865

ADAM'S INTEREST IN ARCHITECTURE STEMMED from his last school year in 1853. He was fortunate enough to have studied under Mr. Smithers who lit in him a spark of curiosity in the field of erecting buildings. Ben was impressed with the teacher who saw Adam's potential and with his suggestion that Adam be encouraged to pursue the best education in that field abroad.

Although it was possible to bypass academic training to be licensed as an architect after an apprenticeship in a professional office, Adam wanted to learn everything he could at a university. After three years of saving money and convincing his father to provide the balance, Adam left for the School of Architecture in London, England in 1856. He returned two years later after having mastered in Drafting and Model Building.

A mature and stoic young man returned to his beloved home, hoping to never be away for that long a period again. But his cultured creativity in the field soon had him drawing plans for a new and modern ranch house. Ben put Adam's education to good use right away and began the process to replace the cabin that had been his family's home for more than twenty years with a larger one with modern conveniences.

In late 1864, Adam heard that Harvard University in Cambridge, Massachusetts, due to open the following year, would be the first institution of learning to offer a formal architectural curriculum. He submitted drawings along with his application to study Visual Arts and Construction Law.

By mid-August 1865, Adam was packing his bags and heading out to Massachusetts. He had been accepted based on his grades from his years at the university in London. He had yet to decide exactly what he wanted to do in the future, but he was excited to investigate his increasing possibilities. Now older and wiser, he would occupy his time with the sights of Boston—and especially Cambridge where old buildings lined the banks of the Charles River.

He was eager to go to university but regretted leaving before realizing his newest design—his brother's house.

Hoss and Evelyn had asked Adam to design their home. The back of the house would contain four bedrooms, one for the parents, one for the girl or girls, one for the boy or boys and one guest bedroom. Evelyn planned on using the guest room for her sewing and knitting projects if the grand room proved to be too busy with meal times and entertaining family and friends. Adam designed it to allow for expansion to include an upstairs loft if there was ever a need.

Their home was to be built on the far-north side of the ranch, very close to where Evelyn's parents live. The properties were adjacent, but the Cartwright ranch was so vast that it would be a fifteen minute carriage ride from the new home to the ranch house.

Even in his absence, Adam's plans were easy to follow, and the building of the house began.

Early September 1865

BEN AND BARBARA TOOK A BREAK FROM THE RANCH life in early September to venture back to Barbara's cave. She wanted to go back and close it up, so to speak. She never wanted to be alone like that again, but she did want to see it at least one more time.

She rode Vincent bareback because he still wouldn't be saddled. He eventually knew where he was headed and didn't need for her to guide him.

When they arrived, Ben said, "I would have just ridden by this rock. I would never think that there is a cave inside. How did you ever find it?"

She replied, "Remember when I said it was pouring rain and I sheltered under these branches, right here?" she pointed. "I tried to get closer to the trunk of the tree because that is where it was the driest, but it didn't exist. That's when I ended up in the cave totally protected from the rain."

She went inside the cave first, followed by Ben, and then by Vincent.

She lit a torch she had brought and was disappointed to find that little animals had located her cache of food. No matter, it would have been ruined anyway, but she at least now knew that it wasn't safe to keep food there if a human being wasn't around to discourage its discovery.

They didn't stay long. She just wanted to be alone with Ben in surroundings that were all too familiar, even for a moment. There certainly were no mementos that she wanted to bring back with her. She suddenly noticed that her tub was considerably smaller than she remembered.

Ben saw something behind the branches that were still leaning on the wall of the cave. A quarter of a cord of wood was stacked there. He knew she had chopped it all and placed it there for cooking and heating the place. Until this moment, he hadn't realized how totally self-sufficient she was. He reminded himself that he needed to stop treating her like a delicate little woman and start treating her like the independent adult that she truly was. She was his equal. No doubt about it.

Before they were ready to leave the mountain, he asked her to bring him to the area where she found him. When she did, they were both shocked to see the barren land that remained after the avalanche. He was still amazed that she had saved him by seeing his waving hand. It was utterly unbelievable that anyone could survive such a disaster.

She dismounted and crept forward until she arrived at the spot where his life would have ended had she not found him. He inhaled fully as if his lungs couldn't believe that they had survived the crushing, heavy, wet snow.

Ben didn't tell her, but he was looking for signs of his bay horse. There wasn't a trace. He was sure the remains would not have decomposed that quickly so the carcass and his saddle and other possessions must be lower down the mountain—probably where all the trees had piled up near the bottom.

No matter now, he thought, shaking his head in disbelief.

She thought he might be looking for signs of his beloved bay horse. She couldn't see any, so she didn't make mention of it.

It should have taken them about a day and a

half to make their way back home from there, but they stretched it out to three. Ben could tell that she was enjoying sleeping under the stars again and he relished the thought of keeping her warm on the cool evenings this high up in the mountain. She certainly was in her element here. There was nothing left for her to learn up here.

As they relaxed near the fire after the last day on the mountain, she hummed the same song that she hummed the first time they had met. He smiled remembering.

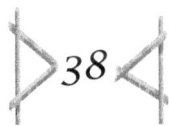

November 22, 1865

FROM HIS PORCH, BEN OBSERVED HOSS AND JOE working together, smearing grease on the wheels of the wagon and carriage in front of the barn. He couldn't hear them but knew that Joe said something in that gifted way he has when Hoss threw his head back and roared in laughter. Then Joe took the wet brush from the grease bucket and started fencing with it, showing Hoss his fancy footwork. Hoss laughed even harder as he lifted a wheel in place.

Ben couldn't help but admire his middle son. Hoss was a genuine man. Never a pretense to be someone he wasn't. Hoss loved life, family and animals. Ben thought, *When did he grow up? Or was he always this way? Evelyn sure adds to his happiness.*

Later, after lunch, the three men rode over to Hoss and Evelyn's place where they spent the afternoon putting up an outside wall on the back of the house. That was the last wall to go up. Next they started on the roof. They would have all winter to finish the inside.

~

Sunday, at the ranch, alone in the bedroom with her husband, Evelyn asked, "Hoss? Are you awake?"

"Miss Evelyn, you know I always nap in the afternoon of the Lord's day. You know I'm asleep."

147

"Then why did you answer?"

He let out a boisterous guffaw. He could never get angry with her. She knew that. She laughed with him.

"What is it? You need my help with something?" he asked.

"No, not really. Well not yet. Remember that day we went fishing in September after a frost and there were no bugs? But the fish weren't biting either so we made love in the meadow instead?" she asked mischievously.

"No. Describe it to me."

"Why Hoss Cartwright! Ah, well then, sure. I will."

Hoss opened his eyes in delighted surprise. Would she really?

"Ha, made you pay attention, didn't I?" she asked.

He laughed again. "What about it?" Suddenly interested.

"Well, I'm pretty sure it caused me to have a reaction."

"A reaction? Like what? Poison Ivy? I'm pretty sure welts would have shown up a while ago." He said, still laughing, loving this game.

"No. I'm throwing up in the mornings kind of reaction."

He was stumped. But only for a moment. "Evelyn, are you telling me you're with child?"

Wearing the biggest smile ever, she nodded.

From his laid down position, he pulled her into his arms. She giggled. They kissed, they laughed, they kissed.

~

With the announcement that their baby was due in May, no one seemed to be in a hurry to help Hoss finish building his house before winter—they were all too happy to keep everybody right where they were— here on the ranch.

Hoss and Evelyn's house was finished by the end of April, three weeks before the arrival of their baby boy. They named him Edwin after Evelyn's maternal grandfather. He was born late in the afternoon as announced by his cries.

Hoss held his son for mere seconds before handing him back to Evelyn. He had never seen a newly born baby and was too afraid of breaking such a small human being. Evelyn laughed and knew that time would change his hesitancy. She smiled and showed Hoss Edwin's ten perfect fingers and toes.

39

July 16, 2019

DOMINIQUE AND MICHAEL SPENT ONLY A COUPLE of days in Sacramento. They repeated the searches and narrowed them down considerably. They knew the exact date to be searched from the information in the letter, as well as the names of all the players.

It was no surprise that in a matter of minutes they found the copy of Mr. Devon's testament that had been held in his lawyer's office, that of Mr. Arthur Richardson.

Mr. Devon indeed changed his Last Will and Testament. He apparently had a change of heart and had included his niece as co-heir. The letter to his lawyer explained that he had left the bracelet in Sacramento to be engraved with the inscription *Annette Devon, beloved niece.* Although Mr. Devon had moved to Virginia City, he did not know of any engravers who could do the delicate job there.

Should the lawyer locate his niece, she would inherit half of Mr. Devon's substantial estate and receive the small gift as a token of his affection for his estranged, late brother's daughter.

Other letters on file indicated that a search was undertaken and after the great sum of $1,000 allotted to the search resulted in zero success, the entire estate eventually went to a half-brother's only son.

When the group of eleven met online the last evening of Dominique and Michael's stay in Sacramento, Jacqueline mentioned, "I wonder what kind of search they could do back then."

"What do you mean, Jackie?" asked Céleste.

"Well, what records did they have?" Jacqueline asked.

"I suppose they had marriage, birth and death records. Why?" asked Philip.

"I don't know. I was just wondering, should we do our own search?"

"Hey, that's a great idea! Why not? We can probably search the entire United States in a fraction of the time that they could search even one state. They would likely have to physically go to a city to do the searches while we can do it with online ancestry sites," said Camille.

"Well that makes sense," said Joel.

"Okay, let's do it—together," said Gabriel.

They agreed that they would meet on the first day that every cousin was off work. As three of them worked shift hours, that day would be August 8th.

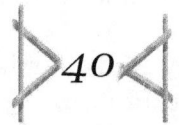

Summer 1866

ADAM'S FINAL YEAR IN SCHOOL WAS INDEED ONE of mixed sentiments. He met nine other equally brilliant men in the architectural field. The class capacity was capped at ten students. Such a small number of scholars enabled the men to bond friendships that would last a lifetime. Their Professor Dawson was truly impressed with the men and constantly challenged them.

Adam had arrived at the end of his studies. Only firsthand experience could advance his knowledge in this field now.

At the beginning of the September 1865 classes, the professor had assigned the students an extracurricular project to be completed over the summer months the following year. During the academic year, a half hour per week was set aside for the students in the class to discuss and write the rules involved in the challenge and on Monday, July 9, the race would begin.

The grading of the competition would not affect final grades. Winning first place of the competition would, instead, provide opportunities.

The challenge:
>   1) The student currently enrolled at the University would take the lead in the building of the proposed model.

2) The project was to begin on July 9 and end on August 18.

3) The student would be assigned a prominent freshman who showed promise in the field of Architecture.

4) The student, assisted by the freshman, would spend the summer building a model of a specific building type that would be judged by the professor.

5) The winner would be nominated to work on the construction of the Suez Canal and the freshman would be assured of a seat in the architectural classes for the following three years.

Over the course of the next nine months, the students would separate into teams to review freshmen's curriculum vitae and discuss and choose building projects. With the exception of which senior student would receive which challenge, all aspects of the challenges were decided by the student groups before they dissolved their teams to begin working on their separate assignments.

Professor Dawson decided which graduate would receive which challenge and created ten envelopes—each contained the name of the student, the name of the freshman selected, and the details of the model to be designed for him to grade. The students had to follow through with the decisions that had been made for them or admit defeat.

When Adam arrived home to the ranch, the envelope detailing his assignment was already waiting for him. He had regularly written his father, Barbara, and his brothers over the course of the last ten months and his family could tell he was thoroughly enjoying his studies and eager for the upcoming summer challenge.

As directed, on July 9th, Adam opened the thick envelope of instructions. He read that he was expecting a freshman by the name of A. J. Simmons on July 12th to be his assistant on this assignment. Gratefully, Mr. Simmons' curriculum vitae showed promise of becoming a reputable architect if provided with this prestigious opportunity. Mr. Simmons was already known to be a top student of his current studies.

Nothing could please Adam more, nor would he expect less. Adam recalled all the summaries of applicants' overview of their life's academic formation he and his classmates had read and vetted in an attempt to only select the best without any face to face interviews. Not all of the successful candidates had acquired top marks in their current studies. He was pleased to have ended up with one who did.

Adam discovered that he was tasked with building a model of a dwelling that could be sustainable underground. Of course, no one was assigned something as easily duplicated as a sixteen-peaked, Gothic twelfth-century church—but an underground dwelling? Challenging, yes. Elegant, no. Out of the ordinary, definitely.

He grimaced and reread the task. He decided that he would make this odd task appealing. He thought it possible that underground dwellings could be built for employees who would be expected to work on and at the Suez Canal. What first appeared to be a boring, useless project suddenly became interesting.

Excited now for the task, Adam soon discovered he had three advantages. One, this project was sure to be judged on its own merit as no one else was likely to have a similar challenge. The second, he had three months' work experience in the silver mines. He had been sent there by his father to determine the feasibility for mines on Cartwright land. The third,

Barbara's former life on the mountain would offer him some insight to draw from. She had lived in a cave for eleven years after all. Surely he could use some of her reality in an aspect of this project. He was starting to devise his plan.

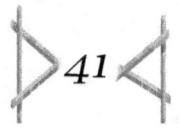

July 10, 1866

BARBARA, EVELYN AND EDWIN WERE ENJOYING A breeze in the shade of the big oak tree in front of the house.

Barbara confided, "I don't want to say anything to anyone, Evelyn, so please keep this to yourself."

"What is it, Barbara?"

"I'm not feeling well. I'm not feeling ill, not all the time, I'm just feeling, oh, I don't know how to explain it, I'm just not feeling like my usual self."

Evelyn asked for her to describe her specific symptoms which made Evelyn suspect Barbara was pregnant.

"Why Barbara, I believe you are going to be a mother!"

Evelyn knew the dangers of an older woman in her forties who was pregnant for the first time, but she kept quiet about it. No point adding worry about something that might not happen.

Of course, Barbara was overjoyed. Ben was shocked at first and then elated. He had embraced and kissed his wife in front of Evelyn. Barbara was more than embarrassed—as she was not yet comfortable with public demonstrations of affection, even within the family—but Evelyn put her at ease when she mentioned that Hoss had done the same thing when he found out about her being pregnant.

Barbara and Ben soon told the rest of the family about the addition expected in March the next year.

Everyone was happy for them. None of the three boys were bothered about the age difference between themselves and of their future sibling and joked about how Edwin would be older than his new aunt or uncle.

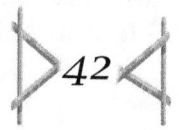

July 12, 1866

ADAM WAS NECK DEEP, LITERALLY, IN HIS MOCK prototype. He couldn't begin to design a model of his project unless he could be sure it would actually support the weight of soil above it. He was not going to build the entire human-size model of his design, just one room of it; that being the entrance and multi-use room. Mr. Simmons couldn't arrive soon enough. Adam very much looked forward to some fresh ideas, recommendations and helping hands.

A. J. Simmons had also been provided with a copy of the assignment. The front of the cover of the envelope read: Do not open until July 12. Obeying the instruction, A. J. had opened it on the stagecoach but found that mixing reading and a bumpy ride resulted in motion sickness, so the envelope was put aside.

Barbara was heading out to Virginia City on July 12 and was tasked with bringing Mr. Simmons back to the ranch with her. Adam had asked Barbara to bring the student over right away to the area where he was building the prototype. Barbara was also asked to instruct him to put on the supplied coveralls, working boots and head gear before nearing the area.

But when Barbara arrived at the stagecoach platform that afternoon, there were no young men waiting. As she turned to leave, not relishing sharing this disappointing news with Adam, she noticed a lovely young lady, looking lost.

In regular Cartwright fashion, she approached

the woman and asked, "Can I help you?"

The young lady nodded and introduced herself, "Hello, my name is Angelina Simmons. I'm looking for a Mr. Adam Cartwright."

Angie looked around at the people walking by. "Would you know him? Is he here?"

Barbara grinned when she said, "Hello, I'm Barbara Cartwright. I am married to Ben who is Adam's father. I'm pleased to meet you," and they shook hands. "I'm going to bring you to meet Adam right away."

Both knew but neither woman mentioned the fact that Angie was not the expected man for the job at hand.

They climbed up in the wagon and were on their way to the area where Adam was working. Between the wait on the platform and the carriage ride over to the site, Angie had finished reading up on the model expected from her and Adam.

Barbara told Angie, "As you could not read the project assignment until now, Adam wasn't sure that you would bring appropriate clothing with you. He has set aside boots, pants and a long-sleeve shirt in case you need them. And because you will be outside all day, he also put aside a hat to protect your head from the sun's heat."

Angie was grateful for Adam's thoughtfulness with respect to the protective clothing.

Barbara dropped off Angie with the promise that Adam would escort her back to the house if she didn't want to walk the short distance alone and pointed out the ranch house just over the hill. She also told her she would look after her bags and that supper was at 6:00 and to not be late.

Angie found the clothing. She removed her traveling jacket and tucked her skirt into the shapeless over-sized pants and donned the shirt over her own.

Lastly, she pulled on the boots and hat provided. Approaching the ground where Adam was working, she saw someone below, standing in dirt next to a wall that had caved in. He was covered in dust from hat to boots. The man was busy clearing the breach when Angie managed to yell out a "Hello" in the quiet moment between his shovels of dirt to the bucket.

He looked up but couldn't see clearly for all the dust in the air and coughed back, "You must be Simmons. I'm Adam Cartwright. Listen, I've had another breach here. I'm sorry there is nothing for you to do here until tomorrow. Go ahead to the house. I'll catch up with you in about twenty or thirty minutes. I'm almost done for the day here anyway." He motioned for her to go and pointed toward the house.

Angie understood and gave him a quick nod, not sure if he noticed. She removed her gear and neatly stacked it back on the wagon from where she had found it.

The walk was very pleasant, but she stopped when the ranch house came into view. She gasped. Even the air was exciting to inhale. As far as she could see there was pure nature in all its beauty. A richness surrounded the house and barn. A few horses were grazing in the deep-green meadow near the house and cattle were visible in the far fields. Ice-capped mountains could clearly be seen on this cloudless day there in the background and to the right. The house was nestled in among giant trees, full in their foliage. She was pleasantly surprised to see such a magnificent house. She may have been misled to believe that most everything in the western part of the country was rough and crude but this house certainly was not.

She deeply breathed in the clean air. She would love her short stay here, she was sure. She would be doing what she enjoyed most in life while seeing the sights on the ranch like Lake Tahoe. What an adventure awaiting her. She was full of excitement and all smiles when she thought about the rest of her life being one treasure to be unfolded after another.

She had always enjoyed her studies and although she was eventually interested in pursuing a marital endeavor, she wasn't planning on one for many years yet. She couldn't let domestic life interfere with her desires to explore this country and possibly even venture overseas.

If only women were accepted into universities in fields such as architecture, I could make a career out of that, she thought.

But alas, she could only hope to meet intelligent, interesting people and continue her education through them. Her studies in university to date indicated she attained high marks in all subjects and showed promise that she would be an ideal candidate for further schooling in topics such as architecture. But alas, she was not the right gender!

Angie had heard a little bit about Mr. Adam Cartwright through her father. Her father was Professor Dawson's former colleague. Her father had since retired but kept in close contact with most professors at the university. Professor Dawson had shared with her father the unique gifts possessed by Adam, as well as those of other promising students. But as Adam was the student who had been assigned Angie as his assistant, he had divulged that Adam was one of the fortunate students to have been schooled in England. She knew, her father knew, they all knew the wealth of education Adam possessed and how fortunate she was to be his partner in the challenge.

Angie made it to the house by 5:30. Once inside, she paused for a few moments to gaze at the high ceiling. She understood the possibility of the loft being supported by the way the beams had been secured.

She intuitively knew Adam must have designed it. She had to admit to herself that she admired him even without having properly met the man.

Barbara entered the grand room from the kitchen and noticed Angie standing there, staring at the ceiling. "Where's Adam?" she asked.

"I've not really met Mr. Cartwright yet," explained Angie. "He was in a hole that I assume is our assignment. He was covered in dirt. Dust covered the air and neither of us could clearly see the other."

Barbara suggested, "Well supper will be served at 6:00. You will meet him then. I believe you have just enough time to change from your traveling clothes but that leaves no time to rest. Come, this way."

"That's all right. The walk here has been refreshing enough," Angie said as she followed Barbara toward the guest bedroom.

~

At precisely 6:00, Ms. Simmons came downstairs. The family had gathered in the grand room and all turned to look at her. All except Barbara were surprised that A. J. Simmons was a woman. Of course, Joe and Hoss raised an eyebrow and gave each other a nod in silent approval at the sight of such loveliness.

But Adam was perplexed and annoyed. Where was Simmons? Hadn't he met him briefly earlier? Who is this woman? Why were there not two extra settings at the table if Simmons had brought a companion? And why didn't his freshman have the courtesy to ask permission to do so? She was certainly a good looking woman, he admitted to himself, but his attraction to her fought with his annoyance at her presence.

Angie almost stopped her descent of the flight of stairs. She was looking at four of the most

162

handsome men she had ever seen. They were truly magnificent examples of the male species and she was dumbfounded. But only for a moment. It would take more than good looks to distract Angie from her goals in life.

Barbara felt a surge of energy from the direction where Adam was standing. She was puzzled by it, but put it down to being caused by her pregnancy.

Adam's flustered look when she introduced Angie to him made her smile even more. She realized that Adam was highly attracted to this lovely, young, smart woman who would become his partner for the next few weeks.

Barbara apologized for failing to mention that she had learned that A. J. was short for Angelina Josephine, but there just hadn't been any time. Ben looked at his wife, surprised by her making fun at their expense. She wasn't known to be humorous, but she was certainly finding humor in this situation.

Adam was flabbergasted and attempted to cover up his reaction. He shook her hand and quickly said, "I read that A. J. Simmons was in the top ten of his, ah, her class. I had not realized that women had been accepted at the university in this field."

He held her hand a little longer than usual. He was so drawn to her that he almost kissed the back of it. He was drinking in her beautiful, flawless, white skin, her perfectly chiseled nose, and her smiling lips, but mostly he was captivated by the biggest brown eyes he had ever seen. She was crowned with lovely, black hair that was so thick she had enough for another person. He was only six inches taller than her, but she was so petite that she appeared shorter.

His perfect and challenging smile, in turn, flustered Angie. She felt drawn to this man even though his eyes were demanding her to accredit herself. She sensed he was as intelligent as her own father and she liked that very much. She had not met any men during all her years at study who could match her academic wealth of knowledge. As she never felt any of those men her equal, she never accepted any invitations to pursue courtship. She knew Adam's knowledge surpassed hers, but she was surely going to be giving him a challenge in discovering that for himself. She looked forward to getting to know this man, Adam Cartwright.

Ben moved to sit at the head of the table and they all found their spots—Barbara to his right, followed by Adam and A. J. Simmons, Joe at the end, followed by Hoss and Evelyn on Joe's right.

Angie laughed as they seated themselves around the table, "Please call me Angie. And no, they have not let women in. But being Theodore Simmons' smart daughter and only child helped me get this far. I may never get a degree in Architecture, but I should because I'm more intelligent than most of the current-year students. My father loves to talk about everything architecture. In order for me to spend quality time with him while growing up, I had to learn to develop smart and challenging questions. So, over the years, I started studying the books he had at home."

Helping herself to some vegetables before passing the bowl, she continued, "Last September, my father heard about your professor's summer assignment and submitted my name using only my initials. Just my father's recommendation alone assured me of a part in this summer's project, but I wanted to be chosen without his endorsement. No one knew I was a woman either. Father knew it would not cause an issue at the university because the rules did not specify men only as the potential student of architecture. Only your professor knew who I was. I hope you won't back out of the competition because of me. I am excited by the challenge of this build. I promise to not disappoint."

"Professor Theodore Simmons is your father? I should have made the connection," Adam laughed, causing her to relax. "Of course, I don't mind, and I would never back out even without an assistant. I look forward to a woman's input on this project. It will not be easy and with the knowledge I am sure you possess, you will most definitely be an asset."

Angie was more than pleased by his comments. She hoped his remarks were genuine and that he was not just being polite.

Barbara was once again surprised at the Cartwrights' ability to accept women in fields normally dominated by men, without prejudice. What amazing men these Cartwrights were. If they truly had biased opinions, they would not have been able to hide them for too long, so she figured they were genuinely impressed with the abilities of the women around the supper table.

After the meal, Adam gave Angie a tour of the house. Joe decided he would help but when her questions were beyond him, he quit following them. He was bored by the topic. Adam couldn't have been happier when Joe stopped tagging along. Angie never even noticed that Joe was attracted to her, he just was not part of her current interests. She was interested in architecture, not romance.

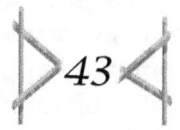

July 15, 1866

DAYS WENT BY WHEN NO ONE SAW ADAM OR ANGIE until suppertime. They would leave early in the morning to work on the prototype model that only they could understand. They often had their heads down after the family meal, fixated on their drawings. The two foot tall model they assembled in the grand room was upgraded on a weekly basis. They occasionally had heated discussions about the direction of the project, but always agreed to try out the potential solutions within the next day or so. They were both headstrong and neither could respect someone who would give way if they thought they were correct about whatever was being disputed.

They spent hours together alone, side by side, day after day. When one of the hands or the cook brought over their noon meal to the site, they would take a break and discuss their project. Once in a while, they would talk about something other than their work.

"I do want to have a future that involves architecture, Adam."

"Me as well, of that I have no doubt. I always dreamed of being invited to a city in Europe to study or work, or better yet, being hired to build a prominent building."

"Oh, that would be so exciting," said Angie, encouraging him to go on.

"When I realized that I loved architecture and

could design and build, I started dreaming about doing just that. I could probably find a job in New York or in another city on the east coast, but my dream is to go to Europe. The history, the people, the buildings are all so rich, old, and exquisite over there, that I can't imagine a better challenge than to build something new and make it look old."

"I agree. I have traveled with Mother and Father to Rome, Paris, Athens and England. I have seen beautiful buildings more than three hundred years old and have always imagined myself there in the midst of erecting something magical like a new castle or church. All the buildings are ornate and have so much character."

"I have only been to England, but I have seen enough to know that I want to see more."

"I'm sure you will," said Angie. She swallowed hard and couldn't figure out why her reply bothered her.

One evening, about two weeks after Angie's arrival, Adam said, "Let's leave the hygienic aspect of the dwelling until the last, shall we?" They had spent the last ten days discussing it and exhausted all ideas on the problem. "We can't spend any more time on it. If we do, we'll be too rushed to do the rest of the design and that would be a disaster. Do you agree, Angie?"

She straightened up from her position at the model and replied with a smile, "That's the smartest thing I've heard all day. I agree, let's not waste any more time on getting rid of odors that can build up in a confined space until we're satisfied with the rest of the project." Adam smiled back and moved on with renewed vigor.

~

Adam and Angie discovered their mutual interest in music one Sunday when Adam accompanied Barbara at the piano on his guitar. Angie began to sing along to their music in her clear alto voice. She then sat next to Barbara, playing the accompaniment in bass on the piano.

She was quite surprised when Adam joined in on the second verse. His baritone easily gave the song the character it needed. She couldn't help but be mesmerized by his eyes locked on to hers that appeared to challenge her to sing solo on the third verse. But instead, he sang it with her by completing the last few words of each phrase. His accomplished voice caused goosebumps to appear on her arms and neck.

Angie had never felt such an attraction to a man. They were so well suited. She could only determine that her growing attraction and interest in him was because of their similarities.

No one was discouraged from singing along, but most wanted to simply sit back and enjoy what they were listening to.

Barbara was elated to learn that Angie knew so many more pieces of music than she and was fascinated to learn that she could also play the guitar, the violin and the flute.

"You are so gifted, Angie. How marvelous to be able to play so many instruments and to sing as well as you do. I wish we had more sheet music we could play together. You could teach me so much."

"Oh Barbara. I will ask Mother to send my music sheets right away. You will enjoy them tremendously."

"Really Angie? You would do that?"

"Of course. It would be my pleasure."

~

Ben was sitting in his favorite chair, enjoying smoking his pipe and drinking a glass of brandy. He reflected on how well his sons interacted with each other. His family had easily grown to embrace Barbara with open arms and then just as easily welcomed Evelyn.

He was proud of Hoss and Joe as they easily pitched in to do Adam's share of the work around the ranch. There was no resentment of Adam's desire to concentrate on his project at the expense of his chores. They were even so generous as to offer one of their Saturday afternoons—after finishing chores—to help Adam put up supporting beams on the dwelling.

Most evenings, Ben watched Hoss and Joe play with Edwin until his bedtime, followed by playing a few games of checkers with his sons while Evelyn and Barbara went to their craft room to do whatever they did there.

Presently, Evelyn was teaching Barbara to sew on the new Singer machine that Ben had purchased as a gift for Barbara. The machine had been invented about twenty years before and when Barbara saw one in the Ladies' Clothing Store in Virginia City, she was thrilled by its possibilities. Evelyn's mother had purchased such a machine five years earlier and Evelyn was determined to teach Barbara how to use it to make her sewing projects easier to accomplish. Barbara often had to be reminded that most women her age had at least twenty years of experience at hand stitching. As she mastered some of the intricate details of sewing with the machine, she was quite pleased with herself.

At the end of the evening, Hoss and Evelyn would take turns carrying Edwin home, usually heading out as late as possible, reluctant to leave the good company of their family.

44

July 19, 1866

LATER THAT WEEK AT THE SUPPER TABLE, ADAM started chuckling and said, "Let me tell you something funny that happened this morning ..."

Angie's face turned beet red. She dropped her fork and said, "You promised, Adam!"

He replied, "I did no such thing. I never said I wouldn't tell anyone how funny you looked coming down the ladder when you tripped on your pant leg that had unfolded and covered your boot just right so you would miss that second step." Holding his sides laughing and then in slow motion imitated her falling and arms flailing.

Joe and Hoss easily laughed along with Adam at the display.

Barbara said, "I hope you didn't get hurt, Angie."

Then turning to her oldest stepson, she sternly said, "Maybe we should do alterations to those pants that were meant for a man. What do you think Adam?"

She shifted her focus to her other two stepsons until all three men ceased their impolite laughter. Ben smiled, all too happy to let Barbara discipline his sons.

Adam cleared his throat and replied, "No she didn't get hurt. I had just climbed down myself and caught her in time. And yes, of course, shorten the pant legs at the very least."

He wouldn't be telling anyone, but would forever remember, how he had caught her in his right arm, steadied himself on the ladder with his left, and kissed her, long and hard, when she was momentarily off balance. She had stiffened in his embrace and he was sure he had offended her with his kiss. He was surprised himself for doing so uninvited and had apologized, setting her solidly on her feet. He immediately turned away and got back to work, but he couldn't fully concentrate on the work at hand. The kiss had moved him; invaded him.

Meanwhile, she was dazed by the fall and especially by the kiss. She knew she had reacted badly. She wished that she would have at the very least, placed a hand on the back of his head or his shoulder. She was then upset at his apology confirming his error in kissing her. How confusing. The memory of the kiss burned her lips the rest of the day. It was like there was a power between the two sets of lips and when they met, they created a force that made the lips reluctant to separate. That was the only way she could have described it. Surely, he had felt it too, hadn't he? But they buried their innermost feelings and got back to the task at hand.

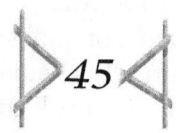

45

Friday, July 27, 1866

ADAM HAD NEVER CONSIDERED THAT ONE DAY HE would feel drawn to someone. It just hadn't played a part in his plans for his future. He always thought that being a scholar would satisfy him. Early on, it was obvious that he loved to study and learn. Unlike Hoss and Joe, who showed little interest in furthering their education once they graduated from the minimum grade decided by their father, he often had his nose in a book and a newspaper nearby.

Adam had never met a woman who could challenge him intellectually, especially one with so much knowledge on architecture. Nor one who was so talented, let alone who could sing like an angel and play multiple musical instruments. She fascinated him.

One morning, halfway through the challenge, it dawned on Adam that he more than admired Angie. He was dreading the day when their project would come to an end. He found himself unhappy at the thought of her going back home. Just the thought of her leaving made his throat tighten and stomach clench.

He was beginning to understand his true feelings for her, yet he didn't know how she truly felt about him. He had not found another occasion to kiss her. They were always working so intently together on the project that the opportunity had not arisen—and a part of him didn't want to risk a kiss or conversation about emotions in case it put a strain on their working relationship.

July 27, 1866

AT THE END OF JULY, ANGIE MENTIONED IN passing that she would miss this beautiful state of Nevada. Most of her time had been spent around the ranch, the site, or the distance in between. Adam had mentioned that he would show her Lake Tahoe when they had a chance.

The morning of Sunday, July 29, she reminded him subtly, "Can you really see the better part of Lake Tahoe from your land?"

"Why, yes of course. I promised to bring you there, didn't I? Shall we go this afternoon?" Adam asked, happily.

The view was spectacular. The water was both incredibly blue and green at the same time as it reflected both sky and forest.

Adam was not going to let this occasion slip by. Now was his chance to kiss her once more. She was so captured by the landscape—it was unlike any she had ever set eyes on—that she hardly gave him an opening.

He finally turned her away from the scenery, pulled her close to him and kissed her. When she moved her arms to hug his big, firm shoulders, she opened herself up for a deeper, more passionate kiss.

His lips slowly, yet eventually, left hers and when he opened his eyes, he saw her beautiful face still tilted upwards. Her lips were slightly parted. Her cheeks were flushed. She slowly opened her eyes as if in disbelief that the kiss awakened feelings in her she didn't know existed. It was more intense and meaningful than the first. Yet, she could never forget their first kiss.

Still looking in each other's eyes, they both heard his inhale of air. He released his hold on her and she reluctantly took her arms off his shoulders and neck. He didn't smile for fear that she might misunderstand that the kiss was a conquest. It wasn't. If anything, she had conquered him. She almost reached up to touch his face, but lost the moment.

He said, "Well, I guess we should be heading back." She nodded.

She had never been so close to another person that she could see her reflection in their eyes. But she had clearly seen her face in his eyes looking back at herself. On the ride back to the ranch, she wanted to ask him about it but was afraid that he might say something deflating like, "Oh, yes. Every time I kiss a girl, I see myself in her eyes."

When they arrived at the ranch house, Angie passed Evelyn and Barbara on the unlit staircase, glad for the low lighting considering her burning blushing cheeks. She thought about sharing her feelings with the other women, but then decided to keep it private. She didn't know them well enough to confide in them. She was on her own with her thoughts and questions. Instead, she only asked, "Do you think I have time to change before supper?"

Barbara replied, "You have ten minutes. Hurry."

Angie rushed to her room before the heat on her cheeks exploded.

Adam had kissed a few women in his life. There was Louise who was really just a friend from their early school years together; then Jenny whom he had courted on and off for three years until she tired of waiting for him to make a decision; and she was followed by Regina who he was sure was that special someone, but their background differed and her religion led her down a separate path. After all these heart breaks, he had decided to pursue other dreams, alone.

Adam was frustrated. Why had he let go of Angie so soon? He may never have another occasion to kiss her. Not like that anyway. Maybe a kiss goodbye at the stagecoach, but not one where they could embrace, and linger ... he stopped himself from thinking further.

~

The following morning, the two felt awkward as they began working on their project, but as neither knew how to address the tension, they both ignored their feelings and pretended to work unaffected. By lunch time, the tension had eased, emotions had calmed, and the conversation went back to its normal pace.

They had returned to the ranch house for the noon meal and while they passed the bowls around the table, Adam asked, "Barbara, could you meet with Angie and I this afternoon?"

"Why, of course, Adam. What do you need me to do?"

"Oh, just answer a few questions."

Shortly after they finished eating, they started the discussion while heading to sit near the model. Ben had come along out of curiosity.

Adam asked bluntly, "What did you do with your waste during wintertime in your cave?"

Angie didn't know if she could ever fully understand Barbara's life before coming to live here. She was very interested in hearing what Barbara had to say and listened attentively.

Barbara described how she would discard her

and Vincent's waste daily. She also remembered the first time there had been a severe snowstorm that prohibited her from exiting her cave for days.

Adam asked, "That is what I am most interested in hearing. So, what did you do? Just put up with the smell?"

Barbara replied, "Yuk, the first time, yes. It took four long days before I could head outside! I would push our waste as far into the snow as possible at the entrance, in the hopes that it would freeze along with the smell. Eventually though, I remembered what my Pa did once when everyone in the house had been sick with influenza. It's not that our being sick did not eventually get cleaned up and sheets put outside, it's just that we all got sick at the same time and he couldn't clean it fast enough, so the odor lingered."

Adam leaned forward, excited with a possible solution. "What did your father do that made you copy his actions?"

"I placed sawdust and leaves that I had gathered over the summer months on top of the waste."

"That's it?" Angie asked, incredulously.

"That's it. It works. You simply place sawdust or leaves, if you have any, or a combination of both, over the waste. Make sure to cover it all and no odor will escape into the air from the area where your waste is. In my case, the entire cave because it was an open space. I think even ashes would work, but I'm not one hundred percent sure on that."

"Throughout the entire cave? That is our solution, Angie. Thank you, Barbara. Pa, did you know that sawdust could smother odor?" Adam asked.

"Well now that you mention it, I did. But it has been so long that we've had need of using sawdust with the flush toilet upstairs and the outhouse, that it must have slipped my mind," Ben replied.

Before adding the information with respect to

sawdust to his design and documents, Adam would test Barbara's solution. It is not that he didn't trust her, he just needed to be sure it worked. If he didn't test it and it didn't work, he would certainly come in last on the competition. Of course, he didn't want that to occur if all it took was a small experiment.

~

When Angie came down the ladder the next morning, she could smell horse manure. It was quite strong and her eyes teared at the repugnant stench. Adam was ready with a shovel of sawdust and Angie pinched her nose as she observed him covering the manure with it. They decided to exit the dwelling and come back in about an hour to see if the odor was less strong.

They didn't expect much. After all, this was an underground dwelling and Barbara had lived in a cave with many openings to allow air circulation. In comparison, they had only supplied the underground room with one air shaft for the escape of odors. Maybe they should have included at least one more. If this strategy didn't work out, would they have time to develop a new one? Time was running out.

When the hour passed, they climbed back into their experiment. The nose test worked! They knew they had completed their biggest challenge. Adam breathed a sigh of relief. Angie was overjoyed as she allowed herself to think that they might just win the competition. They actually held hands and jumped around in glee. They hugged each other and gave a quick peck of a kiss and then just as quickly released each other.

Immediately, a disappointed Adam recalled the conversation he and Angie had shortly after they met. Angie had said, "I want to do something more in my life, certainly something different than most women. I know I will encounter many challenges because I am a woman, but I won't let that stand in my way. Not only do I want to travel, but I want to go to places where I can learn about architecture, designing—even engineering. I want to know more about these crafts so I can better decide for myself where my talents are best suited. Do you agree that everyone should add to their knowledge as much as possible?"

And, he had basically told her the same thing, "Yes. I do. I also want to travel the world and discover buildings of clay or wood or stone, just to be more knowledgeable. I find the more I know, the richer I am in my field. I could contribute so much more to whatever project awaits me with such experiences."

They had both talked about their singular dreams, but in the weeks since had not ventured in discussing them further.

When they first met, Angie was sure Adam wanted to hear exactly what she had said. Their desired futures appeared to be possible only as long as they did not part from their dreams for themselves—and those dreams were on different paths. Now every time they clashed with a difference of opinion or laughed when they agreed, it reinforced their attraction for each other. Then they would pause, often physically, deciding to respect the dreams of the other and not pursue or even discuss their desire to kiss or even hug.

Adam knew in his heart that for Angie to achieve even a small portion of her dreams, she would have to remain unwed or at the very least not become a mother too early.

August 11, 1866

ADAM WENT TO HIS FATHER'S STUDY AND SAT down on one of the chairs in front of the big mahogany desk. Ben was working, his head down, frowning at his paperwork.

"Pa, I need your advice with something," Adam said. His father stopped what he was doing and looked at his son. The worry on the younger man's face made Ben put down his pen and push back from his desk.

Although Barbara was outside tending to Vincent, as she always did this early in the morning, the others living in the house were stirring upstairs and would soon make their way down for breakfast. Adam wanted a private moment with his father, so he lowered his voice and scooted his chair closer to the desk.

"I can't seem to let myself get past the day when Angie won't be here challenging me on the direction I want to go in with some design or model. I like her, very much. She is so much like me. We love all the same things, even music. I can't get over how much I will miss her. But I am torn with the direction my studies are leading me. What do you think I should do?"

Ben sighed. For a few moments, he just sat there, saying nothing. Finally, he knowingly, incorrectly replied, "Let her go."

"What? That's it? I can't do that!"

"What do you want me to say? I can't make a

decision for you, Adam. I suspect you already know what you want to do. Now, leave me to finish these papers before breakfast."

Adam just stood there. "You think I already know what I want to do?"

Ben just gave him an impatient look.

Finally, Adam got the message. "Oh, you're right. I do know. I'm in love with her! This is love, right? Oh, it must be. I don't want a day to go by without seeing her. What do you think I ... ah, never mind. I know what to do. Thanks Pa."

Ben smiled as Adam went off like an excited little boy on his birthday to write Angie's father, requesting his blessing for him to ask for her hand in marriage.

> *Dear Professor and Mrs. Simmons:*
> *I have fallen in love with your daughter, Angie, who is an angel, but you know that already. I admire her talents and in-depth knowledge of things we have in common. She continually challenges me and makes me want to be the best version of myself. She completes me.*
> *Rest assured that I want to help Angie pursue her dreams in every aspect but especially those that involve architecture.*
> *I ask for your permission and blessing to ask for Angie's hand in marriage.*
> *Yours truly and most sincerely,*
> *Adam Cartwright*

Adam knew that it could take up to two weeks for a letter to reach its destination in Cambridge from Nevada. He posted the letter separately and sent a wire with a shorter message.

I love Angie STOP
I promise to make her happy STOP
May I have your blessing? STOP
My letter will follow STOP
Adam Cartwright

Her parents already knew they were perfectly matched. Angie had been writing regularly to them about her summer activities and every sentence or two mentioned Adam. Professor Simmons and his wife gave their full approval by return wire.

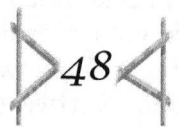

August 16, 1866

ADAM PROPOSED THE NIGHT THEIR MODEL WAS finished. He led her on a romantic walk toward a field that was splashed with wildflowers—where their new home would be built, if she said yes. In his pocket was a ring wrapped in a white handkerchief. It was a family heirloom—the ring his grandfather Cartwright had given to Ben's mother. They had been married for over forty years and Adam thought perhaps the ring would bless Angie and his marriage with the same steadfastness.

He got down on one knee, took out the ring from his pocket and asked for her hand. She emphatically replied, "Yes!"

He stood, placed his arms around her waist while she placed her arms around his neck and shoulders. He leaned forward; she lifted her head up. They anticipated the power that would make their lips reluctant to separate once they touched again. They kissed a kiss that sealed a promise of eternal love. They both felt it and meant it.

"Oh, Adam. Will kissing you always be like this?" she asked, catching her breath and allowing herself to swoon in his strong hold.

He looked at her standing there with her eyes still shut, "I believe so."

When she opened her eyes, she was looking into his dark, piercing, kind eyes. He was smiling. She smiled back. She loved his smile and vowed to make him do so more often.

Suddenly she removed her arms from his neck and pushed him away and exclaimed, "Adam, what about your dreams?"

He replied, "Angie, what about yours?"

She answered him, "I want to marry you Adam, I could forget about my dreams to become an architect. But you!"

He said, "Angie, I love you more than a career and I want you in my future, but neither of us has to give up anything. Don't you see? We both want the same things. I want new dreams with you in it. I want to build buildings with you. I want to travel with you. I love how we solve problems together and find new ways to erect walls and design and ..." he paused, and then continued with a smile, "solve the mysteries of sanitation."

"Oh, Adam. You're right. I need to continue with my passions. What better way than to do them together." She approached him with open arms, and they kissed again.

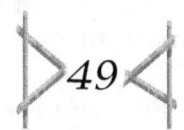

49

August 17, 1866

ADAM AND ANGIE DISMANTLED THE MODEL AND labeled each panel for easy reassembly. The panels were tied together with the instructions and placed in a wooden crate along with the designs and papers. Together they dropped the box off at the stagecoach. They paid the fees for the transfer by train from Salt Lake City in Utah to the professor in Cambridge. And, that's it. They were done.

They reflected on their chances of winning. Adam's initial enthusiasm at winning this competition was replaced with his elation of loving Angie.

He admitted, "I would not wager on having submitted the winning entry."

"Why not, Adam? It was quite a challenge that I believe was achieved in the only possible way. You know that structure will hold underground," she said.

"I don't know why not. I just feel that others may have received a greater challenge and their structure may be more appealing. I do not know under what merits we will be graded, I just have this notion."

But the anticipated loss was not heartbreaking. Adam had lost interest in joining the construction efforts for the building of the Suez Canal. He much preferred working on his new plans for a life with Angie.

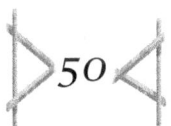

August 29, 1866

ADAM AND ANGIE WERE MARRIED ON AUGUST 29. Barbara couldn't help but think that she was likely never going to err in her predictions that some people belonged together. After all, she had been right about herself and Ben, about Evelyn and Hoss and now about Angie and Adam. She had surmised quite a while ago that Angie's gift was fortitude. She had never met a more determined, self-assured woman and would be a wonderful wife to Adam.

The day of the wedding, Adam received a telegram from Harvard. Their project came in at fourth place. Adam would not be offered the opportunity to work on the Suez Canal project. Angie was secretly relieved that they wouldn't be leaving America for any length of time. Not only did she want to start her life with Adam, there had been reports that the Suez Canal project was in peril. It had begun its planning stages years ago and was experiencing endless difficulties and delays—including a cholera epidemic.

~

Adam and Angie spent their honeymoon night in Adam's bedroom. In the following three days, Angie moved her belongings from the guest room to Adam's and made decisions on which items to pack for their trip to Cambridge.

She had brought a wide range of outfits to Nevada, as she had no idea what to expect, having not opened the envelope until she was in transit. There was no need to take out east any of the work shirts and plain dresses she had packed along with her fancier choices.

In spite of the short time frame, her parents had managed to arrive the day before the wedding, but were looking forward again to traveling back home. They and the newlywed Cartwrights left by stagecoach in Virginia City to Salt Lake City. The four-day coach ride was uneventful. The overnight stops provided the couples with separate rooms except for one station that was so small, the men had to bunk in the same room along with the drivers.

Private cabins for sleeping on the train were paid for by the senior couple as a wedding gift. Angie giggled when they tried to make love on the lower bunk bed, but Adam continued to fall out of bed due to the rough ride. They cheerfully gave up, anticipating a larger and more stable location in the future.

All in all, it was a pleasant week of travel to the east coast, visiting and getting to know each other. The Simmons quickly grew to love Adam and he them.

The newlywed couple stayed for two short weeks, with a promise that they would stay longer on their next visit. Adam met most of Angie's friends and family as well as several of Professor Simmons' colleagues. Adam fit right in with his exhaustive knowledge of architecture and his input on so many other topics like ranching and even politics. He never felt more at home. But he missed the life on the ranch. Angie wanted to be wherever he was.

Many women might have been frightened by the deep, focused, all-encompassing love that Adam lavished upon Angie. But she was as strong as he and didn't know that her own demanding love might have crushed an ordinary man. She was able to love Adam back as fiercely as he loved her. Adam and Angie would dream their dreams for their future together.

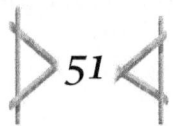

Late Summer 1866

IT WAS SEPTEMBER 4TH WHEN THE FAMILY learned that Evelyn's grandmother was near death. It was thought that she might not live another month. As Mary-Lynn had not seen her mother in nine years, she and Karl decided to go see her one last time.

The Swensons left for Utah the following day. Evelyn wanted to accompany them, but as she had said her goodbyes to her grandmother three years ago on a separate trip, she and Hoss agreed to stay at her parents' home to look after the sisters; Donna who was fifteen, Lisa who was thirteen, Beverley who just turned ten, and Margaret who was only five.

Her parents would be gone about a month. Hoss' routine would not change very much. The Swensons lived only a thousand yards or so away from his and Evelyn's house and he would travel the fifteen minutes to go work on the ranch every day as this was the busiest time of the year.

Two weeks after the Swensons departed for Utah, Beverley complained of stomach pain. At Evelyn's request, Hoss fetched Dr. Grant who determined that she was suffering from appendicitis.

Not many things frightened Evelyn, but seeing a life sentence handed over to her sister scared her very much. She asked Hoss to go back to town to send a wire to her parents:

Come quick STOP

Bev has appendicitis STOP

Grandma Gertrude was not afraid to die alone and sent Beverley's parents on their way as soon as she heard the news about her granddaughter. She died four days later. Mary-Lynn and Karl arrived home on the fifth day of their travel only to discover that Bev had died two days earlier. Evelyn had put off the funeral so they could see their little girl before she was put into the ground. The only consoling thing Evelyn could think to tell her parents was that the doctor had sedated her sister, so she hadn't felt the pain.

Appendectomies were not performed in North America until the 1880s. Many people, mostly children, suffered from the pain of the swollen snake-like appendage of the colon until it burst. Their blood would get poisoned and then they would die.

Evelyn was deeply affected by her sister's death and felt responsible for not having kept her safe.

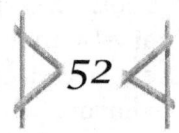

52

September 10, 1866

A FEW DAYS AFTER ADAM AND ANGIE RETURNED
to the ranch from Cambridge, the seven Cartwrights
gathered around the dining room table to catch up
on all their news. Ben suddenly remembered a letter
he had received earlier that day from Carson City. He
excused himself and retrieved the document from his
desk.

Sitting down again at the table, he explained,
"I have received a letter from an old friend. I spent a
good deal of time with her husband when we needed
good working horses for logging. He sure knew a lot
about horses, both buying and selling them."

Turning to Barbara, he continued, "We became
good friends and we even had their daughter spend
a couple of springs with us when their business kept
them both so busy. The poor girl would not have much
to do otherwise."

To his sons, "You boys must remember her,
little Jeannie?"

Ignoring the gasp from his youngest son sitting
at his right, Ben opened the letter, skipped the greeting
and began to read.

> ... *Martin, bless his dearly departed*
> *soul.*
> *Our house sold quickly. I need to*
> *tend to Martin's business affairs with*
> *the lawyer for the next few weeks. I sure*

would appreciate it if you would accept
having Jeannie stay with you during
this time. I'll fetch Jeannie later and we
will move to Virginia City as planned.
The house there won't be ready for at
least two and a half months and there
is nothing for her here until I'm ready to
leave.

Martin always trusted and
respected you. I hope you can render this
favor to us. My hands are tied here until I
can join Jeannie. I don't necessarily want
to leave her in a hotel or boarding house
there in Virginia City, but will if I must.
I fear, probably unreasonably, for her
safety; and she did enjoy the few visits
to your ranch as a child before we moved
away. You and your sons are the few
people remaining there that we are still
acquainted with.

Please wire back if you are able to
do this for us, but do not rearrange your
schedule just to accommodate my request.
We will manage.

Mrs. Laura Matheson

Before asking anyone else, Ben looked at Barbara and said, "I want to consider what you want to do, my dear. If in your state this will become too much for you, I will accept to look after Jeannie, but in Virginia city. She is about Joe's age and should do all right mostly on her own if need be."

Barbara was always surprised at Ben's tender concern. She had never known anyone who cared for her entire being like he did, and it always astonished her.

"And before you answer, there is something you

should know about Jeannie," said Ben.

But Joe interrupted, "Hey, is that the same Jeannie that was in my school but at least three or four years behind me?"

When his father indicated so to the positive, Joe started laughing and let everyone in on the joke, "She was the clumsiest girl and always got teased for her goof-ups. One time she tripped on her own feet and somehow pulled a stack of papers off the teacher's desk with her to the floor. Paper was flying everywhere. Everybody laughed. I don't think she had many friends. She had big teeth and wild hair and had crooked eyes, so she wore glasses with real thick lenses to correct that. I can't believe that she has fond memories of this place. She was often on her own, even when she was staying here at the ranch, wasn't she?" he said, looking toward Hoss and Adam to support his story.

But Joe was at least three years older than Jeannie, Hoss was six years older, and Adam had already left grade school. The two older sons' responsibilities on the ranch would have been greater than Joe's and they would not have spent any leisure time with the little girl.

Joe continued, "I only remember spending a bit of time together with her at meals and that she wasn't very talkative. We weren't in the same grade and had nothing in common."

Ben said, "You also spent all your free time with horses from the age of seven to—heck—even to this day! She mostly stayed in the house and played with her dolls. She was a loner."

Ben was already acting protectively toward their impending guest, "You are not going to be bringing any of those things up when she gets here, are you Joseph?" he challenged.

Joe swallowed hard, relieved that he had not

mentioned the rest of his thoughts, *She was the fattest kid in class. Just an ugly girl nicknamed Fatty Jeannie.* He apologized and said of course he wouldn't. He would be grateful though, to be out helping Adam with the building of the new house and wouldn't have to stay behind to entertain Jeannie in the coming weeks.

Hoss asked, "Wasn't there a rumor of her being a witch, or something like that?" Joe sat straight up, hoping he would finally learn the truth about that weird girl.

Adam nodded and said, "Years ago, I heard something like that too, Hoss. Is it the same girl, Pa?"

Ben made a noise, "Phew," but decided to tell them the horrible truth about Jeannie.

He started, "That was what I was beginning to explain to Barbara before she makes a decision. You see, Jeannie was about two years old when she was found on the steps of a convent in Reno. The nuns called in the priest who noted the poor child had scars on her back. He examined them closely and instructed the nuns to fetch the doctor. Which they did. He confirmed what the priest suspected. They believed she had been burned by someone putting out a cigar, or rather several cigars, on her flesh."

Everyone gasped.

One said, "Oh, how awful."

Another said, "Poor child."

A third said, "It takes a monster to do something like that!"

"The doctor took her into his office as it was his duty to try to find a family who would take her in. My friend, Martin, was present in the doctor's office that day, I forget why. He decided to bring the girl to their childless home. They raised the girl, but I'm afraid that Laura never really warmed up to Jeannie. Apparently as a child, she was very difficult to handle. I'm sure they took pity on the girl and tried their best.

I suspect things are not as stressed between mother and daughter anymore. They moved to Virginia City shortly after they took her in and moved to Carson City because of Martin's work when Jeannie was nine or ten years old—so seven or eight years later."

"Nobody knew where she came from or what happened the first two years of her life?" asked Evelyn and Angie practically at the same time.

"No one knows. I do know that the Mathesons didn't keep her adoption a secret. They tried to raise her with the knowledge that she was chosen and loved by them. I guess it was also because she would know they were not responsible for the scars on her back."

Although Barbara was still experiencing morning sickness, she replied, "Why Ben, I'll be all right. We are not talking about a child Edwin's age who is so active I could not keep up. We are talking about a grown woman. No, she can most certainly come here to the house. I insist you reply by wire tomorrow and put Mrs. Matheson's mind at ease so she can concentrate on her other matters."

"Good. I just wanted to make sure. Now, for the rest of you," while he concentrated his gaze upon Joe, he instructed, "even though Jeannie has always known about her past, we can show her respect by not mentioning her childhood unless she brings it up first. Understood?"

Everyone nodded.

On the sixteenth of September, Jeannie arrived. Originally, Barbara was tasked with picking up their guest when she came to Virginia City, but she had been asked by Evelyn to help the younger woman treat a sick animal. Joe was sent in her stead.

Out of curiosity, he very much looked forward to seeing her again. But when the stagecoach arrived, he couldn't see anyone who remotely resembled Fatty Jeannie or even looked like a Jeannie Matheson.

Maybe someone got her arrival date wrong. Too bad, what a waste of his time.

Oh, but he did notice a lovely, slender, woman with a perfect smile waiting patiently on the platform. Her hair was neatly combed and tucked underneath an emerald green hat. Her traveling clothes matched the hat. He figured he could at least enjoy the company of a stranded traveler and make this trip to town worthwhile. So, he approached her to strike up a conversation and offer his assistance if she needed any.

"Excuse me. I'm wondering what a lovely lady like you is doing all alone in a place like this?" he asked politely.

She had seen him approach and recognized the boy she once had a crush on. She could tell he hadn't recognized her. At his question, she replied, "Why Joe Cartwright, I'd recognize you anywhere. Glad to see your pimples cleared up!" said Jeannie with a wry smile.

When she stepped forward to greet him, she tripped on a cracked board and started to fall, face first. Joe quickly threw himself in her path and broke her fall. Placing her back on her feet, he burst into boisterous laughter. She was embarrassed and could not find anything funny about her mishap.

He finally said, "Jeannie, Fatty-Jeannie, Matheson. I'd recognize that clumsiness anywhere. How are you?"

Revolted with the fact that he remembered the despised nickname of her youth, she replied, "Anxious to get to the ranch so I can rest from this horrid trip. Do you mind if we get going?"

She was incensed with her foiled attempt to provide an impeccable first impression. She was so upset, she didn't speak another word to Joe all the way to the ranch. He hadn't changed one bit. He was always so nice at first and then would laugh at her about something. He bothered her so much. He was incorrigible.

After several attempts at conversation, Joe rolled his eyes and stayed silent. He wanted nothing to do with her if she couldn't be friendly. What was the point? He didn't recall her being so stuck-up, but then again, he and his school friends had never really bothered with the younger kids.

When they arrived, she turned her charm back on when Ben, Hoss, Adam and Angie came out of the house to greet her. As she proceeded toward the house, she stepped into horse manure. She was disgusted! Everybody else there tried to hide their giggles to her chagrin. Joe eventually said he would clean her boots, to which she replied, "Of course you will. I wouldn't expect anything less." She sat down on the step, removed her boots, and pushed them into Joe's hands.

The Cartwrights looked at one another and raised an eyebrow or two, but the expression on Jeannie's face made them keep their thoughts to themselves. *She is going to be difficult and challenging*, thought Adam.

Hoss, happy that they did not live at the ranch house anymore, grabbed her bags and showed her to her room. Angie brought Jeannie hot water for the basin so she could freshen up and rest before dinner and then quickly escaped to her own bedroom. Ben did not expect any difficulty from Jeannie; after all, she was his guest. Joe and Adam took care of the horse and buggy, chuckling all the way to the barn. Later, when Joe was cleaning her shoes, he freely laughed through the smelly chore while thinking about her misstep.

Barbara and Evelyn were laughing when they came into the house shortly before the supper meal was to be served. "What's so funny?" asked Ben.

"The sick cow's calf, who is not so little anymore, kept butting up against us the whole time we treated its mother. It was as if he was protecting her and showing us he was in charge. It was so endearing," replied Evelyn.

"Oh, hello," greeted Barbara when she noticed Jeannie sitting on the sofa. Jeannie stood now and approached the two women. It was apparent that they had been inside a barn for a while and Jeannie scrunched up her nose at their pungent aroma.

Barbara may have been remiss to not have had the opportunity to change before meeting a guest, but Evelyn wouldn't let anyone make her feel out of place. She extended her hand toward Jeannie and said, "Would you rather wait until I have freshened up and changed before shaking my hand?"

"Ah, no. Of course not," replied Jeannie as she shook Evelyn's hand.

Ben said, "Allow me to introduce you to our guest. This is Jeannie Matheson. Jeannie, this is Hoss' wife, Evelyn. And this beautiful mother to be is my wife, Barbara."

Jeannie turned to Barbara, eyeing up her belly, smiled and shook her hand. She politely said, "Pleased to meet you Evelyn. Barbara. Did you say you were both treating a cow? You are veterinarians?"

"No, not quite. I learned from my father how to treat animals and as he was called to be elsewhere, Mr. Fergus asked me to come to his ranch to take care of the problem. I've done work for him before and he was accepting that I take care of this one, too."

"And I went along because she needed me to shoo away the calf and keep him occupied while she worked," Barbara said, still laughing.

"Well, if you will excuse us, we'll quickly change and then we can eat," Barbara said as she and Evelyn headed upstairs.

No one missed seeing Jeannie wipe her hand on her dress. But that wasn't enough and she excused herself to go wash her hands again before supper.

Another guest for the guest room, another chair at the table, another family supper meal. Barbara was quick to notice that Jeannie and Joe did not appear to like each other. She thought that Joe would have been under a spell from such a beautiful house guest, as he was with most beautiful women. But disappointingly, he was not. He wasn't paying attention to the conversation if it involved a reply or comment from Jeannie. Barbara actually saw Joe roll his eyes several times during dinner.

Jeannie was self-centered and talked only about herself and her achievements. When Ben asked about her mother, she answered as briefly as possible, before turning the conversation back to herself. She did not show any interest in her hosts either, neither asking about their well-being nor what they had been up to in the past ten years. Barbara sensed that Jeannie was a difficult character, but there had to be something deep inside worth knowing.

Evelyn was somewhat bothered that Jeannie showed little interest in Edwin. But she dismissed the thought when she remembered the details of Jeannie's upbringing. After all, the young woman was an only child in a household with older adopted parents.

Jeannie loved to cook and promised to prepare special meals that she hoped would appeal to her hosts and in the following days, she fulfilled that commitment. The food Jeannie prepared was certainly tasty, but it was a bit too rich for the hard-working ranchers. They needed food that could sustain them, not tickle their palate.

The cook didn't mind the free time and suspected that the guest would eventually get tired of preparing meals. Jeannie would have tired preparing meals sooner had she been required to clean up after herself. Lee was not impressed with her messes. He would rather make the meals and clean up after himself.

One day near the end of the first week, Joe barged into the kitchen where Jeannie was baking a batch of cookies. She was standing on a chair and reaching for the jar of honey and was startled by his abrupt entrance. Her foot, which was too close to the edge of the chair, slipped suddenly and she fell to the floor with the jar of honey as well as the one containing the flour. Of course, both containers exploded and covered her in white dust that stuck to the places where the honey had landed. She gasped and exhaled a huge breath of white powder.

Joe couldn't help himself and howled at the sight of her. He pointed at her, laughing at the situation. He couldn't even speak, as he laughed so hard.

Jeannie wasn't hurt physically, but her pride certainly was. She shook her head, got up and stormed to her room. He left the kitchen to find someone to share this comedic sight with, but no one was around.

Once everyone had gathered at the supper table later, Joe finally had an audience to share in the funny story. Jeannie did not grin. She was angry that her hosts all laughed at her expense. She wondered if her coming here was a good idea. She pursed her lips and childishly quit speaking or responding to any direct questions. When asked to pass the food, she excused herself and left the table to go to her room.

She convinced herself that Joe was the root of her problems. How could he tell all of them about her clumsy moment and laugh about it? To her face as well! She hated that she often felt embarrassed, especially when she hadn't really done anything to deserve blame. Nothing had changed. Even now when she had the perfect opportunity for a new beginning, nothing changed. People were still laughing at her. Nothing funny ever seemed to happen to someone else. She could not ever remember laughing at something that had happened to someone else. He hadn't changed. He was still laughing at her, still embarrassing her. She hated being here.

By the next day, she had forgiven everyone except Joe, but he didn't care. She had to forgive the rest of them. She had a long while to wait before her mother would come fetch her and she needed to be friendly, didn't she?

53

September 20, 1866

ADAM EXCITEDLY APPROACHED HIS BRIDE. "YOU won't believe what I have in my hand."

Angie coquettishly played along. "A letter?"

"Ha ha. Of course, it's a letter. What's in it? Where is it from?"

"The King of England? No? The President of the United States?"

"Seriously, Angie!"

"Seriously, Adam. I am never going to guess. What is it?"

"It is an invitation to attend a meeting in New York where an architectural symposium will be held in April next year."

"Oh Adam, how exciting! Can we go?"

"Absolutely. Even if you became pregnant between now and then, we would be back here in time and we could even fit in a side trip to Cambridge and visit with your parents."

"Wonderful! I want to start packing already."

"Hey, now that is more than six months away. Glad to see you so excited but don't you think you are a little early for that?"

"Look who's excited. I suppose you want me to help you purchase new luggage?"

"Well, yes." They both laughed with glee.

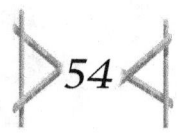

54

September 22, 1866

JEANNIE BECAME BORED SPENDING ALL HER days with the pregnant Barbara and with Evelyn and the very active Edwin. Even Angie who was usually wrapped up with conversations about babies was now becoming annoying with her constant bragging about the imminent trip to New York City. Jeannie announced that she would like to go for a ride on horseback.

Barbara said, "That is an excellent idea, but keep to the ranch as the weather is unpredictable. It may be an unusually warm 60 degrees now, but it can quickly dip to freezing in the shade or as you go higher up a mountain." Jeannie agreed to dress accordingly, but then didn't bother after all as she didn't want to get her jacket dusty. She wasn't planning on riding for more than an hour, she justified to herself.

At supper time, the family were still waiting for Jeannie to return from her ride. When she hadn't returned by quarter after six, Ben asked Joe to saddle up his horse and go look for her. Joe was reluctant, but he didn't want to experience Ben's wrath, so he dressed himself warmly, grabbed Jeannie's cloak, and went to look for their guest. The rest started in on their meal.

Even though daylight was disappearing, Joe was able to track Jeannie's general direction. He was disappointed to see that she had turned towards the mountain. It could get colder up there especially if she went beyond the tree line. He braced himself for a long ride.

About forty-five minutes into his search, he came close to where she had finally accepted that she was lost and decided to stop.

She could hear horse hooves and called out loudly, "Hello, anybody there?"

Joe called back, "Stay put, I'm coming."

Jeannie became even more embarrassed at hearing Joe's voice. He was so detestable, she thought. He called out to her a couple more times for her voice to guide him to her. The disappointment on his face was visible to Jeannie. She tried to apologize for getting lost as she gratefully put her cloak on over her shoulders, but he wouldn't hear any of it.

He wasn't angry. He could have chided her, but he didn't. In the past few days, the two had developed a silent understanding to not say anything to each other, good or bad, unless absolutely necessary. He didn't see this situation making any difference to that arrangement. He didn't care about anything except getting back for a late supper.

As far as Jeannie was concerned, he would be wasting his breath if he tried. She wasn't going to become friendly all of a sudden just because he had come to rescue her from her own foolishness. She had liked him once, but that was a childhood ago.

They both admitted to themselves that they had no common ground.

It was past seven by now and as predicted by Barbara, the winds were blowing stronger, colder. When they came upon an open rocky range, the winds increased further, driving directly into their faces. Joe decided to go back into the woods for the shelter of the trees and the warmth their covering provided.

Jeannie eventually showed her intolerance in his choice of routes, but he just curtly shot back, "You can't even navigate an afternoon ride; how can you possibly be qualified to judge the warmest way back home?"

She reluctantly kept her mouth shut. No use adding to the dispute. They had arrived at the edge of the woods again. They would have no choice but to face the cold, strong winds now. But when they were out of the woods, it felt like the temperature dipped to freezing so Joe decided to lead them back up the mountain to a cabin about a fifteen-minute ride away.

"It is easier to see where the horses are stepping from the shine of the moonlight on the rocks. Grass only grows in patches along the boulders. There is too much risk for one of the horses to break a leg in one of the countless holes dug up by groundhogs in the meadow." He just mentioned what he was doing. He did not expect her input and he would have ignored any response had she provided one.

55

September 22, 1866

WHEN THEY GOT TO THE CABIN, THEY FOUND IT
had been ransacked and stripped of all comforts.
There was no kindling for a fire inside, nor any logs
around outside for chopping. Even the door and
window shutters had been used for firewood. There
were no blankets, food or supplies.

Joe shook his head and muttered under his
breath. It was too late to go anywhere else. Without
a lantern it would be difficult to find firewood. The
little moonlight filtering through the trees would mean
searching with his fingers instead of his eyes. He didn't
relish that option, especially when it may be futile in
the end.

Jeannie was standing and shivering. Her teeth
had begun to chatter, and she coughed out, "Wh-what
nnn-ow?"

He said, "I'll go look for firewood."

She quickly said, "Nn-no. Pp-please don't. I dd-
don't want to bb-be here all aa-alone in the d-dark."

He replied, "Well, fine then. I guess I'll stay
here." He gave in, as much to her request as his
own realization of the futility of finding wood in the
dark and starting a fire without matches. He couldn't
believe he had neglected to bring a lantern with him—
but then he hadn't thought he would be spending the
night on the mountain either. He thought he would
have quickly found Jeannie and been home by now.
If there had been a lantern left behind in the cabin in

the spring, it had certainly been stolen along with the rest of the supplies.

Jeannie might not know how to survive a cold night, but Joe had an idea. He didn't like it and suspected neither would she. But they had no choice if they were to live to see tomorrow.

He looked around the dim cabin while he devised the plan to execute his strategy to stay warm through the night. "I know what we can do to get warm. Please do everything I say, and we won't freeze to death tonight."

She replied, "How cc-can you bb-be shhuure?"

He said, "It will work. I know. I've heard of it."

She asked, "Yoouu nev-vver act-tually ee-even test-ted this theee-ooo-rry?"

He said, "No, but it will work. We have no other choice. Please, just do as I say and we'll both wake up tomorrow."

Curious now, she agreed by nodding her head up and down. Her teeth were chattering more audibly, and she just wanted to be warm. She watched Joe move the bed springs to the north wall. He removed all objects off the east-side floor as he hoped it was the warmest part of the room. Then he unsaddled both horses and placed the saddles on the floor on top of each other in the cleared space. Then he placed both horse blankets on the floor, in opposing directions and barely underneath the saddles that held them in place.

He considered bringing in the horses for their body warmth and breath. He didn't but would later if his plan didn't exactly work to his liking.

He then asked Jeannie to stand facing the south wall. At this point she thought he was being stupid, and she told him so. He let out a tired sigh, regretting skipping supper for her.

Without any gentleness in his voice, he told her, "Just do it."

He then stood facing west and crouched down to sit on the blanket. He asked her to now sit down on the floor still facing south. Then he instructed for her to reach for the other end of her blanket and place it on top of her. He reached for his own blanket and did the same. The two were soon cocooned under the two horse blankets in the small space hemmed in by the east wall and the two saddles.

He said, "Now this is going to be the hard part. We have to, um, hug."

"Wh-whaat?"

"Hug. You see, our combined body heat will keep us from freezing to death. I assure you I don't like it any more than you do."

Even though she closed her annoyed eyes and rolled them up in their sockets, she did think this might just work and decided to lean back as instructed. She then scooted over onto her left hip and awkwardly hugged him around his neck. He decided that was not comfortable enough for the both of them. So, she sat up again, he undid the opening to his jacket and motioned for her to try again but to place her bare hands around to his back where they could at least get some warmth. As he wore gloves, it was likely that his hands would not chill as quickly as hers. She reluctantly did as she was told.

It didn't take Jeannie long to realize that she was getting warmer. She wasn't entirely spiteful and thanked Joe for his insight, and he said, "You're welcome."

Before long, he was laughing. He figured he did so because of how much they tried to avoid each other and the unbelievable nearness of their bodies at the moment. At the sound of his contagious laughter, she started giggling but she couldn't tell why. She was not as astute about it as Joe was. After the laughter died down, so did the tension between them. Joe tried one more time to have a conversation. It would be an extra-long night if she didn't join in.

Joe started on a polite and safe subject, "So, have you always lived in Carson City after you moved away from here?"

She said yes and told him about her last twelve years. She had a few friends, or rather acquaintances who were presently being courted.

When he asked if she herself was also being courted, she responded, "Me? No, I've not met anyone special. You?"

He didn't find her last twelve years very exciting. *Come to think of it*, he thought, *mine doesn't fare any better—especially compared to the lives of Pa, and my brothers.* He replied, "No, me either."

Then she asked, "Why don't you like me?"

Joe thought a moment before speaking. "I don't dislike you. I just got the impression that you didn't like me, so I decided to not bother trying to be friendly if it was going to be a waste of my time."

Although this was true, he also couldn't admit— especially to her—that he was in awe of how beautiful she had become. He was embarrassed by his earlier childish rantings to his family of when she was a young, seemingly ugly girl.

But in spite of all that beauty, Jeannie's disposition was off-putting and he didn't want to pursue her if she was going to continue to be unreasonable and mean toward him. But now that he had her in his arms—a necessary physical nearness to save their lives—he thought they could at least be on speaking terms.

"Funny, I thought you didn't like me. You always laughed at me in school and you're still doing it." In spite of the fact that they were forced to spend the night in discomfort, she felt safe with him and was happy they were having this time together. She ached for a friend.

He marveled at how she didn't realize how she was coming across. He replied, "Well, you must admit, you do some pretty funny things."

She huffed, "Well, I don't think I do funny things—and I think it very impolite that people, that you, laugh at me!"

"I'm not really laughing at you. I would hope that I am laughing with you. You just don't see the humor in what you do. That's all. I'm not laughing to be mean. I'm truly laughing because whatever has happened is funny."

"Really? Honestly?"

"Yes, of course Jeannie. You have to learn to laugh at yourself if you are ever going to make friends. I will often create my own fun just so I can laugh. For example, I played a prank on an older couple about twelve years ago. It was summertime and at around four o'clock in the morning, I got up and hard-boiled half a dozen eggs and sneaked out of the house through the kitchen door. I had wrapped the eggs in a cloth and I held onto those six eggs like they were treasure. I headed out on foot to the Watson's farm. I didn't take my horse 'cause I didn't want to be heard—nor seen and identified. I hoped to be back in time for breakfast so no one would ask me about my little adventure."

"When I got to the farm, I walked as quietly as I could. The animals there knew me and didn't alert the owners. You see, I had come by every day the week before and made friends with them. The horses didn't neigh, the dog didn't bark, even the pigs didn't sound the alarm at my arrival."

"I walked straight to the chicken coop. I entered and opened my precious package. Two minutes later, I left the coop. My bag now held six fresh eggs which I placed in our own coop. I made it back home without being detected, even before the cook started working on breakfast. For a decade, I never told anyone about my excursion of that morning."

"One day, two years ago, the Watsons were over at our place visiting and I asked the Mrs. if she ever figured out how her chickens could lay hard-boiled eggs."

"She pointed at me and said, "It was you!" then Mr. Watson said, "You rascal, Little Joe, you!" That's when I laughed. We all laughed. It took me ten years, but I haven't laughed like that before nor since."

"That is funny, Joe. But that poor couple, how could you do that to them?"

"Well, I don't like to laugh at other people, but I sure love laughing with them. They laughed. I assure you," he finished.

"You think it's okay to laugh as long as you do it with them?" Jeannie asked.

"I know so. Try laughing along next time. You'll see. People will be pleased that you see the humor in whatever it is and that you are gracious enough to laugh at yourself. That helps them feel better about themselves in that they are not being impolite by laughing at you."

"Huh, I'll be sure to give that a try. Thanks for telling me this, Joe." It was like she had received a gift.

She had always been self-conscious and eventually became self-centered. No one wanted to be her friend because she was so wrapped up in herself. Her teen years were no better. When she outgrew her childish, chubby appearance, she hoped that would all change, but it turned out she couldn't make any friends as a grown woman either.

Her one true friend, her father, convinced her that she had grown into a beautiful young woman who was also the smartest one in the county that he knew personally. Then he died. She no longer had anyone to help build up her self-esteem. But now it seemed that Joe might want to become her friend. She hoped it was true. She couldn't stand it if he didn't like her.

They fell into silence for a few moments. They certainly had misunderstood each other.

"Do you think we are being immature?" she asked.

"Oh definitely," he replied and they both laughed at his response. He laughed his usual laugh where the left side of his mouth reached up higher than the right.

She was, for the first time, listening to herself laughing. It was an odd sound.

Joe was relieved that she could be nice after all—and decided he liked her laugh. He hadn't believed his eyes when he saw her again after twelve years. She was a lovely girl. She had beautiful, shiny auburn hair and mysterious hazel eyes, a perky little nose and a charming dimple on her left cheek. He was glad they were finally putting their animosity aside.

For the next hour they learned about each other's likes and dislikes. They caught up on people from Virginia City they mutually knew. They even gossiped about the people they had heard stories about in their youth—both truth and hearsay. When there was a new burst of laughter over a juicy detail, they caught themselves, Jeannie tucking her face into his shoulder and Joe saying, "What would your ma or my pa call us if they could hear us now?"

"Wicked!" Jeannie cried, and they both laughed.

He told her about Pa, Hoss and Adam meeting and marrying their wives.

Jeannie said, "That's amazing about Barbara living all alone for twenty-three years. How awful. I'm glad you told me more about Angie and Evelyn too. I feel closer to them now that I know their stories."

211

She was astute to recognize—but wouldn't be saying out loud—that the three other women had strong characters, strong enough to become Cartwrights.

After a lull in the conversation, she asked Joe, "Why is there a cabin way up here on the mountain? I mean, it's lucky that you knew about it, but why have one out here? Did someone live in it and desert it?" She was having difficulty concentrating on anything but how warm his chest was and how alluring his wide shoulders were. She shivered.

He absentmindedly rubbed the shivers off her arm with his free hand and replied, "It belongs to the ranch and is one of many. Every winter we have the hired hands take turns staying in these cabins for three or four months at a time. It is a very lonely time but most of them like that about this job. They have to go out every day when it is not storming and hunt for mountain lions or wolves or other big predators that might feed on or injure the cattle in the valleys below."

How utterly smart, she thought.

Joe added that he would remember to tell the man who was coming here to bring, along with his own mattress, a door and shutters and a full restocking of tools and supplies. *Not to mention a lantern,* he added to himself, ruefully.

A silence came between them. Her hands were innocently moving up and down his back, trying to keep warm. He could sense the quickening of her breathing from the sensation of her chest on his. She happened to look up just then while he looked down and they kissed. It was ever so sweet. They kissed once again and then, looking at each other for a brief moment, continued, their arms tightening around each other.

He had planned on kissing this attractive woman from the moment he saw her on the stagecoach platform, but she had discouraged that and him in all ways. Kissing her was different from all the girls he had kissed before. This time, he hadn't planned on it. It just happened. And it was the softest kiss. His kisses normally made young women want more than his lips—like his arms around them—and he would oblige. But this kiss was sweet and kind. He was not expecting anything in return.

She, on the other hand, was grateful that she was already sitting on the floor because she felt so weak she would have fallen. She was bewitched by his kisses. She had wanted to kiss him since fourth grade, but never dreamed that it would actually happen. How different these kisses were to her fantasy. The real thing was so dreamy and much more romantic. His lips were so soft and yet demanding.

They were growing ever mindful of the warmth of their bodies so close together. They stopped kissing and smiled at each other.

Jeannie took in a huge breath of air. She nodded and decided to say, "Joe, have you heard about my being found by the nuns?"

Incredulous that she had gone from kissing to the story of her youth, Joe replied, "A little bit from Pa. Why?"

She thought, *Just a little bit? I wonder if he and his family knew the whole story, would they still treat me like I'm normal? Shouldn't I feel pitied? If they know even a little part of my secret, how can they treat me no different than other people? Can they really be that kind? I will tell Joe just so I can find out if he acts differently toward me.*

"Oh, I just thought you should know. I would have told you if you didn't know."

"I don't know a whole lot. It's none of my business. But Jeannie, if you want to talk about it, go ahead." He replied politely and as encouragingly as he could. He had been curious.

Jeannie paused a moment, as if to get her thoughts in order. "I was only two so you can imagine I don't remember much. I had nightmares for many years about cigars being extinguished on my back by a big, ugly man who held me down so I couldn't run away. When I was seven, Ma and Pa told me that the dreams were not nightmares, they were real. They helped me see my bare back by holding a hand mirror in front of a big mirror."

"It was awful to realize the truth! I didn't know why someone would do that to me. What could I have ever done to deserve it? But Ma and Pa tried real hard to explain that the man wasn't well in the head because no child deserved to be punished like that. I don't remember a mother before Ma, but I always thought that cigar man couldn't possibly be my real father. I will never know for sure. But in my heart, I just needed to believe that he couldn't be. You know?"

Joe nodded sympathetically.

"Some time after Ma and Pa told me, I told my friend Maggie about my scars. We shared a desk at school. She asked to see them, of course. I was reluctant to show her, but decided to trust her. That was my mistake. I thought I could trust her, after all, she had let me play with her doll. She wasn't a nice girl. She began to tell other kids that I was from the devil. I mean, who else could be my true father if I could have scars like that and live? Right? I'm sure she was just scared by what she saw but the lies just grew into nasty rumors that I should be feared. Sometimes I played along with the lies just so the kids would leave me alone. And it didn't make any difference where I was. The same thing happened one spring when I was here with your family. Another girl I thought I could trust knew, but then there was more gossip." She sighed. "That is why I can't trust that people like me or aren't laughing at me or telling lies about me."

"Oh, Jeannie," he said, holding her closer.

"All my childhood was spent thinking that people believed those awful lies about me and would look at me wondering why I could be punished that way. Well, it took me years to finally realize that people didn't think that at all. But it was too late. By then I didn't have any friends, and I was so lonely ..." She started to cry. "I didn't know—I still don't know—how to make friends. Nobody likes me."

Joe stayed silent. He had no idea what to say.

She appreciated he kept his comments to himself. She needed to just say things and not be judged. He was a good listener. She rested her head on his shoulder and sobbed. He stroked her hair and held her.

"I'll be your friend, Jeannie."

She sighed, looked up at him gratefully. "Thank you, Joe. I'd like that very much."

She rested her head on his chest again. Tears subsided. They both soon fell asleep.

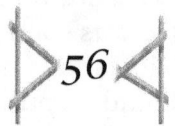

September 23, 1866

BY MORNING, ALL BAD FEELINGS BETWEEN THE two young people were in the past and the excitement of their first kiss was fresh on their minds. They were happy to be alive and hungry to get off the mountain. Like old friends, they helped each other saddle up the horses and set off toward the ranch house.

They arrived just as the household was cleaning up after the breakfast meal. Ben was happy that Jeannie was back. He had never worried about Joe. He had just hoped that his son had found Jeannie and managed to get her to a warm place for the night.

Barbara and Angie were happy to see the change in Jeannie as they spent hours each day with her. The conversations were suddenly lighter and Jeannie's contributions bubblier. Barbara noticed that Jeannie was smiling more and seemed less tense.

Although Barbara thought that Joe was too young to fully settle into his character as an adult, many times, she thought Joe's strongest virtue might end up being humility. If it was Jeannie's as well, she had a greater distance to go before achieving it.

Joe and Jeannie began spending more time together now that they were enjoying each other's company. Joe was no longer using the building of Adam's house as an excuse to be away from the ranch. Barbara, Angie and even Evelyn rarely saw the youngest woman except at mealtimes and even Ben noticed that Joe stayed around the ranch house more.

Jeannie gladly joined Joe on his chores. His afternoons were usually spent with the horses. She loved horses and he was pleased that she could tell the difference between the pintos, mustangs, palominos, bays and the prized thoroughbreds. He discovered that she knew as much as he when it came to horses.

On one of their afternoons riding the horses together, she told him that for two summers she had worked on a ranch that bred racing horses. This surprised Joe, as he didn't think of Jeannie as an independent kind of woman.

Occasionally she would do something that caused Joe to laugh—like getting down off a horse with a foot landing right into a full bucket of water, or slipping on fresh horse dung, or even walking into a post. She would give him that stern look of hers, but that only brought on more laughter from him. He wouldn't stop until she changed her attitude and found the humor in what had just happened. She noticed that laughing made her feel differently. She pondered why she felt differently, separating her feelings for Joe from those of her changing self.

One day, she placed a hand on Joe's arm, interrupting him from doing his chores and said in a serious tone, "You were always laughing at school and I always wondered why you thought so many things were funny. I never laughed. Certainly not at home. I didn't have any siblings and it wasn't my parents' nature to tell a funny story or see humor in a situation, so I guess I never learned to laugh. I brought that attitude to school with me. It didn't get me many friends. Joe, I just want to say thank you for laughter."

He smiled, lovingly put his arm around her and tenderly kissed her. As he reluctantly returned to the task at hand, he shrugged his shoulders, smiled a half-crooked smile—the one she liked very much as it made him even more appealing if that was possible—and said, "You're welcome!"

The next couple of weeks were filled with romance. No one else existed. If Joe saw her a short distance away, he would approach her just to smell her lavender-scented hair. Whatever little gesture she made would cause him to utter an involuntary deep-throated moan with his eyes shut as if in a trance.

He would also tease her. Caressing a cheek with the pretense of a prelude to a kiss, he would place a hand on her cheek and jawline and lure her face closer to his. When their lips would touch, he would back away as slowly as he had approached.

She found Joe to be even more handsome when he smiled and certainly when he laughed. She was attracted to his physique and never tired of looking at him. She hungered for his kiss. She felt more attracted to him with each of his advances and he to her by one of her reactions. He would often touch her hair, her shoulders, the small of her back, or a cheek.

Their intimacy came on gradually. At first, she could feel his hand on her neck. The next time his hand would move down a little bit toward the middle of her chest as if he was reaching for the lace trim on her collar. Another time his hand would wander over a breast and she would push it away. She would always stop him, but he wasn't easily discouraged. She no longer felt the shock and excitement by his hand on her cheek or neck or arm or back. But when she no longer reacted to the feel of his hand on her breast, he was encouraged to go even further. Eventually, she would push his hand away.

One night they were kissing, her body swaying to the movement of his hand on the outside of her dress on top of her hip. His thumb was dangerously close to the top of her thigh. She caught her breath and pushed him away hard, close to tears.

He was wild with desire. It took all of her energy to stop him. She began to cry at the thought of what they had almost done.

Joe apologized and she said, "How would you feel if no one respected me, Joe? You would probably consider never seeing me again!"

"I said I was sorry, Jeannie. It's all my fault. Besides, I don't know why it would be you who would feel the shame and get the blame. It won't happen again."

"There, see? I don't want you to stop kissing me. I love being kissed by you, Joe. You just need to control yourself. And, I don't want you to be angry with me for saying those things to you. I'm afraid you won't want to see me again."

"I'm afraid you won't want to see me again too, Jeannie. You are so beautiful that I have great difficulty in controlling myself. I don't want to cool things with you, but if I have to, I will."

Still crying, she straightened out her dress. She didn't want to have this discussion with Joe. She didn't want to stop what they had been doing. She loved him enough to think that he would do the right thing by her, but she didn't want him to feel forced to do so either. She was very confused. Neither wanted to lose the respect of the other, nor have their actions affect the rest of their lives.

Two very frustrated young people went to their separate bedrooms that night.

~

They were determined to behave as mature adults and decided to cool the kissing part of their relationship and give each other more physical space. Yet, they found themselves standing and sitting close to each other, in unconscious defiance of their spoken promise to each other and the silent one to themselves.

Eventually, Joe had had enough.

Ben was not surprised when Joe came to talk to him about how serious things were between him and Jeannie.

"She is beautiful, Pa. Full of surprises, knows a lot about horses, is a great cook, is super smart and I'm crazy about her. I can't stand not being near her."

It was not clear to Ben why Joe listed Jeannie's attributes as he certainly didn't need convincing. He fully supported their courtship. He had been younger when he had first married and told Joe as much, "If you know in your heart that you want to spend the rest of your life learning everything there is to learn about Jeannie, then you must ask for her mother's blessing and marry that girl. You don't have to wait until you are Adam's age or even Hoss'. Joe, you know about her past and her troubles. If you two can handle that together, you can probably handle anything."

"Joe, there is something that belonged to your mother that I would like you to have," Ben added.

"What is it Pa?"

Ben opened the middle drawer to his desk and retrieved the ring he had purchased more than two decades ago and handed it to Joe. He looked at the pearl set in silver and surrounded by a ring of diamond chips.

"Pa, I don't know what to say. I love it, Jeannie will love it. Thank you very much."

Ben reflected then on how different his sons were. Hoss never looked for his father's opinion, he just knew what he wanted to do and did it. Adam looked to him to confirm what he felt. Joe needed his father's approval.

~

Mrs. Matheson arrived at the ranch a couple of days earlier than expected. She had not wired Ben of her arrival as he no doubt would have insisted meeting her at the stagecoach platform. She didn't want to impose any more on the Cartwrights' hospitality, so she had instead hired a buggy to bring her to their home.

Jeannie had come rushing out of the house when she learned who was in the carriage and ran into her mother's surprised arms.

"Oh my, Jeannie. I am truly happy to see you. Did you miss me?"

"Oh Ma, I did not have much time to miss you. I have been busy helping out around here." Ben raised both eyebrows at Jeannie's statement, but didn't comment. This gal was going to be his daughter-in-law soon and he wasn't going to criticize her in front of her mother. She had already come a long way in becoming a pleasant young woman since she arrived and had promise of being a wonderful member of the family.

Arms around each other, the daughter and mother began to walk inside the house. Jeannie clumsily tripped on Laura's luggage. Laura held her breath, waiting for one of her daughter's usual temper tantrums. Instead, Jeannie laughed! Out loud! And then she just apologized to the luggage and pretended like nothing had happened. Laura looked at her daughter and smiled. Something has changed in her daughter, and it was definitely for the good.

Shortly after her arrival, Joe came in from the stables. Laura instantly knew the reason for the change in Jeannie. Her daughter beamed with a smile at the sight of Joe, even wider than when mother and daughter had reunited! *Ah, this is the reason for her change,* the older woman thought with a nod.

Joe was elated with Laura's early arrival as he wouldn't have to wait any longer to ask for her approval. He waited a day for his prospective mother-in-law to get to know him, making an effort to show her his horses and explain his plans for his present and future stock.

Jeannie's mother provided her acceptance. She had always had a great respect for the Cartwright men—from Ben down to Joe. Jeannie had changed from a girl to a young woman in these few weeks at the ranch. She had developed a maturity since they had seen each other last. And the love and passion the two young people had for each other was indisputable.

~

Joe planned a romantic evening, just the two of them. They started with a fine meal accompanied with wine at the International House Hotel—in the exact dining room where Barbara had worn her special coming-out dress. Joe had been waiting for a private moment, but by the time dessert was served, he couldn't contain his impatience. He got down on one knee—in front of strangers who might overhear—he asked for Jeannie's hand in marriage.

She didn't hesitate in replying, "Yes."

They shared a quick kiss while still at the hotel and hurried through the rest of their meal. On the carriage ride home, they stopped in a field and duplicated the positions of their bodies of their first kiss, their favorite way of kissing.

They hadn't kissed since the night they had agreed to cool their relationship. But now, as newly engaged, their first kiss was particularly special. Even so, they put a limit on their kissing, stopped at the agreed time and then happily rode back to the ranch house. They committed to restraining their passions while they waited patiently for their wedding day. They knew the wait would be worthwhile.

57

October 25, 1866

PLANS FOR THE WEDDING QUICKLY UNFOLDED. Everyone wanted to hold the wedding before the weather became unpleasantly colder. Jeannie certainly wanted that too, Joe even more so.

Now that he knew Jeannie would soon be his wife, he became impatient with routine and chores that separated him from his wedding day. He would finish his daily tasks in record time—as if he were in a race. Even working with his beloved horses in the field, he would gulp down his packed meal and hurry on to whatever else was needing done on the ranch— like fixing a broken fence or stocking hay in the loft. He tried to keep busy to hurry time along. He was so much in love with Jeannie that he tried to rush the passing of time until they could be husband and wife. The days before the wedding ticked by, but much too slowly for him.

Only during evening meal times, surrounded by the women of the family and his future mother-in-law, would he slow down and simply watch the beautiful woman who would soon become his wife, and dream about the kisses they would share before they parted to their separate bedrooms.

In town to pick up supplies a couple of days before the wedding day, Joe's dreamy demeanor came crashing down. He had loaded up the wagon with his purchases and was ready to head home when he overheard a woman's laughter that sounded like

Jeannie's. He looked back toward the sound coming from the stagecoach platform and couldn't believe his eyes.

Jeannie was in another man's arms! The tall, dark-haired man took hold of Jeannie and swung her around like they were a couple in love, happy to see each other again. The man leaned over as he settled her back down on her feet and kissed her on the cheek! She removed her arms from around his neck and moved them to his waist. He released hold of her waist and placed an arm comfortably on her shoulder.

Joe took a few steps back. His heart felt frozen. Then beat furiously. He couldn't watch any more. His spirit was crushed, his heart shattered. How could she do that? Had she led him on all this time? What kind of a woman was she? She was supposedly spending the day with her mother! LIAR!

He jumped into the wagon and quickly drove back to the ranch. He left the loaded wagon in front of the house, the horses untied, uncaring whether they took off or not. He searched for his father, but by the time he found Ben, he was more than wounded, he was blind with rage. He was ready to hit something, preferably the man embracing his bride to be.

From the kitchen, Barbara and Angie overheard Joe yelling in the study as he told Ben about Jeannie's betrayal—as by now he was yelling out his story. "I saw Jeannie in another man's arms, kissing! How could she do that Pa? I wouldn't have believed it if I hadn't seen it with my own eyes!"

Barbara and Angie approached but didn't venture into the grand room past the end of the dining room table. They could not move any closer to the heartbreaking scene that was unraveling before them.

"Is there any way you are mistaken, son?" Ben asked hopefully, as he stood from his desk to comfort his anguished son.

"Pa, I saw it. Agh! It wasn't just a casual greeting, it was a warm embrace, a really long one. It was disgusting, I tell you!" cried an incredulous Joe.

Hoss and Evelyn came into the house from the garden at the back at the same time that Adam came in from the barn. They had overheard Joe. Surely, he must be wrong. Everyone but Joe thought that there must be a logical explanation.

Their conversation fell silent with the sound of Laura and Jeannie's wagon pulling up into the yard. Everyone went outside. Adam and Hoss were signaled by Ben to stand on either side of Joe in case he did something stupid. By now, Joe was almost in tears.

58

October 25, 1866

LAURA WAS THE FIRST TO GET OFF THE WAGON with Ben's help and said, "Oh, I'm so glad you are all here. There is someone I want you to meet."

Jeannie had excitedly jumped out of the wagon and to everyone's astonishment, placed an arm around the waist of the man who was by now standing next to Laura with an arm around each of the women himself.

"Oh Ma, let me. Please!"

"All right, Jeannie. Go ahead."

"Everyone, I'd like to introduce you to a man that just came back from spending ten years in Europe."

Joe stiffened. Everyone was staring at Jeannie who seemed much too comfortable with the stranger.

She gave the stranger's arm a squeeze and gave him a big smile. "He is my mother's brother ..."

"A much younger brother, I might add," said a smiling and proud Laura.

"My uncle, James Carruthers, arrived just in time to walk me down the aisle. Uncle Jim, this is Ben Cartwright, my future father-in-law," said an oblivious Jeannie.

Introductions were made all around. You could see relief on the family's faces. By the time Jim was to shake Joe's hand, Joe had practically melted into the ground with embarrassment.

Later on that evening, Ben found a private moment alone with Joe to discuss the day's discoveries and misunderstandings.

226

"It is perfectly natural to react the way you did," the father said. "But if there ever is a next time, you should approach Jeannie right away to find out what is going on before reacting so strongly."

Joe sheepishly nodded.

Before retiring for the evening, Joe stole a moment alone with Jeannie. Without uttering a word about his upsetting afternoon, he gently grabbed her face with both hands, drew it nearer to his and placed a most grateful and seductive kiss on her lips. She didn't know what she had done to deserve such a taste of passionate tenderness, but it made her tingle from head to toes.

In bed that night, Joe relived the day and decided that he did not like being jealous. He vowed he would never be that way again. It was a trait that made you do stupid things. Besides, he knew Jeannie loved him as much as he loved her. What had he been *thinking?*

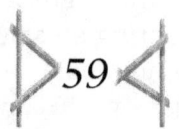

59

October 27, 1866

"I, JOSEPH CARTWRIGHT," HE BEGAN HIS VOWS TO his bride and the assembled guests, but then added to himself, *can't believe I fell for you, the weird girl from grade school.*

"Take thee, Jeannie Matheson," *who made me want to scream when you weren't talking to me.*

"To be my wedded wife," *and to teach me everything there is to know about you.*

"To have and to hold from this day forward," *the only woman I will ever love.*

"For better, for worse," *to help me hold back my temper.*

"For richer, for poorer," *to help me not jump to conclusions.*

"In sickness and in health," *to help me to not react without thinking twice first.*

"To love and to cherish," *I can't wait to shower you with those words.*

"Till death us do part." *Forever.*

"I, Jeannie Matheson," and added to herself, *who is grateful that you never gave up on wanting to talk to me.*

"Take thee, Joseph Cartwright," *who is the handsome, laughing, carefree boy of my youth.*

"To be my wedded husband," *and man of my life.*

"To have and to hold from this day forward," *I will embrace no other, my darling.*

"For better, for worse," *to be patient when I falter.*

"For richer, for poorer," *to give me children and enrich our lives.*

"In sickness and in health," *to teach me to laugh always.*

"To love, cherish, and to obey," *always love, I already hold you dearly.*

"Till death us do part." *Forever.*

Ben observed during the wedding toast to the couple and guests to never give up on finding love. "Why, all four Cartwrights were bachelors a mere three years ago." He wished the newlyweds a long and happy married life.

Adam and Hoss stood. They moved to stand behind their brother as if preventing him from running away. Adam said, "Jeannie, if you don't know yet, you will soon learn that our brother is a brat. He will play pranks on innocent people, including you. Beware."

Hoss said, "Yeah! Years ago, every day for about a month, Joe changed the location of the salt and pepper containers in the kitchen. He drove our cook crazy."

Everybody laughed, including Lee who was standing at the entrance to the kitchen. This set the mood for the musicians to start playing their music and for people to get up, stretch and find their dancing partners once the grand room's furniture had been pushed to the side.

Joe and Jeannie would not be leaving to honeymoon anywhere because they wanted to save all they had to build a house. As the evening wore on, Joe regretted not planning on spending at least the first night at the International House Hotel.

The festive occasion lasted into the wee hours of the morning. Even the musicians were reluctant to leave such an enjoyable celebration. To Joe, the clock moved painfully slow. He was anxious to be alone and romantic with his new wife. While dancing, he whispered in her ear, "I can't wait to kiss you without obstacles."

Surprised by his comment, Jeannie said, "What exactly does that mean, Joe?"

"I mean, we are married now, there will be no reason to stop at kissing."

"Oh, Joe. I know what you mean. When do you think would be a good time to go, ah, kiss?" she teased.

"Oh, Jeannie," he moaned. "Not yet. But soon. I promise."

Evidently, his father and brothers were thinking the same thing. Ben approached Joe and said, "My son. Did you know that it is normal for the newlywed couple to be the first to leave their wedding party? I think it is time for you two to leave."

Joe grabbed Jeannie by the hand and headed toward the stairs. But everyone was in on delaying the exit and giving him a taste of his own pranking spirit.

Mrs. Matheson was the first in the path of the happy couple. "This was such a lovely wedding. So romantic. Oh Jeannie, dear. You have a strand of hair that has come loose. Let me help you with that."

"It's okay, Ma. I'll get it myself," and she followed Joe a couple of steps.

But he was stopped by Adam, "Joe, earlier today I noticed a mare that appears to be limping. I put her in the barn. Shall we go see her together? It will just take a minute."

"Nah, Adam. You can handle it. I'll check in on her tomorrow," and he caught up with Jeannie.

"Just a minute, Joe," exclaimed Hoss and Evelyn. Hoss had grabbed him by the arm and was turning Joe back towards the dancers. "You don't want to leave before second helpings of cake, do you?"

Joe laughed, finally catching on to the joke. "Ha!

I know what you're all up to. So," and he freed his arm from Hoss' grasp, backed up to where Jeannie was standing just a step away, grabbed her by the hand and picked up their pace, saying, "but it won't work. Goodnight everybody."

December 13, 1866

BARBARA STARTED FEELING CONTRACTIONS DEEP in her back after the family supper.

Everyone knew it was too soon.

Joe was sent to get the doctor.

Ben didn't leave his wife's side until the doctor arrived. He told Ben to go be useful elsewhere. The doctor asked Evelyn to stay behind to assist. The other women left the room with Ben.

Barbara kept crying and Evelyn couldn't seem to comfort her. Listening to his wife's pain and aware of the potential outcome of these early complications, Ben was beside himself. He couldn't contain himself to the main floor, climbing a couple of stairs only to be pulled back by his sons to the great room.

Adam poured out glasses of brandy and they all drank, even Angie and Jeannie joined them. The two women and the men waited together. Ben paced.

An hour after the doctor's arrival, he came downstairs to announce that Barbara had lost her baby. With great sorrow, he looked at Ben and said, "A girl it would have been. I'm so sorry, Ben." He motioned with his head toward the staircase, "You can go see her now."

Adam and Hoss were deeply saddened as they had so looked forward to a sibling and to know now that it would have been a sister made it especially painful. Joe was easily brought to tears and this moment was no exception. Angie and Jeannie tried to console their husbands, holding them close. All five wept.

Other than the doctor, Evelyn was the only one who saw the deformed corpse of the baby girl. The babe had been quickly wrapped up and was certainly not to be shown to anyone.

Evelyn escaped Ben and Barbara's intimate words as she left the room with the lifeless body. The doctor said he would take care of finding a casket. The three brothers said that it would be their responsibility. They immediately left for the barn to build the casket for their little sister.

The doctor approved and asked Evelyn to place the wrapped baby in the box. "Make sure it is nailed shut and put in the ice house or cold storage until the funeral. Barbara will be strong enough to attend it by the day after tomorrow."

On his way out, the doctor motioned for Angie to come with him to the door.

"I received the results of your tests," he said, quietly. He shook his head. He told her that she was probably never going to be able to conceive.

Angie nodded with a new sadness added to her eyes, wondering how she would tell Adam.

As Doctor Grant left, he said in a louder voice so he could be overheard by the other two women, "No warm bath until after tomorrow." No one suspected that the doctor had delivered a separate message to Angie.

Upstairs, both Ben and Barbara, in tears, rocked back and forth in each other's arms.

In between sobs, she expressed words of sorrow, "I am so sorry Ben. I lost your little girl. Oh, how I loved our child already." She sobbed, "I ... am so, so ... sorry."

He was as sorrowful, but replied only words of comfort, "It's okay Barbara. Everything will be all right. Shush now. Please don't worry. I love you, Barbara.

I'm truly grateful that you are all right. It's going to be all right. We will get through this together." And then he cried, too.

Barbara couldn't decipher why this was the moment she suddenly remembered the day she saved Ben, but it was very important that she tell him.

She inhaled deeply, "Ben, the day of the avalanche started off funny. I was never one to dawdle or be absent-minded, but that morning, I forgot to pack things and had to go back for them. I had one mishap after another—I didn't put water in the kettle and even muddied a clean garment, and on and on. My leaving the cave was delayed by at least a half hour and I always thought that there must be a reason why. You were my reason why."

Ben shook his head wondering why she was talking about that day now.

"You see, when the mountain released its snow, Vincent quickly became agitated, so in order to calm him down, I circled back to safety. When the snow had finished rolling by, the trees that had been just three feet in front of me were no longer there. I was at the edge of the slide! There were no more trees to obstruct my view and that was why I could see your waving hand."

She continued, "For the first time in my life, I knew I could have died. I had come that close. I also realized that *no one* would miss me. No one." She repeated almost in a whisper, shaking her head.

"Ben, since that day, I have known love! I have laughed and danced."

With glee, she said, "You have three wonderful sons that I am proud to embrace into my life along with their wives, and they treat me like family!"

She gulped at the next sentence, "I have even felt life inside me, ever so briefly, but still, I felt her move."

"I owe you all my happiness. Don't you see? I would give up everything to hear one child call me grandma. You have given me that and so much more. I am quite content to love you with all of my heart—forever."

Ben, speechless and yet smiling, looked into her eyes, tears falling off his face.

61

July 31, 2019

NATALIE DROPPED OFF THE LEATHER REMNANTS at the friend of a friend's place of business. She wasn't expecting much, nor a timely response. But two weeks later, there was a message from the company's leather expert waiting for her when she came out of a meeting.

Full of excitement, she called him back immediately and was invited to come see the process that was used to evaluate their items and to hear the final outcome of the investigation. They were open until nine that evening, so she called Céleste who agreed to go with her.

The company's expert on old leather, Gerry, was eager to report that the material was indeed leather. He explained that it should have deteriorated to dust, but as the stitching at the seams was made doubly strong, it slowed down the process of decay.

"This product was of the best workmanship at that time," Gerry said. "If it had been made for riding a horse, it had to survive all types of weather and even jaunts across rivers where the leather would get thoroughly soaked. This bigger piece is part of the saddle, this long piece is definitely the sheath for the rifle, and this smaller piece could be part of the satchel. I believe they were sold as a set and that they were likely from the same manufacturer or craftsman. My estimate is that these are 150 to 160 years old."

The girls got giddy at that comment.

"Well, if that information makes you happy, you

are going to love this. I found traces of what I believe to be a mark. A brand or logo of sorts!"

"Ack!" both women yelled out.

"Hold on. I can't identify it. I also don't have more than about an inch of it. It is quite small and is so faded that I'm afraid it won't be useful."

Céleste was excited for any progress on the brand, and said quickly, "Show it to us anyway. We'll show the others."

Gerry went to his desk to retrieve a piece of paper. He placed it on top of the plastic bag that held the remnants of saddle and said, "This is the best I could do. As I said, there is not much to it. See here, on the bottom of this piece of leather," he said, pointing, "it was branded like this. The part of this circle would have been what I believe to be the top right side of the circle. Then this part of the brand would have been part of a letter, I think, or drawing of the logo of the owner. I'm sorry I don't have more to offer."

"You have more than we thought possible," said Céleste. "You have confirmed it is leather, that is old enough to be from the story we heard as kids, and that it was branded. This is much more than we thought we could confirm!"

"Thank you again, Gerry," Natalie said, paying their bill. Before leaving the parking lot, they texted the nine others of their findings.

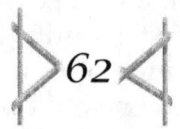

December 21, 1866

ADAM AND ANGIE MOVED INTO THEIR NEW HOME before Christmas 1866. Angie had initially been jovial about furnishing their home, but after she learned the bad news the doctor had divulged, she found it difficult to keep up her happy demeanor in front of Adam. She wasn't ready to tell him what was making her so melancholy. He knew there was something amiss but respected her to tell him in her own time.

The front door to their home was located in the center of the building. When she entered, there was a wall on her right and behind that wall was a guest bedroom. In front of her was a short corridor leading to the kitchen, a pantry and an area for doing laundry and having baths. She was very excited that Adam had incorporated all of her suggestions. To her left was the grand room where they would share meals and entertain guests. As well, on the back wall in the middle of the room was the staircase leading to their loft bedrooms. Past the stairs to the far left, was an empty room meant for Adam's study. The only rooms currently furnished were their bedroom, grand room, kitchen and dining area.

The unfortunate loss of Barbara's baby and the burial that followed added to Angie's indecisiveness. She thought that she should hold off telling Adam until more time had passed. Telling him now would not change a thing except make him sadder. Grieving was new to her. Adam had the experience of grieving for the loss of his mother and now for his sister. She didn't want to add grieving for a child they could never have. Different situations but similar emotions made Angie want to wait. But still, she was tormented as she kept this burden to herself.

Ben and Barbara had Joe and Jeannie living at the house with them, so their days were at least filled with some form of varying conversation. Hoss, Evelyn and Edwin would visit with her parents more regularly in wintertime than with Barbara and Ben at the ranch house. But Adam and Angie lived in a remote part of the Ponderosa, isolated from people occasionally passing by.

Ben's three sons would work at the ranch most mornings of the week and spend the rest of their time on their own chores and projects.

Adam had patiently waited to have a house to themselves, to really give themselves that unsupervised freedom to get to know each other on new levels of intimacy and help their love grow even more. Their first couple of weeks had provided all that and more. Just the other morning, no-inhibitions-Angie had joined him for breakfast wearing a robe that easily came undone and revealed her nudity. Adam had gladly ignored his chores in return for more of her surprises.

Later that week on a clear morning, Adam happily got the horse and wagon ready to go to the ranch house to fetch their mail; do some work he promised his father he would do; and, to pick up some scraps of good wood he thought he could use to finish the back of a cabinet he was building. Angie assured him that she had enough to keep herself busy until his return and declined to spend the day with Barbara and Jeannie. They kissed their farewell.

She was looking forward to being alone with her thoughts. Should she change her mind and tell Adam about her barrenness sooner than later? It was on her mind constantly and she sensed that he knew there was something she needed to tell him. She would take this time when she was alone to ground herself.

She was preoccupied in those thoughts when she heard footsteps on the front porch early on that evening. Expecting her husband's return, she rushed to open the door to find a couple of strangers there on the front step. She quickly noticed that the skies were cloudy, and the temperature had changed to a colder, blowing wind.

Disappointed that Adam wasn't at the door and that the men who were there wore dirty and torn garments, she asked about their business, "What is it?"

The men pushed past her.

"I will thank you for removing your boots. As you can see, I have just washed my floor," but they rudely ignored her.

The second man, called out to a third one back at the barn and said, "Hurry up Ernie, it sure is cozy in the house. We'll let the storm pass us by in here."

"Sure smells good, Missy," he continued. "Get me a plate of whatever you've got cooking in your kitchen."

"Me too," said the first fellow.

"I will gladly give you something to eat, if you will kindly remove your soiled boots. Both of you," she stubbornly insisted, crossing her arms.

Ernie had by now come through the door and watched the agitated woman hold her ground. He slapped her.

"Make that three plates, bitch. Now git!"

She quickly ran to the kitchen holding her aching cheek. The men burst into laughter and started trashing the place. They celebrated when they discovered Adam's liquor cabinet and immediately started in on that. They were on their way to drunkenness when Angie came out with a tray holding three plates and set them on the dining room table. The men ate sloppily but Angie didn't make any further remarks about their bad manners. Her cheek was still stinging.

She had never felt frightened in her life before now and didn't know how to cope with this new feeling. No one before had ever given her reason to feel in danger so she didn't take flight.

All hope that Adam would show up in time to help her vanished when she heard the whistling winds outside. There had always been an understanding that neither would risk their own safety if they had a warm bed to sleep in where they happened to be stranded for the night. Each trusted that the other could take care of themselves alone on their ranch. She knew now he wouldn't come home until the following day—and maybe not even then if the bad weather continued.

She instinctively tried to make herself invisible but when the men finished eating and had polished off a great deal of Adam's liquor, they started to eye her for their added pleasure. She realized that it was too late for her to slip out the back door. She panicked and ran toward the front door to get to the barn. She screamed when they caught her, and they laughed louder at the cat and mouse game. They shoved her back and forth, they hit her, she cried out, they laughed some more. They called her unspeakable names she had never heard aloud before.

When one of the men tugged too hard and ripped the front of her dress, exposing her creamy white shoulders and bosom, they became like animals. She fought back, but barely scratched whereby they punched, leaving painful bruises.

She tried to cover herself up. She cried out loud, but they didn't hear or care.

She told them, begged them to stop, but they were beyond reason.

They had lost all control. They were in a drunken frenzy.

They had cornered her into Adam's study and threw her down on the bare floor. Her face was wet with tears. Her face was unrecognizable from fear.

By then she had only snippets of clothing hanging onto her thin frame. They were in a drunken stupor. She was in hell.

They held her down on all fours.

They were all so anxious to immediately satisfy their needs that they took her all at once. One vaginally, one sodomized her, and one forced her to perform fellatio.

The man who sodomized her used his spit as lubricant. It was insufficient and the pain of the assault almost knocked her unconscious.

The man who was forcing oral sex thrust himself into her throat. He reeked of body odor and she gagged and threw up all over him, and on the man underneath her.

They slapped her off of them onto the floor.

They avoided her face and head covered in vomit and her backside smeared in blood. They took turns at the missionary position, beating her and repeating the offenses until they were spent.

She was shocked by their indecency. They hurt her deeply inside. They were vicious and brutal. She would never have imagined that humans could do such disgusting, dirty acts. Acts that would totally violate another human being, void them of their dignity and decency. Terrorized, she was stunned beyond awareness.

The men slept wherever they fell while she cried like a wounded kitten. She didn't dare cry too loudly in case they woke up and wanted more of her. Eventually, she lost her ability to fight them and in their inebriated state, they lost all interest in her abused body. Her mind strayed to a numb place and felt safe there.

They left as soon as the winds died down just after dawn. Her nightmare had finished. Now, she needed to wake from it.

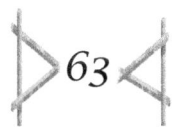

January 8, 1867

BEN HAD DECIDED TO RETURN WITH ADAM AND help him with his cabinet project. There was nothing much to do at the ranch and Barbara was recovering well and was perfectly fine being left at home with Jeannie while Joe busied himself with a repair job on his saddle and reins.

When the men arrived at Adam's house, they noticed the opened barn door and several tracks in the yard. Adam's gut told him to run to the house before Ben could stop the wagon. He called out Angie's name but stopped abruptly when he saw the disorder inside. He quickly ran up the stairs in search of Angie. Not finding her there, he ran back down the stairs to the kitchen and back room.

Ben on the other hand had followed a trail of muddy boot marks to the room at the far end. He discovered Angie there. She was naked, curled up in the fetal position, automatically recoiling at his tender touch and bleeding in several places.

Backing into the great room quietly, he took two blankets that had been tossed over the back of a chair. Slowly, as not to startle her, he covered and tucked the blankets around his daughter-in-law. He noticed that she was aware of the blankets because she grabbed onto them with the little bit of dignity she had left. When he lifted her close to his body, he could smell more clearly the urine, alcohol, vomit and other bodily fluids dried or drying on her body. He

243

swallowed down his own bile as it rose in the back of his throat.

Adam came upon him near the front entrance.

Ben said, "Jump in the wagon. I'll hand her to you." Ben quickly climbed up on the other side of the wagon and whipped the horses to hurry back to the ranch house.

Adam whispered to his wife, "Are you all right Angie? What's wrong? What happened? Angie, can you hear me?"

Ben felt he needed to get a hold of the situation, so he told Adam, "You need to do what I tell you to do. Everything will be all right. But you have to do what I say. Do you understand, Adam?"

Adam didn't understand anything. He was almost panicking. But he trusted his father to know the right things to do, so he nodded.

When they arrived at the ranch, Ben yelled out to one of the foremen, "Pete, ride into town, get the sheriff and the doctor here right away. It's Angie, she's hurt." Pete didn't hesitate.

Hoss, Evelyn and Edwin were also in the yard just approaching the house. They hurriedly followed Ben and Adam with his precious package into the house. A flurry of activity followed.

Ben instructed Adam to take Angie upstairs, but to come back here immediately. He sent Barbara and Evelyn to tend to Angie but to not bathe her until the doctor arrived. He told Jeannie to start boiling water for the bath that the doctor was sure to request later.

While sitting on the bed trying to sooth Angie, Barbara suddenly recognized Angie's stunned stare. The look resembled the one Barbara's mother had on her face when she died. One of a helpless hunted animal who had no hope of escaping her predicament. She now knew for certain what had happened to her mother. She still didn't know what killed her, but she thought it might have been related to the violations.

The women tried not to show Angie that the strong, disgusting odor emitting from her body was making them gag. They didn't want her to see them turn up their noses. But Angie was beyond the moment and couldn't have distinguished their disdain, nor cared.

Mark, the other foreman, had joined the family in the house when he heard all the commotion to find out if he could be of any service. Ben instructed Hoss and Joe to ride out to Adam's place and start tracking right away. He asked Mark to wait for the sheriff and then to follow the trail that his sons would leave for them leading away from Adam's house. He couldn't be sure how many men there were, but he was sure he counted at least three separate horse tracks.

He then told them what they were looking for and why, "Angie has been badly beaten, I think she may have been raped too."

Realizing what his father had just said must be true, Adam sank down on the closest chair. He had recognized the smell of the bodily fluids coming off of Angie on the ride over here but at the time could not believe it to be so.

Upon hearing what Ben said, the three men quickly looked toward Adam who started gritting his teeth. He said slowly and deliberately, "A bullet is too fast, and a hanging is not painful enough for those savages. If I see those men alive, I swear I will beat the breath out of them."

Hoss and Joe immediately redirected their eyes towards their father and shook their heads, indicating that they wouldn't let that happen.

The three men started towards the door and Adam moved to join his brothers.

"Where do you think you're going?" Ben asked, pulling on his arm.

"With them—to look for those sons-of-bitches."

"But what if Angie needs you?" Ben didn't want his son going after those men. Not now. He wasn't sure what Adam was capable of. Ben may have lost a daughter today, but he couldn't risk losing a son too.

Adam was torn between staying behind and going with his brothers. "Of course, Pa," he sighed. "I wasn't thinking straight."

His brothers pledged to avenge Angie on his behalf and left.

January 8, 1867

HOSS SAID, "MARK, GO TOWARD VIRGINIA CITY to meet the Sheriff on the way. That'll save time as you'll be able to head toward Adam's place instead of starting off at the ranch house."

Mark took off but slowed a bit when Joe yelled out, "If there are three of them, you won't have to slow down and track them. It will be easy for you two to catch up to us as we'll add two more sets of prints to their trail."

Mark nodded and sped away.

Once at Adam's place, Joe and Hoss didn't even have to get down from their horses to pick up the tracks. Like Ben and Adam, they saw the open barn door and horse tracks leading east. The rapists had not bothered to sweep away their route taken. Hoss and Joe hoped that meant the three men thought the snow would melt their chosen direction by the time Angie was discovered. Fools. Hoss and Joe confidently quickened their pace.

By noon, the two brothers slowed down as they were certain they were near the culprits. That also gave Mark and the Sheriff time to catch up to them. When the trail turned south toward Paiute land, Joe started to devise a plan to avenge Angie and mentioned his plan to Hoss. Hoss added some of his own thoughts to Joe's plan. When Sheriff Roy Coffee and Mark caught up, they were told about it and thought that was an excellent plan. The Sheriff had one more suggestion to offer. All agreed and so they then set it in motion.

Joe veered to the right and quickly rode farther south. Mark and Roy veered to the left. They quickened their pace to go around and ahead of the men. Hoss continued to follow them at their apparent leisure pace. Minutes later, he overheard them talking while they were resting their horses. Hoss figured they thought no one would ever follow them on Paiute land.

He watched them from a distance. In his mind, Hoss had already named them, Red Scarf, Brown Jacket and Grey Hat.

He waited for signs of Mark and Roy. When he noticed that they had reached their posts, he made his presence known to the three bastards. He cocked his gun and said, "Get your hands up where I can see them. Reach with your left hand and drop your guns to the ground. Now!"

The three men would have nothing of it and raced to reach for their weapons. They knew Hoss would not have a chance at surviving, being only one against their three. But when they heard two more guns being cocked and Roy and Mark came into view with their rifles pointing at them, they acquiesced. Without a fight, the men were soon tied up. Their hands were placed behind them, they were made to kneel in a circle facing away from each other and then their hands were tied to their ankles. There was no getting free.

Red Scarf started off by saying they were innocent—but was told to shut up. Brown Jacket then said there was nothing tying them to whatever crime they were being held for. But Hoss wouldn't hear any of their pretended innocence and simply said that the tracks from the house led them straight to this spot.

Grey Hat, still in a drunken stupor, said "Well, you can't rob us that's for sure, we've got nothing.

We drank all the good stuff." And he and his friends laughed.

Then Grey Hat stupidly added, "She's not worth all your effort, boys. She wasn't much of a spitfire," and the other two laughed at the inappropriate comments.

Red Scarf said, "Which one of you is her husband?"

He looked up at Hoss, "Is she yours? Juicy, ain't she?" and the three laughed anew.

Trying not to fall over, Brown Jacket said, "Whacha gonna do to us now? Can't undo what's been done. Me? I'll remember it for a long time." More bursts of laughter followed.

Hoss couldn't bear to hear anymore and almost shot them right there and then. He couldn't do that—but he needed to do something—so he punched Brown Jacket in the mouth and busted his lip. He remembered their plan for these bastards and replaced his scowl with a knowing grin. Had Joe been here instead of Hoss, there is no telling what he might have done as his temper was on a much shorter fuse.

After a ten-minute wait and countless unanswered questions from the tied-up men on what their captors were waiting for, Joe rode up to the group. The men assumed that he must be the husband. Joe was followed by Chief Yellow Quill and six of his warriors.

As per their earlier agreement, Roy stepped up and—mostly for the benefit of the three kneeling men—explained to the Chief, "I am Sheriff Coffee of Virginia City. These men are guilty of brutally beating and raping Ben Cartwright's daughter, the wife of his son Adam. They have even confessed their crimes to me just a few minutes ago. My job is to bring them to face justice. But, as we are on Paiute ground, I do not have the jurisdiction to remove them from your land without your permission. I will let you decide if they should be punished according to the white man's law or by the standards of the Paiute according to the seriousness of their crimes."

The men in bondage quickly sobered up and started pleading to the Chief for their worthless lives. If the Chief released them, the Sheriff knew he would have no choice but to take them in. White man's law meant jail, but Paiute law meant an eye for an eye and that their punishment wouldn't be one borne out in a jail cell.

"Silence!" shouted Chief Yellow Quill. Joe had told the Chief what Adam had said about a bullet being too fast of a merciful death and that a hanging couldn't possibly hurt them enough for the pain and lasting damage they had inflicted. The Chief assured him that he would deliver in the proper fashion of retribution for such a crime. "I have decided," his voice clear and strong.

"The Paiute knows that the woman is the heart of his family and of the whole tribe. He provides for her so she can make his life full. My people do not tolerate bad behavior toward any woman. In this case, for my friend Ben Cartwright, I will let the women of the Paiute decide the fate of these men. From now until tomorrow morning, they will suffer at the hands of our women and then they will be dead. This Chief thanks the white man and his friend Ben Cartwright for this opportunity to show that the Paiute is master on their own land."

He motioned for his warriors to throw the three men, still secured with rope, over their horses and take them up to the camp where they were to be tortured and killed.

Before the men were carried away by the warriors, Joe took a swing at Grey Hat and Hoss plowed a fist in Red Scarf's face. A black eye and another busted lip were not satisfying, but certainly helped release some pent-up tension for the brothers.

The Chief offered them the horses, but the gesture was refused. They knew that like themselves, Adam would not want a reminder of any kind.

Everybody knew that the native women were skilled at skinning animals and that they had an unmatched knowledge of anatomy. They would intuitively know how to administer pain, make the criminals bleed and beg for a quick and merciful death. The men may even be reminded that they gave Angie no mercy in the hours that they had abused her.

When they arrived back at Adam's house, the Sheriff returned to town and Mark went on ahead to the ranch. Joe and Hoss separately and in silence, wondered if they had done the right thing or if it had been too harsh of a punishment. They entered their brother's new home and were shocked to see the damage to the house and furnishings. When they came to the spot where the floor was smeared with blood, vomit and urine, they thought they should clean up but decided against it. Doing so would not benefit anyone at this time nor erase the obscenity.

The dirty floor and the crime that occurred there eventually worked its way into their minds. They imagined Angie fighting for her safety and dignity. They became somber when they envisioned her in the losing battle. They closed their eyes, blocking out the image.

They never even warmed up the cold house. They knew Adam wouldn't want them to waste any time or energy on the task, but to return to him and Angie.

Their ride back to the ranch house gave them time to realize that they had done the right thing by their sister. Joe couldn't help but think that had this happened to his own wife, he would now probably burn the house down and the bad memories with it.

It was dark when they reached the ranch house.

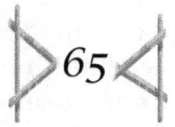

65

January 8, 1867

THE EVENTS AT THE HOUSE HAD BEEN MUCH different than the men's on the trail. The doctor quickly determined what had happened. He gently tried to connect with Angie. He asked a simple question, "How many were there, Angie?" But she didn't reply. This gave him some indication as to her mental state. She was in shock.

The doctor then asked the women to give her a bath and to put her to bed, naked for now and under a loose sheet. He left the room. They couldn't relieve her of one of the blankets that was guarding her broken body without upsetting her, so they placed her in the tub with it. They started by washing her hair and when she started gargling with the tub water, they realized that no one had offered her clean water to drink, which they did now.

The women tried to be gentle. They also talked to her like she was a child saying things like, "Adam loves you Angie, we all do. He wants to be here helping us take care of you. Everything is going to be all right now." But Angie couldn't hear them.

After the bath, she was reluctant to release her blanket, but the women reasoned with her that it was all wet and she would be more comfortable with a dry one. She let them carry her to the bed after they dried her. She took the dry blanket and curled back into the fetal position and the three women didn't want to agitate her so they let her hang onto the extra blanket.

They called the doctor back in.

Doctor Grant insisted that the women stay near during the entire examination. He had briefly spoken to Ben before being called back into the room and proceeded with the knowledge that there were three sets of horse tracks and footprints in the yard, so quite possibly all three men had assaulted Angie. Even though Adam was present for that conversation, he was also in shock and couldn't process any questions asked of him enough to answer.

The doctor examined Angie by uncovering a small part of her naked body at a time. At many instances the women would find themselves wincing during the examination, but Angie just laid there motionless.

The doctor was alarmed to find that even Angie's genitalia had been bruised. He had never seen a beating such as this. He thought, *Sick! What kind of men can do such unspeakable things like this to one defenseless woman?*

She had a bit of fight left in her when he had applied the medicated salve on her bleeding rectum. He kept telling her that he was sorry if he was hurting her, it would be over soon, and that he was trying to help her heal. He talked throughout the entire examination trying to reassure her that he was only being helpful. The women present were encouraged to support the doctor's necessary actions.

Since her arrival at the ranch house, Angie had not stopped her audible meowling. The doctor gave her a sedative so she could sleep. He knew that sleep was the best thing for her body to recover. He knew that time was necessary for her other internal injuries to heal. As for the whole woman, he did not begin to guess if she could ever recover from such trauma. He gave Evelyn enough laudanum—which was opium mixed with alcohol and taken orally—to last Angie a week, even though he promised to return before it ran out.

The doctor then went downstairs to speak to Adam in private. Once alone, Adam learned of the atrocities his wife had endured and he broke down in tears. The doctor tried to assure him that her body would heal quickly because she was young and healthy.

When asked, the doctor could not indicate how long it may take her to recover mentally. He said, "All people go through stages of recovery differently, Adam. I have not personally witnessed many such attacks to be able to estimate the length of the recovery period for Angie. Let me know if you want me to do some research and write to other doctors for documentation on these kinds of injuries and recovery." He didn't know if the young woman would survive this tragedy. Her body might heal, but would her mind? However, he wanted to give her husband hope. And why not? She just might completely recover, and so why not let Adam think that she could come out of it?

Adam replied, "Heaven forbid that there are other women who have suffered from something like this for there to be documentation."

He thought about how much he wanted to know about other women who might have gone through the same terror that his wife had. "No, at least not now. I'll let you know if I change my mind on that though."

The doctor proposed a sedative to get Adam through the night, but the offer was declined. Adam decided he needed to be in control of his thoughts and feelings.

The doctor had a fourth-time expectant mother a few miles away waiting for him to come and assist in the delivery—if it hadn't occurred already. He bid them goodbye after promising to return in a few days.

Ben and a subdued Adam went to join Hoss and Joe in the bunkhouse. The two younger men chose this place away from their wives to recount the events of their afternoon to Ben and Adam, with the exception of the part where they had stopped at Adam and Angie's home on the way back. Adam perked up when they told him of their good fortune when the bastards had ridden into Paiute territory. They told them about executing their plan and that by morning, the men would have suffered a long and painful death at the hands of the capable women of the tribe.

Ben was truly happy to hear that. Adam exhaled a breath he had not realized he was holding and nodded in satisfaction. He was relieved that the men wouldn't have to go to trial and the doctor would not have to tell anyone about the extent of Angie's injuries. It was going to be bad enough to hear the rumors that were inevitably going to spread.

Adam said, "Thank you all, including you Pa, for keeping me back. In my rage, I am sure I would have killed them with my bare hands."

Later when everyone was asleep, Adam went to the barn and saddled up his horse. He took a lantern and rode all the way to Paiute land. He needed to hear the culprits scream and beg for their damned lives. He stayed long enough to know that the pain the women were inflicting was more than he could ever have administered himself.

Adam spent the rest of the early morning sitting on the chair next to Angie's bed. She wouldn't be stirring for a few more hours due to the sedative, but tomorrow and all of the tomorrows for a long time after that, would be different.

January 8, 1867

BARBARA CONSOLED BEN IN THEIR BEDROOM that night where he allowed himself to break down and cry for his broken daughter and son. He had never been so afraid in his life. How could such a monstrosity occur? Barbara knew first-hand what people were capable of doing.

She had never seen Ben so distraught. She knew he would not rest until he found some way for Adam and Angie to find a path out of this hell. But what could he do? As a father he was helpless. Barbara vowed to help her husband help his children if there was any way to do so.

Much later, Ben would think of this moment and be in awe of Barbara's strength. How had she, as a woman, been able to hold it together after learning what had happened to Angie? Wouldn't most women be terrified and at least break down in tears or seek some reassurance from their husbands? He couldn't understand her courage but was marveled by it. He was grateful that she was by his side.

~

Hoss embraced Evelyn and they snuggled deeper into the bed in his childhood room. Neither could sleep. He was saddened by the nightmare his brother and sister were facing; and he felt sorry for Adam and Angie.

But he was secretly grateful that Evelyn was safe and unharmed, right here by his and Edwin's side. He wrestled with his mixed emotions and told her so.

Evelyn helped him realize that if the situation was reversed, if this had happened to her instead of Angie, Adam would be feeling the same as Hoss.

Hoss nodded. His wife was pragmatic and so matter of fact. No use dwelling on the "what if," she would often say.

They decided they would stay here to be of service to Adam and Angie and the whole family in any capacity for as long as they were needed.

"You amaze me, Miss Evelyn."

"Why? What do you mean by that, Hoss?"

"You are very strong in character, my dear. You hold it together for my entire family. You never shirk away from anything no matter how difficult or distasteful it may be. You don't break down and cry, not even later on when we are alone."

"Well, I will share something I have observed. I think it will make you feel better in a way. Events that make a woman powerless, or in Angie's case abuse of her body and mind are normally harder to bear and to endure by the man who loves her than by the victim herself. Not always, but often."

~

Joe waited for Jeannie to come to bed. She had been pacing the floor. Alone in their bedroom, she could finally let her guard down and say what was on her heart. She suddenly buried her face in her hands and fell to her knees crying. Joe quickly went to console her. She had grown very fond of Angie—of her husband's whole family. She had never felt so close to other people before, not even her own mother. She couldn't get past this evil that Angie and Adam were forced to face.

She had also become fearful for her own safety. Joe tried to calm her, lifting her up to sit on his lap on the bed, and then holding her.

"Don't be afraid Jeannie. The men won't come back. Hoss and I made sure of that. Angie and Adam won't have to face this hell alone. We are all going to be here together. We'll listen to them, cry with them, get angry for them and whatever else is needed. We'll tell them and each other, every day, that they are loved and that we pray for their recovery from this hell," Joe said.

This day made Joe grow up quickly. No more would he have that innocent and idyllic outlook on life. He would forever be changed by the reality of life's atrocities. He also vowed to always love and protect his wife. She needed reassuring and he could easily give her that, all she needed, everyday from now on.

~

Adam didn't sleep. He sat in the chair, watching his wife sleep. Each time he imagined what the three men had done to his petite wife, a churning rage in the pit of his stomach would overcome him. Only when he thought of the torture the savages were enduring themselves at this very moment did he not give in to the need to vomit. By morning they would be dead.

At sunup, Adam heard a call. A whistle. He went out to the front porch to investigate but no one was there. The only evidence that anyone had been was the package on the step. There were three right-sided ears wrapped in a remnant cloth. Adam was now reassured that the retribution was finished.

He picked up the package, went to the barn for

a shovel and then disappeared into the woods behind the house. He buried the ears, tears falling off his face. He was grateful the ordeal was over. Now maybe he would sleep.

He returned to the chair beside his wife's bedside and nodded off.

January 22, 1867

FOR THE FOLLOWING MONTH AND A HALF, Barbara, Evelyn and Jeannie would take turns sleeping in Angie's room, soothing her when she would scream in the night. But on the second night after the attack, Angie woke from her shock, yelling in terror. Adam had been sleeping in the chair beside the bed and tried to console her, but she was too frightened and fought back fiercely. Her screams roused the entire household and the women ran into her room. They held her and pushed Adam away when Angie screamed, "Make him leave!"

In silence and alone later in his father's study, the stunned Adam helplessly cried.

The following day, the women suggested to Adam that it may be best if he only sat in the same room as Angie if one of the other women was present. He agreed, praying it wouldn't be a situation that continued for long. Sitting in the chair in the corner, he kept an eye on his wife, while keeping himself busy with paperwork or playing the guitar or reading a book. But if the last of the women had to leave, he left with her. He did not want Angie to feel threatened by his presence again. Ever.

Five days passed. Adam wasn't aware of them. He was neglecting everything—even his personal hygiene. Everyone noticed but no one said anything in the hopes that he would eventually come around.

On the sixth day, Jeannie was helping Angie sit

up in bed when Adam walked in. Angie's eyes suddenly saw what the others had not and she screamed to the top of her lungs, "No, don't let him near me. Stop! Get out." Then she whispered, "Please don't. No more."

Jeannie tried to calm Angie, unsure as to what had caused the agitated outburst directed at Adam. She looked at her stricken brother-in-law and shrugged her shoulders. But Joe, who had just finished with his toiletries, came running into the room. He took one look at Adam and knew why Angie had been so upset when she saw her husband.

Joe put an arm around Adam's shoulder and led him to the hallway and shut the bedroom door behind him.

"Adam, all three men had a beard."

That was all Joe needed to say.

~

Ben did not know if anyone could help Angie, but if there was one person who could, it had to be Adam.

One afternoon during the second week after the attack, Adam was with Angie, so Hoss was working with his father to complete the papers needed for the upcoming cattle sale. Ben asked Hoss a question and after sorting through a couple of papers, his son replied that it sure was beneficial that they kept such good records of all their dealings. "I know that Adam is more organized than I am and quicker to calculate numbers," he innocently said, "But even if he were doing this with you right now Pa, I'm sure he'd have to refer to what you wrote in last year's log to come up with this year's answers."

That night, Ben was restless until he finally figured out why he couldn't sleep. He got up to get himself a glass of water. When he passed Adam's room, he noticed the light under the door from the lantern burning inside. He knocked, waited to be called in and asked Adam to come downstairs to his study as he needed to discuss something with him.

Adam put his housecoat on and followed him, curious as to what subject would be so important his father wished to discuss it this late into the night.

Sitting behind his desk, Ben asked Adam to sit down. "I believe that you will eventually be able to help Angie get beyond this."

"How, Pa? I'll do anything," a now fully alert Adam said hopefully.

"I want you to keep a journal."

"A what? How in hell will that help her?" Lately, Adam had taken up a bad habit of cussing and was quick to anger.

Ben snapped back, "Watch your language in this house. I don't care if you are a grown man." Ben quickly calmed himself down. He felt an overwhelming compassion for his son and looked upon him with pity. He was sorry for having disciplined Adam just then.

Adam, however, had—for a brief moment—felt the normalcy of his father's discipline and was glad for it and nodded his head.

Ben gently explained further, "You need to write down everything you have felt since discovering her at the house. Write down all the darkness, the anger, the hurt, the hopelessness, the feelings of despair, your loss, your love. Write it all down. Everything, every thought and every emotion. Even if you think she couldn't take it if she ever got a hold of your book and read it."

"For now, write in her presence. Let her see that you are writing in a journal. One day she may need to know what you went through. She may even discover that you both went through a similar darkness and feelings of helplessness. She may draw strength from it one day. Adam, if you can't survive this, what makes you think she can? This will take time. You will be tested."

Ben said, coming from around the desk and placing a hand on his son's shoulder, "Angie didn't choose this test. She will resent it, and you for that matter, even if she knows in her heart you are not to blame."

Adam had figured out most of what his father was telling him, but the older man's voicing of his thoughts confirmed what the future might hold.

He took a journal from a stack he kept to write down business dealings, brought it to his room and started to write.

~

Every day, for almost the rest of the year, he wrote. Some days contained just a short message representing some small event and other days contained repetitions as there were no new emotions. Some messages would occasionally appear stale and at a stand-still, just like Angie who was not making any progress or showing any promise of moving forward. At the beginning the hurt was too unbearable to describe on paper. His thoughts were all over the place just like his disrupted life. Just little snippets of words put to paper.

My dearest Angie,
This is my first attempt to put into words what I feel. I cannot imagine what hell you have been through. I can only tell you about mine. I feel rage. Total anger. But mostly frustrating helplessness. I am blind with pain and desperately want to wake up from this nightmare unscathed.

You recoil at the sight of me. I understand. Believe me, I do. But you must know that I would never hurt you. I love you more than my life. I would die for you.

Can you see me? Do you care what I'm doing? I feel I no longer have a purpose. I am living day to day without a reason, aimlessly wandering the hallway until I can come into your room. Tearfully, Adam

Angie, my love,

When we found you after the attack, Pa handed you to me. Even holding you close, I could not imagine the state you were in. I could only see the blood on your face and smell a putrid stench coming from you. But when I learned from the doctor about the attack infringed upon your petite body and the pain it caused you, my knees buckled from underneath me. I was swept into an abyss of despair and hopelessness not knowing if I could ever claw my way out. I wanted to vomit. I wanted to weep like a baby. And then I wanted to kill. But I couldn't breathe, still can't. Someone has punched me in the gut and my lungs have collapsed.

I went back to our house on the pretense that I needed to pick up some clothes, but I really went there to freely destroy things so I could demonstrate my true feelings. I had a physical need to express my anger. I needed to work my frustrations out. I started by ripping the curtains, blankets and pillows and

*I tossed every dish and then I threw
furniture and even busted up some walls.
I couldn't stand having anything survive
that place, so I destroyed it all.*

*I was broken and eventually ended
up on the floor in desperate tears. Why?
Why? Why? I kept asking myself.*

*Then I went upstairs. Except for
my dried footprints on the floor from that
day, nothing had been disturbed. They
had never ventured upstairs. I hadn't
remembered that. They didn't find your
jewelry or the chest that holds treasures
from our wedding gifts to each other. I
couldn't destroy the place where we made
love and whispered in the night to each
other our innermost feelings. I vowed to
pack everything from the second floor and
bring it over with us to a new house.*

*I know the men who did this are
dead, yet I still have this unsatisfied need
to avenge you, my most precious love.*
Adam

My dearest Angie,

*I come into your room and watch
over you only to discover that I upset you
with my presence. I'm sorry. I only want
to show you that I love you and I am here
for you. I am so sad with it all. I cry tears
that no one will ever notice, tears that I
want you to console but you can't. I cry in
silence when all I want to do is scream to
the end of my voice.*

*I want to show you that I am
capable of being the most tender man you
will ever know. Please let me sit with you.*

THE CARTWRIGHT MEN MARRY

*I miss you. I hurt because you hurt. I want
and need to be consoled by you.*

Oh, how I love you. Always.

Desperately, Adam

Angie, my love,

*I often reread what I have written.
I find that I sound more like a victim than
the loved one of a victim. But then again,
maybe I am a victim! After all, my whole
life has been shattered. Like a mirror! Can
we ever put it together again? Will we find
all our missing pieces? I wonder. You need
to know that I hurt—maybe as much as
you do. In different ways, but still hurting.*

Help me help you, please. Adam

*P. S. Today, I regrettably canceled
our travel plans to New York. I can't and
won't leave you to go alone.*

My dearest Angie,

*Part of me wants to stay away
from you and the room that you have
made your whole world. But today, I
made a promise to myself that I would
not. Although you don't allow me to get
closer than the chair in the corner without
screaming or whimpering—and only allow
my company in general when one of our
sisters is in the room—you have to adjust
to my presence if we are ever to live
together again one day.*

*Your bruises that are visible look
very painful on your beautiful skin. I want
to kiss, ever so tenderly, the hurt away.
Of course, I know that you will not let me.
But just knowing that you know I would*

266

do that if I could, helps me cope and gives me hope. I still can't help feeling frustrated with my helplessness and uselessness. I love you, always. Adam

Dearest Angie,

I'm grateful to have had the opportunity to sit in your room with you today. I played my guitar but when you shouted for me to stop, I picked up my journal and wrote this instead.

I cannot begin to understand what demons you encounter. I can only hope that you will let me go through this with you. I pray that you will let me help you.

We will always have music though, won't we? Will we get anything back? I often wonder if you wonder the same things I do.

I'm very confused about God right now. So confused that I can't write about it. Not yet. I love you. Adam

P.S. I think you frightened Evelyn! I know you frightened Jeannie right out of the room when you yelled at me to quit playing. It almost made me laugh out loud. But then, it wasn't funny.

My dearest Angie,

I can hardly contain myself to stay away from you when you cry out at night. I want so badly to be the one to hold you and tell you that everything will be all right. Please remember that I love you and would never hurt you. Please let me in, soon.

I love you, Angie. Adam

My love, Angie,

I have stopped writing down which day it is since you were violated. It does not matter how many days pass. It only matters that we face this darkness together.

My message is short today. I am at a loss for words. I can only say that I am numb. I love you, always. Adam

He wasn't just numb. He was depressed. He had started grieving for his losses. He couldn't stand to be in the room with her, the non-Angie. This other non-person didn't even care if he was there or not.

He found himself heading for the guest bedroom that had become his and found that place to be void of all warmth and comfort. He ran down the stairs and his father watched him flee towards the barn. He had reached the end of his despair. Once he thought he was alone, he freely started to sob, his entire body giving up whatever was restrained.

He inhaled huge gasps of air and let out his sadness. His sorrow came out in the loudest of painful wails. His body looked as deformed as his heart by the pain it was expressing.

But he was not alone!

Joe could hear Adam sobbing uncontrollably. He decided to come out of the stall he was cleaning and in response to Adam's heaving, he tearfully squeaked out of his own constricting throat, "Adam?"

Adam quickly stood up and shook his head, trying to put his feelings back in check. He truly thought he had been free to express his grief. He turned away to go look for another place of solitude and was caught in Hoss' strong, yet trembling arms.

He willingly gave in to his brothers then. He let it all out, as loud as his pain. Joe joined his embracing brothers and together they sank to the barn floor and wept together. Hoss held both brothers in his arms barely able to keep them from toppling over. They found their solidarity and drew strength from each other.

Minutes passed and eventually Adam's sorrow became a hiccup. The men began to rise, giving each other pats on the back to bridge from the intense emotional moment to one of normality.

They felt no shame with their tears. Without uttering a word, Adam knew he had their full support and love. He was not alone after all. He should have known. He did know. He had probably run to the barn subconsciously knowing they were both inside.

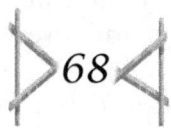

Late January, 1867

WHEN ADAM WASN'T COMING BACK TO THE HOUSE, Ben decided to follow him. As he entered the barn, he witnessed the greatest example of love his sons had ever demonstrated. They weren't speaking yet, they were still arm in arm, in unison, and red-eyed from tears. They seemed determined and ready to face this darkness together.

Ben approached them as they were getting up, finding a chair, a stool, a bale of hay and a barrel to sit on. They finally spoke.

Joe started, "I love you and Angie, Adam. You know that. I'm going to say something that may sound mean-spirited, but hear me out. If this evil had to happen to someone, I think it happened to the two of you because of all the couples I know, I believe the two of you are the only ones strong enough to get past it. Had it happened to me and Jeannie, well I don't know for sure but I'm afraid I would be too weak to live up to my vows and would end up giving up on her. I would probably fail her. Or worse, she would probably have let herself die. For one-hundred percent sure, I would have killed those men in a blind rage."

Hoss agreed, if only to support Adam, "I think I would fail Evelyn too. I think I would move on if she ever gave me any indication that she doesn't want me in her life anymore. I would grieve, but eventually I would try to move on without her. I know she comes across as very strong, but I'm not sure she could survive something like this any more than I could."

Ben could see right through his sons, but added anyway, "But you Adam are the strongest of us all. You love Angie with all your being. We know that because you were not what most people would say was "the marrying kind". Angie's love was God-sent to you as a gift. You treasure that gift and realize that it is as close to God's love as you will ever get here on earth. She will know that too one day and she will rejoice in your love for her. Just never stop praying. All of you."

"You really think so, Pa?" Adam asked.

"I know so, son. I know it."

Adam wasn't fooled one bit. He said, "Thanks for lying, all of you. Oh, I'm sure there is some truth to some of what you said, but I know how deeply Cartwrights can love because I am one, remember? I know you two would both be true to your vows. But I thank you for picking me up today. I need to know I am not alone in this mountain of pain I have to face."

His brothers smiled for a very brief moment. Then they sighed.

Ben told them they had better get into the house for lunch otherwise one of the women would come looking for them. They left the barn, arms circling backs, a wall of men.

~

Adam was healing. When he wrote in the journal, his written thoughts would no longer be all over the place. He was healing. Oh, he would still have his moments, but he only had to think of his brothers and father that day and he would remember the path he chose to take. The difficult one. The one that God wanted him to take for Angie. God didn't confuse him anymore.

Ben felt reassured that Adam had no doubt that

he could rely on their love, on God's love, and mostly on his own undying love for Angie.

After the first month and a half, Hoss, Evelyn and Edwin went home to sleep in their own beds.

Angie started to sleep through the night alone, knowing that Barbara and Jeannie were nearby, but she was still responding negatively to all the men in the house. Even the dear man she once called Pa caused her to become agitated and afraid.

February 27, 1867

ON A WINDY WINTER DAY TWO WEEKS AFTER HOSS
and Evelyn returned to their home, Hoss was working in
the southwest forest with his team of horses. The task at
hand everywhere in the region at this time of year, was to
gather dead wood to use for heating and cooking for the
following year—during the warmer months. With their
busy ranching season, men could not afford the time to go
out and cut down dead trees and branches for firewood.
Adam would not be going out this year to chop down
dead branches. He wanted to stay near Angie. Joe was
in a section southeast of the ranch with Ben. Working
together, they would keep the ranch well supplied.

Men everywhere would make their own trails.
They each sectioned off a five-mile radius in order to not
deplete the entire range nor interfere with another man's
work area—unless invited, of course. The logs would be
brought to their homes and sawed and chopped down to
size and corded into long rows at the back of the house
for use throughout the rest of the year.

At dawn, able-bodied men would leave their homes
after a huge, filling breakfast. Their steady attention to
the task at hand quickly brought on the lunch break. But
all men would have to quit working shortly after three
o'clock in order to find their way out of the woods before
dark. Some men worked in pairs; some worked alone.

Hoss always enjoyed this task. It was hard physical
work, but he couldn't feel the cold from the chilling winds
as they could not reach deep inside the forest due to the

insulation provided by the density of the trees. Other than the echo of Hoss' chopping and the occasional chirping of winter birds and squirrels, the forest held no noise. He breathed in the cool winter air and felt at peace. He often thought himself lucky to be alive when he was in the woods doing his favorite winter task. Time would go by unnoticed. Only the sleepy sun and his growling stomach would remind him when it was time to go home.

His whole day would be spent in prayer. Today his meditation during this peaceful time would be on his brother, Adam and his and Angie's needs. He wouldn't be solving all of their troubles, but he would often resolve a problem just by praying on it all day. On the days where nothing was solved, he would still find peace because he had spent it with God.

When he arrived at his destination with many fallen trees, he began to unharness the horses from the sleigh. He would use the horses' strength throughout the day to pull on dead trees that were bogged down in holes or stuck on other trees.

The branches of the trees above shut out some of the sun, yet the physical work quickly drove Hoss to shed his outer coat and drape it over a stump. He tied up a broken branch from a dead ash. Ash and birch trees were known for their pleasant scent, but ash had a longer burning time. He moved towards the front of the team of horses to lead them to the right. This would enable him to pull the tree away from the hole that was preventing him from getting a good footing to chop it down to a manageable size.

The high humidity of the past few days combined with the dropping temperature had made the snow heavy and wet. A squirrel busily running back and forth—from a stash of her food to her nest—caused one of the overburdened branches to suddenly release all of its snow. It landed with a thump on the backs of the horses below. Spooked, they took off. The sudden momentum easily lifted and freed the tree that Hoss was trying to control.

The ash was holding up a much larger tree, one his family would refer to as a giant. The giant had been uprooted in the past summer storm. It was deceiving as its branches still held on to hundreds of leaves. Hoss had assumed incorrectly that the larger tree was still living. So, when the smaller tree that was holding it upward rolled toward Hoss, the giant tree followed. It was too late for Hoss to react to the huge tree coming his way.

"AAAHHH!!!!" Hoss yelled.

Birds left their perches because of the unexpected outburst. Squirrels froze in their tracks and looked toward the source of the sound. But no human being heard Hoss scream. The tree came crashing down on top of Hoss. He fell backwards and the tree bounced once and fell again, settling once more and pinning him underneath it. Only his right arm and head escaped the prison.

Hoss tried to concentrate on anything but the pain. He tried to think about Adam and Angie again, but that didn't work. He tried to think about what Evelyn might be doing, but that only made him worry about what she would do when he was late getting home. He slowly moved his head up and to the right and from his position which was slightly elevated, he could see that the horses were nowhere in sight. He couldn't even try to think of a way to enlist their help getting him out from beneath the crushing weight.

Hoss tried to push himself up but couldn't. He then tried to push himself away from the tree and succeeded in freeing the left side of his upper body including his arm. It was numb and when blood finally started to circulate once more, pins and needles wouldn't let up for a couple of minutes. As the pins and needles eased, Hoss shivered. Cold started to set in. He realized he was trapped.

February 27, 1867

EVELYN HAD HUNG BED SHEETS ON THE LINE outside. The temperature was a favorable 25 Fahrenheit and the sunshine encouraged drying. She had hung Edwin's clothing on the inside line and then fed him and settled him down for his nap. She sat down to darn a pair of socks. She didn't expect Hoss to return for another couple of hours, so the hair on the back of her head rose when she heard the neighing of horses outside. With the assault on Angie fresh in her mind, she became afraid. She suspected that something was wrong even before she rose to see who came to visit.

Then she recognized the team of horses as theirs. Hoss was nowhere in sight and the sleigh was not attached to the team. Instead, a lone ash tree had left a long trail in the slush of the lane. She pushed her fears of personal safety deep down into the pit of her stomach and went into fast motion. She gathered the sleeping Edwin, bundled him up and put on winter clothing. Before leaving the house, she gathered every available lantern and blanket she could find. She went outside to the barn and picked up two more lanterns.

Evelyn didn't bother with separating the horses and saddling one up. She absentmindedly released the rope that had dragged the log all the way to the house and eased the burden on the tired horses. She tied all her gear as best she could on the horse beside the animal she chose to ride. Countless times, she bent over to put something on the ground, bent over again to pick it up and tie it to the horse. She lifted the last bundle, held her baby tight, lifted up her skirt and mounted the first horse bareback and rode it while leading the other toward her parents' house a thousand yards away.

"Ma, Pa" she yelled out. Her father came out of the house and her mother soon behind him.

"What's wrong, Evy?"

"Take Edwin," she beckoned her mother from on top of the horse. "I don't know what's wrong. The horses came back to the house alone. I don't know what happened to Hoss. Pa, could you get the Doc and follow the path of lanterns that I will make from my house to the woods where Hoss went this morning? I will be able to tell where he went but you won't because it will be dark by the time you get back. Could you send one of the girls to get the Cartwrights to come help?"

Mary-Lynn said, "Margaret can go get the Cartwrights and the girls can look after Edwin. I'll go get the Doc and your Pa will go with you."

"Oh, that's a better plan. Okay, let's go. Hurry." Evelyn turned back, very close to tears yet relieved for the quicker plan. Karl went to saddle up three horses while Mary-Lynn and Margaret put on boots and warm jackets.

Evelyn was in worry mode, but not yet panicking. She soon found the trail that Hoss took that morning. She could easily see the tracks from the sleigh and the returning tracks from the same horses along with the trail of the dragged tree. When she was about two miles into the woods, she started yelling out, "HOSS!"

"Hoss, can you hear me? Hoss, where are you?"

He had been pinned down under that tree for almost an hour. Cold and fatigued from attempts to free himself, he couldn't force his lungs to yell loud enough for Evelyn to hear. He waited for her to get closer before exhausting his voice, "Here. Evelyn. I'm over here. To your left. That's it. Can you see me now?" He held a weak arm up and waved a cold, tired hand.

She ran to her husband, slid down to the ground near him and started pushing on the giant tree. "No use, Evelyn. It won't budge. Stop. Come here."

"Hoss. Oh Hoss. What happened? Are you okay?"

"The horses spooked and when they ran off, they brought down this monster that was being held up by the smaller tree that I was after. Stupid thing. I guess I was too much into my thoughts and didn't notice that this tree had been uprooted. I'm sorry if I frightened you."

"Oh my. You were lucky that it didn't hit you on the head! You can't get out?"

"Well, I'd be dead if it got me on the head and I'm pretty sure you wouldn't have found me until spring." He smiled at her, trying to make light of the predicament. "No, I can't get out. I got my arms free but I can't feel the parts of my body that are still trapped and I can't budge anymore. I'm also cold."

"Where is your coat?" she cried, removing the blanket from around her and placed it over him.

"Over there," he said, nodding to the stump where his outer coat lay.

She jumped up, retrieved the coat and placed it over the blanket.

By then Karl had arrived. He got to work lighting the lanterns he had brought. He assessed Hoss' predicament and said encouragingly, "The way I see it Hoss, we'll have to cut the giant at both ends and then slice it in the middle to be able to lift what's left off of you. All I have is an ax. I'll get started at one of the ends while we wait for more men."

"Who's coming?"

"Your Pa, Joe and maybe even Adam. I've also sent Margaret to get Doc."

"Oh, swell." Hoss said faintly. He could see that his wife and father-in-law had taken up the task of worrying about getting him out, so he allowed himself to rest.

Evelyn gulped and even cried a little. How long would it be before he could be set free? How difficult would it be to get him out? Would the cold temperature and frozen ground cause him more harm than the tree? She could panic but decided that it wouldn't be helpful. Instead, she built a fire nearby. She gathered more blankets and placed one on the ground as far down her husband's back as she could in the hopes that he could warm up. She knew it would not warm him as much as he needed, but she had to do something.

Hoss stirred. He could feel the heat from the fire. He looked into his wife's eyes who had sat up against the tree facing him, less than a foot away. She had nothing to do but wait. He opened his arms and she gladly leaned into him, resting her head lightly on his shoulder so as to not inflict further injury.

"I love you Miss Evelyn, have ever since you took hold of that second calf and I could clearly see how much you wanted those poor little critters to get better."

She smiled, turning her head to wipe a tear into his thick winter jacket. "Not at the first calf I treated?"

"Naw, well I was falling but I wasn't in love until the second one." He kissed her on the head.

"Listen," he said, pushing his forehead against hers. "I want you to know that if I don't make it out of here, that you have been my reason for living. You have given me everything."

Karl was within earshot and wanted to disappear. This was going to be a private moment that he didn't want to witness. He wished it didn't have to occur.

"Hoss, please stop."

"Evelyn," he scolded, "let's be reasonable. I need to say these things just in case. Don't get me wrong, I don't want to die. It's too soon. I have a whole lifetime that I want to spend with you and Edwin. You are a marvellous wife and mother, but you are so much more to me. You are my strength, my friend, my reason for being. You are my sunshine in the morning and my north star at night. You are my happiness and a blessing. I ... have ..." and he drifted off.

Evelyn knew what cold could do to a person. She let out a sob, but didn't give in to the panic. Not yet. She tucked the blankets tighter around her husband.

Karl was in a sweat from chopping away at the giant tree. He had hardly carved into it. He was desperate to get his son-in-law free. Evelyn had just found love. He didn't want to see her lose her husband so soon.

A half hour later Ben, Adam and Joe arrived with Pete and Mark. Karl explained what he was doing. They couldn't come up with a better plan so they also started chopping and sawing away at the giant. Margaret had found them just as they had reached the ranch house. Not knowing what the situation might require, they only released the one wagon with the chopped wood and continued on with the other wagon and their equipment. Their saws now would make quick work of setting Hoss free.

Hoss woke and said to no one in particular, "I'm cold."

The men huddled for a brief discussion and then changed their course of action to trying to dig him out. But after seeing that he was lying on a bed of rock, they realized digging him out was not an option. Evelyn placed the blankets from the Cartwrights' wagon under Hoss' head and shoulders, and the men doubled the speed of their sawing.

The men could finally see the fruit of their labors

when Doc arrived. He began to examine Hoss and the men stopped working to give him space and silence—but he insisted they continue with the chopping as time was of the essence.

When the giant was chopped down to seven feet in length, Doc said, "Hurry. I don't know how much more he can take."

Ben looked at his oldest and youngest sons, registering the fear that mirrored the emotion on his own. He urgently motioned everyone to put down their tools and move to the sides of the tree. All men, Doc included, moved up to the log, applied their weight and pushed with all their might—and succeeded in rolling the giant off its victim.

After Hoss was free, everyone relied on their adrenaline, ignored their exhaustion, and quickened their pace. The doctor along with Ben, Karl and Adam wrapped Hoss up in blankets. Joe and Evelyn hitched up the horse team to the sleigh while Pete and Mark picked up tools, blankets and lanterns. The men then carried a frozen Hoss to the sleigh and made haste toward the comforts of home.

71

February 27, 1867

AT THE HOUSE, KARL AND THE DOCTOR TENDED to Hoss. Evelyn was finally in panic mode. Adam added wood to the stove and started to boil water that he assumed would be needed. Joe came into the house after tending to the horses. Pete and Mark were sent back to the Swensons and to the ranch house to give the families the latest news.

"What's taking so long?" Ben asked no one in particular. Evelyn stirred at his question and rose to make coffee.

"ARGH!!!" Hoss yelled from the bedroom. Ben caught Evelyn as she tried to run to the bedroom.

"Let the Doc do his job. He can't be worrying about you too, Evelyn. Come sit down with Joe."

"Let me go, Pa! Let me ..."

Adam moved to stand in front of her and didn't speak until her eyes met his. "There is nothing you could do for Hoss that the Doc isn't already doing. Let's wait for him to finish his examination and tell us what he knows when he's done."

She tried to stare him down but then nodded and slowly went to sit with Joe at the table. She stood up again a moment later. Ben moved toward her, extended his arms and she embraced him.

He patted the back of her head, lifted his face toward the ceiling and prayed, "Lord, spare my son. My family cannot endure his loss. We pray that you provide Evelyn the strength and courage she needs to get through this, whatever Your plan is," with tears pooling in his eyes and wetting his cheeks.

"I need to nurse Edwin," said Evelyn to no one in particular.

Ben looked at his worried sons and said, "I'll go get him." He retrieved his horse from the barn, trotted away and was back with the babe in no time.

Moments after Evelyn came out of the baby's room who was now sated and happily sleeping, Barbara arrived with a food basket.

"Barbara, how did ...?" asked Ben, then stopped. Of course, Barbara would have thought to provide food.

"Thank you. How considerate." said Evelyn. Barbara and Evelyn started unpacking the basket and getting plates and utensils out of the cupboard.

"How are Angie and Jeannie?" asked Adam and Joe.

"They'll be all right. Truly. Besides, Pete and Mark are back at the ranch. We had all this food ready and just us three to eat it, so I thought I would bring most of it over," she smiled reassuringly.

The men didn't think they could eat, neither did Evelyn. But they did, in silence, each deep in their own thoughts or prayers.

~

Finally, Doc and Karl emerged from Hoss' bedroom.

"Now before you go in there Evelyn, I should tell you that I don't know the extent of Hoss' injuries. His legs are frostbitten. Thawing will cause him a lot of pain, but he should take this medicine until the worst is over. It will help with the discomfort. He might lose some toes. I can't be sure. He has a broken pelvic bone that I know of and because he is so cold, I can't tell if he also has a broken back or not. I will be able to know more in a day or so."

"Can I go in now?"

"He's asleep. I gave him a dose of laudanum. But yes, please go in. You can all go see him if you want."

Evelyn went in first and looked back toward Ben. He took that as an invitation and followed inside. Adam and Joe couldn't stay back. Barbara put food on plates for the doctor and Karl.

Evelyn moaned and silently started crying when she set eyes on her gentle husband. Ben stood at the foot of the bed and placed a hand to his forehead. He almost touched his beloved son's foot but didn't when he remembered that it was frostbitten. He knew that just a feathered touch could be painful.

Joe knelt down on the floor by his brother's bed and reached for his right hand. He brought Hoss' hand close to his face and freely let the tears streak down his exhausted cheeks.

Adam was already emotional from his personal trauma and could not endure another one stoically. He fell to his knees beside his brother's bedside and sobbed, leaning his head on the quilt close to Hoss. Joe put an arm around Adam to comfort him. Adam lifted his head off the bed and turned toward Joe to cry in his arms. The two reeled from the tragedy that had struck their loving brother down. They were inconsolable.

A teary Ben had to gently urge them up and convince them to go home to their wives and get some sleep. Hoss would not be waking until the next day and they should be rested if they wanted to be there for him.

Adam and Joe left soon after with Barbara. Doc promised to come back in the morning. Karl also went home after hugging his oldest daughter.

Ben would not leave his son's side. Neither would Evelyn. They watched him all night long.

~

None of the rest of the family would ever know that Jeannie had actually loaded a gun and sat with Angie in her room. Jeannie was worried sick that doom was hanging over the Cartwrights. One more bad thing had to happen. Didn't bad luck come in threes? She knew she was perhaps being unreasonable, but stayed wary until she heard Pete and Mark returning to the bunk house.

Angie was oblivious but Jeannie felt silly and embarrassed about her actions as the evening went on. She swore she wouldn't mention to her husband what she had done. He didn't need to worry that she had needlessly panicked.

When Jeannie next set eyes on Barbara, she realized that her miscarriage had been the first bad luck that struck the Cartwrights. That meant three bad things had already happened. Jeannie let out a sigh of relief. She never considered herself as superstitious, but a rush of adrenaline does funny things to a person.

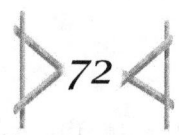

March 2, 1867

EVELYN WAS BEYOND FATIGUED. SHE HAD constant visitors, one after another, all day long. One of the brothers or sisters or the father or the ranch hands or friends from town would come by to visit with Hoss.

If Hoss was ever going to recover from his broken pelvis, he needed more rest than he was getting, but he was too polite to turn away company. He was fortunate to not suffer from a broken back, but it could be months before he could get around again or longer if he didn't repose.

Everyone said they wanted to help. She didn't know how to tell the well-intentioned guests that they were *not* very helpful if they were just going to sit with Hoss and rely on her to feed the stove, feed them, feed the animals in the barn, and then feed the baby. But she didn't know how to ask for help.

One afternoon, while she was outside gathering more firewood, she tripped and fell down hard on the freshly snow-covered ground. When she pushed herself up, blood dripped from a cut above her right eyebrow. She dabbed the blood on a cloth once inside the house, then forgot about it in the rush to get all her chores done.

Hoss was the one to notice it. Ben was the one presently visiting.

"How did this happen, Evelyn?" asked a concerned father-in-law.

She burst into tears. She let out her frustrations, "I can't do this anymore. Either everyone will have to stay home and let me help my husband in peace, or I ... I don't know what I'll do. Maybe I'll go back home to my parents' house. How can people be so rude? Can they not see how much work I have to do? Can they not see that I have double the work? The laundry is piling up. The house needs cleaning." Evelyn's voice was rising in tone and volume.

"I'm so tired, I fell. I came within inches of hitting my head on the ax instead of a piece of firewood lying on the ground. Then who would take care of the baby? And Hoss? I need to bake bread and, and ..."

Ben had his arms around her now. She was freely crying into his chest. "You're right. We have been so concerned about Hoss' well-being that we forgot about you. How can we fix this, Evelyn?"

"I don't know. I need to think but I worry and then I can't sleep," she sobbed.

"Evelyn, come here. Pa, let me ..."

Ben nodded and left.

Evelyn laid her head on the bed beside her husband and he stroked her hair.

"I'm sorry Hoss," she said. "I'm not as strong as I thought I was." She half sat, half lied down on the bed, next to him.

"Nonsense. You are still the strongest woman I know. You just need to sleep."

"But my mind won't let me. All kinds of worries keep me up."

"Like what? Let me share in that burden. I can still do that," said a medicated Hoss. He might never stand again, but he could help make decisions.

Burdens shared are burdens halved. Evelyn must have heard that a hundred times growing up.

She slept easily in the chair next to his bed after spilling out her frustrations. Meanwhile, Ben had stacked the wood box to its limit and brought in the cold-stiff clothing that had been hanging on the clothesline since the day of the accident. He tidied up the kitchen and checked in on his grandson.

When Ben heard stirring in their bedroom a couple of hours later, he knocked and entered when Evelyn said, "You can come in."

"I have a solution I would like to offer you both," Ben said.

"Oh? We also came up with one," replied Evelyn.

"Well, I'd like to hear yours first."

"We'll hire a man to come do my chores around the house so Evelyn can concentrate on Edwin and me." Hoss said.

"That's certainly an option," said Ben. "But I would like to suggest one that won't cost you anything and give Evelyn more time to help you and Edwin. She won't even have to make meals. If you will permit me."

"Sure Pa," they both said curiously. "What is it?"

"Come live at the ranch house. Now, I know we can't have Hoss stay upstairs, especially when he starts getting better and needs to walk around. You could stay in the craft room downstairs. We can exchange those furnishings with Hoss' bedroom. What do you say?"

"Oh, Pa, what about Edwin? That room is not very big. We would be in everybody's way!"

"Yes, I know. I thought about that too. Adam would probably look forward to putting together a plan to rearrange the storage room and alter the back entrance to give you both a more private place. We all would benefit being together again. I'm here every other day and so are your friends and family. This arrangement would save everybody a lot of time. What do you say? Can we do this for each other?"

Evelyn jumped at the chance to leave behind household responsibilities, allowing her to focus all of her attention on her most precious husband and baby boy. Hoss agreed, not as quickly, but he did see a lot of benefit from the plan.

73

March 10, 1867

ADAM COULD NOT WRITE ABOUT HOSS. IT WAS too sad. His brother had been pushed down and there was no telling if he would ever get up again. Adam couldn't cope with any more sorrow. He tried to be positive for everyone's sake, but simply wanting it didn't mean it was achievable. He could hope for nothing in his future without Angie.

Ben was fraught with worry. He knew Hoss' mental health at the moment was as fragile as his physical health. He could see that Adam, already withdrawn, now barely interacted with the other family members since Hoss' accident. He could also see that his youngest son was close to tears at the smallest of events, even a broken teacup. As a younger man, Joe had always left the room whenever things weren't going his way. But now, the challenges facing the Cartwrights were out of their control and Joe didn't know how to cope. None of his sons did.

Ben called Adam and Joe into his study.

"Do you remember when you turned twenty-one years old, Adam? Joe? Remember what I said to you then?" Adam and Joe looked at each other and shrugged shoulders.

"Let me refresh your memories. I told you that every year or so, on or around your birthday, you should examine what you accomplished in the past year, what you liked about it and what you could have done better. Then I also said that you should envision where you plan on being next year, or even five years from then. Remember?"

"Yes, Pa. Sure, I remember." The two replied.

"Now sons, this is going to be one of those terrible years. We can't expect a miracle overnight, can we? These tragedies will take time for our family to recover from. Together, with our wives and each other, we will get through this. Hoss will come around probably before his body does. He *will* be all right. When we feel that we are fighting a losing battle, we need to come together and encourage each other. We'll ask Barbara, Evelyn and Jeannie to join us."

Ben looked at them and added, "Do you want to ask them to join us now?"

Adam replied, "No Pa. Angie can't be left alone, not yet. But I would like to have a family meeting with as many as possible. I need to draw from their strength."

"Me too. I'd like that Pa," said Joe.

Ben breathed in and out. He was feeling too much stress himself.

Over the next three months, their frequent family meetings were always absent of Angie, Hoss and one of the women. But they proved to be beneficial to everyone. They soon became a gathering for prayer.

74

March 24, 1867

HOSS AND EVELYN WERE CRAMPED IN THE SPACE of the craft room for the first couple of weeks. Evelyn spent all of her time doting on Hoss and Edwin. She flourished. Hoss became smaller and smaller—and more and more frustrated.

After two weeks into their new accommodations at the back of the ranch house, he let his rage show through. "Stop asking if I want a blanket, or a book, or whatever. I'll ask if I need anything. Gee, I wish I could just get away."

"What do you mean by get away? What does that mean, Hoss?" asked a puzzled Evelyn.

"I mean, I don't like being looked after, not being able to do anything for myself. I don't like having you serve me hand and foot like this. How much longer is this going to take?"

"I really don't understand Hoss. What exactly is the problem? Am I not looking after you all right?"

"Oh, you know what I mean!"

"No, I don't. I really don't." Evelyn was becoming very frustrated.

Just then, Ben came in for his daily visit with Hoss.

"Is this a bad time?"

"Pa, I ah, er ..." Hoss muttered while Evelyn left in a huff.

"What's going on Hoss? No, actually, it's none of my business. Do you want to skip our visit today?"

"No, I don't. I, we need to talk." Hoss told his father about his frustrations with the outcome of the accident, how he felt diminished as a man, how he felt guilty skirting his responsibilities, and how he didn't know if he could ever be even half as strong as he once was. He was angry at himself for lashing out at Evelyn just now. And yet, he was angry at her because she could do everything she was doing. He was angry with the pity he saw on his friends' faces. He was angry at everything and everyone.

Ben just nodded his head until he realized Hoss had stopped talking.

Hoss looked at him with a scowl. "Well? Don't you have words of wisdom for me, Pa?"

"As a matter of fact, I do, Hoss. I believe you have been grieving for your losses. It is quite normal. You can't use your legs and you're angry about it. You take it out on the people you love the most and you can't help it. Stop me if I'm wrong."

Hoss shook his head side to side.

Ben continued, "You pull away from Evelyn when you need her the most. There are many stages of grieving and many reasons to grieve; not just death you know."

Hoss nodded, giving himself a chance to think about this new information.

"I also believe that you are almost done with your grieving. You are close to being over your losses and are ready to move on to embracing your blessings. I suggest you get on that and make peace with your devoted wife before she hits you over your hard head with the frying pan." Ben didn't know if it was wise to tell Hoss that he was near the end of his grieving period. What did he know? But he hoped that it were true and that saying so would make Hoss believe it too.

Hoss pouted as Ben left the room.

It took all afternoon for his father's words to sink

in. He still felt helpless. He prayed for God's help. When Evelyn came in with his supper, he asked her to stay and talk to him. She willingly stayed. She was not at all reluctant to discuss his issues.

He apologized, "I'm not sure I know how to behave, Evelyn. This is new to me and I am probably going to slip up again and again in the future. Forgive me?"

She softened. Yet another way presented itself for her to help her husband. "My darling, Hoss. You must know that I love you. I didn't marry you for your physical strength."

"I don't know how to go on being the man of our family, Evelyn."

"Oh, I realize that, but I believe in you. You will be the father who will teach his children how to respect, love, and have faith. You are so much more than your limbs. I married you for your integrity, thoughtfulness and honesty. You will teach Edwin all about your virtues. Being a husband and a father is not about being able to walk and do physical things. It is so much more—and that, you can give us."

A moment of silence passed. He looked deeply in his beautiful wife's eyes. He touched her face and said, "Thank you, Miss Evelyn. You have built me up and I thought it was my job to do that for you."

"Oh, but you do, Hoss. Every day I am married to you I feel like I'm someone special. Every single day. I should tell you these things more often. It works both ways, Hoss. You don't always have to build me up. It feels wonderful when you do but I forgot that you need to hear it too."

They both said, "I love you," and kissed.

Hoss pulled away from the kiss first and said, "Children? You believe we can have more?"

"Well, one can always hope." She smiled and they kissed again.

75

April 2, 1867

LOVE OF MY LIFE, ANGIE,
More than two months have passed.
There has been fading of your bruises,
but no fading of the true hurt. As usual, I
cannot speak for you. I can only say what
I feel and see. I am hurting.
I am still very angry at the total
destruction caused by those three
animals. They have violated your body,
yes. But they did much more than that.
They got into your mind. Kick them out!
They have taken away your
independence, your carefree attitude,
and even, dare I say, your desire to go on
living.
Your body can heal but I worry
that you may wonder why to go on? You
should know that I question my own need
to be here too. Why am I alive when I feel I
have no hope, no future?
I only surmise that if I didn't love
you, I could not breathe. You and the hope
that you will come back to me is my only
reason for living. I have hope that we will
find each other again. I love you, always.
Adam

Adam realized his responsibility toward Angie's parents. It had been three months since the attack. He had hoped that he would never have to write about the assault—that Angie would come back to him and they could continue on with their lives, turning the page and beginning anew. However, he knew now that the situation was not going to change quickly enough to avoid informing his in-laws of Angie's condition. He sat down with pen:

> *Dear Professor and Mrs. Simmons:*
> *This is truly the most difficult letter I will ever write. Do not be alarmed, Angie is physically fine. But a few weeks ago, she was brutally beaten and raped. She is in a state of shock to say the least. Her body is healing but I am afraid that it is taking her mind more time to recover from this unspeakable attack.*
>
> *I cannot tell you enough how sorry I am that I was not at home protecting her, but my guilt will never fix this wrong or make it go away nor help her get better. Thankfully the three men responsible for this heinous crime have been apprehended and are no longer living.*
>
> *If you can manage, please come to Virginia City. Wire me of your arrival and I will meet you at the stagecoach. I know that she will benefit from a visit with two more people who love her with all their hearts. I look forward to your reply.*
>
> *I can feel your prayers already.*
> *Adam*

My dearest Angie,

I wrote your parents and, as conservatively as I could, told them about your state of health and the cause. They are coming west in the hopes of providing you comfort.

I tried to tell you, but I was not sure you heard. You stared out into space and made no eye contact. Why do you not speak to me? Are you afraid to say something you will regret? Are you afraid you would ask me to leave you and I would? Well don't be. I'm not going anywhere, no matter what you say.

I just imagined us having an argument and you are annoyed with me and therefore not speaking to me. I wish we could make up. I love you, Angie.
Adam

My dearest Angie,

I have never known such darkness. Such despair. I feel like I'm on a merry-go-round that belongs to the devil himself. I want to hit a wall. I want you to hit a wall. Get angry! For God's sake, Angie, show some emotion. Yell, cry, scream, fight. Something.

Do something other than give blank stares at the wall. Do you talk to your sisters? Or do you just reply one or two words to their questions? I see you move around your room, but you don't sit and read a book or reply to a letter from your friends. You do nothing. Is even that too much?

I wonder at times, do you ever think of our life, our love, the way it was just months ago?

The doctor came by again today, the fifth time this past month. He said you were physically so much better that he would only come over now once a month. Well, at least your body has moved on to the next stage.

I am picking up your mother and father off the stagecoach tomorrow. I hope you will be encouraged by their presence. I miss and love you so much. Adam

My love Angie,

Apparently, your father and Pa had some words today. Your parents were adamant that you belong with them until you are fully recovered and can decide for yourself if and when you want to return here to me.

How could that possibly help you make a full recovery? Even if you do leave the ranch, why would you want to come back to me if you think I was willing to let you go in the first place? No. I would not allow it. I could not go on living day to day without knowing you were there in the next room.

I would die for you. I will say this once again—I cannot breathe without you. I do not allow myself to dream without you in my future. You are my wife, in sickness and in health.

Understandably, your father was hurt and defensive, just like the rest of us when we learned of the assault.

He lashed out at the hurt and pain you endured, still endure. He couldn't stand to watch you like that any more than the rest of us could.

I wasn't there in the room with them and I do not know what else Pa said exactly, but I believe he had both our interests at heart. I hope you see it that way too one day. He made your father understand that we all went through what he was going through at the moment.

I think the best place for you is right here. If you ever get out of this nightmare or once you are back to some form of normalcy, if you still decide to go to your parents, I will have no choice but to let you go. I will take you to them myself. But until then, I will fight for you.

My love for you is not ready to die. You will have to be the one to kill it because I will love you even beyond our physical death. Adam

Dearest Angie,

Your parents' visit was two of the longest weeks of my life. I was saddened to see you throw yourself in your mother's lap when she sat on the bed beside you. That should be my lap. I am jealous of the little bit of affection you show others. You show me nothing and my anger grows. I fight it. I know it is not healthy. Oh, but I want you. I want the Angie that wore those shapeless working pants last summer. I want to sing our songs together again. I want … you, all of you. The good and the recent bad. I feel such despair at

times.
But still, I love you so. Adam

My sweetest Angie,
You let me bring you a bowl of soup today. I sat on the edge of my old bed and could feel a bit of normalcy beginning. But it didn't last. You just as quickly turned away, pointed at the door and said, "Go." That's fine. I'm just grateful for the small steps in what I am presuming is in the right direction.
I wonder, do you pray for yourself? For your recovery? Do you even know to do so? Can we do it together? Should I suggest it and try?
I love you, always. Adam

Angie, my love,
You came downstairs with Barbara and Jeannie today. You ran back upstairs when Pa stopped in his tracks at the surprise of seeing you. Tomorrow you may be even braver. I am rejoicing at your progress.
I wonder if you noticed Hoss' absence. I'm crying for my brother. We all are. I need you. Adam

My dearest Angie,
It is extremely difficult being positive when you are so unresponsive. I am tired of watching you give up and walk around like a rag doll. You make me want to shake you and then I realize that I would be demonstrating behavior that would remind you of those bastards and I give

*in. Should I be tired of giving in? I want
to shout at you. You should know that
I've had enough. Snap out of it. Come on.
Get angry. Not at me, at them! Please.
Don't let the bad guys win. Don't let them
control you. Take a hold of yourself and
show them who you really are.*

*Wait, are you angry with me
because I wasn't there? You should
be. I certainly am. I would have died
in my attempts to protect you from this
unspeakable harm. I do love you and I
miss you terribly. Adam*

Dearest Angie,

*I meant every word I wrote
yesterday. I am still on a short temper. I
hate that I have to go through this. I have
a fresh hatred of those thieves. Yes, that
is what they are, of the gravest kind. They
stole you from me. They stole you from
yourself. They stole almost everything we
had and I'm not talking about the material
things. I am talking about everything
beautiful and innocent that we once had.*

*But I love you with all my heart.
They couldn't steal my love. Did they
destroy yours? Please come back. Adam*

76

May 4, 1867

"I DON'T THINK WE SHOULD GO!" EXCLAIMED JOE.

"But you promised me. We promised Ma, Joe!" Jeannie said adamantly.

"What's going on?" asked both Ben and Barbara who overheard the argument as they were coming down the stairs.

Jeannie replied, "Remember the invitation Joe and I got a few months ago? My father was the best at buying and selling horses for ranchers and farmers in Carson City and countless counties around and there are many people who want to honor his memory. We promised my mother that we would escort her to Carson City for a celebration being held in his name. We already replied we were going!"

"That was before Angie's attack and before Hoss' accident. We can't leave here when the family needs us! Besides, it's just a dance. They were probably just looking for any old excuse to hold a dance," Joe replied back just as adamantly.

"Now listen, both of you." said Ben. "You can't put your life on hold forever. Joe, I understand your sentiments and I appreciate your sense of responsibility, but Barbara and I can handle things here."

"We sure can," Barbara agreed.

Ben continued, "There may never be a good time to be away, but what might happen when you are away would happen even if you stayed here. Now I say go and enjoy yourselves. I don't mean that you should pretend

301

that nothing has happened, only that you deserve to go and have a good time."

That's all Joe needed to hear. "You're sure Pa, Barbara?"

"Of course, we're sure."

"Okay, Jeannie. We'll go."

"Yippee!"

"When do you leave?" asked Barbara.

"We leave day after tomorrow," replied Jeannie, focusing her smile at Ben. Ben didn't say anything new that she hadn't already said to Joe. Joe just needed the assurance from his Pa that going on this trip was an appropriate thing to do.

Three days later, in the late part of a somber morning, Joe and Jeannie drove the carriage to Laura's home in Virginia City. The farther the young couple rode away from the ranch, the more carefree they felt. They soon relaxed and enjoyed their adventure.

Thirteen scenic miles and a little over an hour later, they arrived safely at their destination—a hotel called the Ormsby House, in Carson City. None of the boarding houses or hotels had any suites available. As the three would not be spending more than three nights they decided that taking two bedrooms and going out for every meal would be a welcomed change to their daily routines.

Jeannie felt nauseous after the buggy ride and decided to stay to rest in their room. Laura and Joe, assured that it was just motion sickness, decided to visit the dance committee at the hall to see how the preparations were advancing and if they could be of assistance. They were surprised to find twenty citizens, who were involved in the planning of the festivities, there to greet them.

Laura reacquainted herself with many of the ranchers that her late husband had done business with. She introduced her son-in-law to them and communicated her daughter's regrets for the evening assuring them that Jeannie would be at tomorrow's dance after a good night's rest.

As Joe and Laura left the hall to head back toward their hotel, Mona, an old acquaintance of Jeannie watched them leave.

How could such an obviously vibrant, manly man, be happy with a stuck-up woman like Jeannie? she thought. *He deserves a taste of Mona,* she thought with a smile. *A taste of excitement, adventure and even lust.*

Mona had her eyes set on Joe. She pitied the man, imagining that the self-centered Jeannie she knew from the past may be selfish in bed also. He obviously was virile and exciting. *He likely is fantasizing of a fun and buxom woman just like me,* she thought.

Mona enjoyed the game of luring seemingly happily married men to her bed. However, it wasn't long before she quickly became disappointed with weak men who let themselves be led by their sexual desires. She would grow tired of them as soon as they were hers and would focus her sights on a new prospect. The man would inevitably destroy his marriage before he figured out what his side venture had cost him. Her life was a turmoil of ups and downs with the vicious game she played with the lives of others.

Mona was difficult to resist and using her feminine attributes to capture a man excited her. Her couture was the latest style, with modern lowered necklines. She had a fine bust; and, unlike a lot of other women, wasn't afraid to show it. Jeannie was not a top-heavy woman and Mona thanked God for small mercies. She giggled at the intended pun.

But the ample Mona knew she was a handful that many men wanted to seduce and even control. She was on an upward swing with respect to her mood lately and decided that Joe could keep her there for quite a while. She would give him a long deserving taste of her gifts. She only had to be alone with him and let her attractiveness and willingness do the rest. She wasn't going to waste any time on child's play.

She started forming a plan that involved a couple of her female friends, Rita and Violet, who would keep Jeannie busy. Then, when the time was right, one would ask Jeannie if she could meet Joe, the other would send her looking for him in the right direction and Jeannie would walk in on Mona with Joe. Oh yes, that would work.

Mona knew from experience that she would end up with Joe on the rebound. Men were stupid. She didn't want him permanently, of course, only until she tired of him. Then Jeannie could take him back or not. It wouldn't matter to her one way or another.

~

The following evening, the night of the dance, Mona wore an elegant dress adorned with lace and pearls that showed plenty of her cleavage. She certainly turned heads when she arrived at the hall. There was no doubt that she was the fairest of them all. Jeannie saw Joe staring at Mona but easily dismissed it. Everyone else was looking too.

As planned, Rita and Violet caught up with Jeannie. They got her talking about the boring journey to Carson City, what she was studying now if anything, her home, horses, her courtship with Joe ... anything to make her believe that they were genuinely interested in what she had done since her father's demise. Jeannie was seemingly oblivious, absent of any suspicions and enjoying the attentions of the two women who had apparently overcome their dislike of her.

Joe tried to steal his bride away for a dance but every time he headed her way, she was talking to the two women. He knew that Jeannie had issues with making friends in the past and he wanted her to enjoy any attention she was receiving, so held back from disturbing her socializing. An outgoing fellow, he found several men to discuss horses with—one of his favorite topics and he even danced once with his mother-in-law.

Mona had the pleasant occasion of dancing with him twice. As Joe had not dissuaded her flirting in any way during the two dances, Mona was further encouraged to follow through with her plan. In Joe's mind, although it was easy to set eyes on such a beautiful woman, by the end of the second dance he was put off by Mona's overly flirtatious manner and quickly registered her lack of depth of personality. Yet, he felt he must be courteous to all of Jeannie's friends.

Finally, Mona made her move. Rita and Violet knew the signal. They witnessed Mona coax Joe into the storage room behind the hall's kitchen on the pretense that she had a surprise for the committee and desperately wanted a strong man to carry it into the main room.

While in the dark back room, Joe asked, "Where is this thing?"

Mona called from deep inside the room, "Over here."

Joe said, "Let me turn up a lamp so I can see it better."

Mona quickly said, "There are a couple of lamps by the surprise. Come on over here. You can see well enough by the moonlight."

Joe, although curious, reluctantly followed her voice to where he could see a shadow of her in the moonlight shining in through the window. Mona knew that Jeannie would be walking into the room at any moment, so she had to act fast. As he got closer, she flung herself at him, while pretending to trip. She swooned into his arms and grabbed one of his hands and pulled it toward her bosom. She was shameless and without boundaries. She hoped the fall felt just like an accident to Joe and that she would be able to act a bit shocked in case he didn't lust for her instantly.

Over the music drifting in from the hall, Jeannie's voice clearly reached the two in the corner. She turned a lamp up and saw Mona throwing herself at Joe. "What is going on here?"

Joe, surprised, could now clearly see what Jeannie was obviously seeing as well; his hand covering Mona's right breast. But even more surprising was Jeannie's reaction. She burst into laughter. Joe couldn't see the humor in it and frowned. The woman in his arms was obviously in need of attention. Had she tripped and hurt herself? He was awkwardly trying to figure out what happened.

Finally, he asked his wife, "What's so funny?" as he pushed Mona, who obviously had been off balance, back to her feet.

Jeannie replied, "You Joe. You should see your face. I'm sorry, I couldn't help laughing. And you, Mona, you are a whore. Get away from my loving and loyal husband. Joe, you poor dear. Did she ask you yet to be her lover?"

"What? No!" replied a flustered Joe. "Was that what this was all about?" he asked, looking at Mona.

Mona blushed for the first time in years, huffed out an excuse and exited the room. Jeannie laughed even louder as she made her way to Joe. She explained that she knew what Mona was up to the moment Rita and Violet showed too much interest in her life. Those two had never given her the time of day before this evening.

Jeannie explained, "I also knew that Mona would stop at nothing to get what she wanted. This morning while you were checking in on the horses, Ma told me that Mona has already broken up three other marriages, or at least severely shaken them to their core. I knew she might have selected her next adventure to be you, so I kept my eyes open."

"Me? Why?"

Jeannie paused, "Why Joe Cartwright! Are you fishing for compliments?"

"Ah, no, but sure. Tell me. Why me?" He smiled now, that crooked smile that she loved so much. "Couldn't she tell that she bores me? Couldn't she tell that I would never stray from you?"

"No, she couldn't tell that she bored you. You were probably too polite to let that show. Her pride and vanity would not allow her to conclude that you would never stray. In her eyes, all men stray or can be persuaded to. The more devoted the husband, the bigger the challenge for a woman like her. I don't know how to change her and I don't really care to try. But I feel sorry for her. Her looks are going to fade one day and she will be all alone and miserable. Don't you agree?"

"Of course, I do. But laughter? Really? Couldn't you have shown me some jealousy, woman?"

"I'm sorry, are your feelings hurt?" she asked, stroking his cheek. "You looked like the kid who got caught with his hand in the cookie jar, literally! But I knew you wouldn't take a bite. She, on the other hand, deserved my laughing at her failure. She has no idea how much we love each other. What we have been through as a family. You are like your Pa and brothers. You are that rare breed of man who obeys the vow you made to God and me. Aren't you?"

"Yes, I sure am. I love you. Only you. Forever and beyond. But only because you give me all the right reasons to do so." Already in each other's arms, they kissed. And they danced in the back room.

77

May/June 1867

LOVE OF MY LIFE, ANGIE,

I had an awkward few hours in Virginia City today. A couple of ladies approached me and after polite questions as to the state of your health, asked me if you were ashamed! I was totally surprised by their blatantly personal question and must admit that I probably answered too quickly. I was almost incensed when I replied, "Why the hell should she be? She has done nothing wrong! Would you rather she had died?"

I do not know why I said those exact words. I just reacted and came to your defense.

Now I can't help but think that you might feel shame. Please don't. I am not ashamed of you nor of what happened to you. I would be ashamed of being kin to the bastards who did this to you. But as I am not, I can only say that I am proud of you. You are fighting for the return of your health, both physically and mentally.

I love and support you, one hundred percent. Adam

P. S. I was in town getting supplies for our new house. It will be built on the hill overlooking the northern valley.

We will be able to see Joe's house and Hoss' backyard from that distance. Our neighbors will be much closer than before and we will all feel safer.

The grand room will hold the main fireplace and will be a much bigger room. Believe it or not, I'm thinking of placing the staircase to the loft in the center. The study would be next to the guest bedroom on the left of the entrance as you come in and the laundry and washing area would then be to the right next to the kitchen. There should be plenty of room for the piano. With us both enjoying music so much, I want to give us more space to play music together. I hope you will like it.

My love, Angie,

I heard you got upset today when you overheard laughter coming from downstairs. It was innocent, I assure you. After lunch today, Pa was playing with Edwin and when he asked the little fellow "Do you love me? Do you love your grandpa?" he replied, "No" clear as a bell. Well, we all laughed. We know the boy can't speak yet. It was purely and simply an accident. It was good to laugh again. I wish you were here downstairs with us and that you would have found it funny. I wish ...

Remember that the rest of the family cannot stop living just because you are in a dark place. I love you. Adam

June 6, 1867

THE CARTWRIGHTS DID NOT HOLD THEIR ANNUAL spring dance. It hadn't even come up for discussion.

Evelyn was so attentive to Hoss' every need that she stopped helping her father treat sick animals. She focused on Edwin and Hoss.

Evelyn measured every minute improvement. If he felt a twitch, she would massage and encourage the muscle. She accepted a used invalid's chair the doctor provided, but when Hoss showed that he could push himself up and into the chair from his lying down position on the bed, she scrambled to write Angie's parents in Cambridge to be on the lookout for a stronger chair, to purchase and send it. She forwarded them the money three short weeks after her request.

She pushed Hoss to try harder. She cheered when he wanted to rest. Evelyn never let on that she was tired of the routine. She outlined goals and tasks to accomplish daily including working his muscles out of atrophy.

"Aren't you tired of all this?" asked Hoss.

"Not really. Not when I measure the differences I see in you," she replied. "Why? Are you tired of this?"

"It is boring."

"Yes, well. Let me show you what I see." Evelyn had anticipated this day. She left the room and didn't come back for several minutes.

Hoss turned toward the bedroom entrance

when he heard a noise. Lee was pushing in the old wheelchair, which Evelyn was sitting on.

"What's this?"

"There is something I need to show you and I don't know any other way." She indicated for Lee to stop when she was in the middle of the room and said, "Thank you, Lee. I'll return the chair to the shed later."

"No problem, Evelyn. Glad to help. Oh, just leave it outside, Mark or Pete will put it back," said the cook, and he left.

"This is what I saw two and a half months ago when we started this, this—what should we call this? Our health work—routine?"

"Yes, that sounds about right. Our health routine," replied Hoss.

"Fine. When we started in March, you couldn't lift yourself up." She lifted her lower half—with her legs rigidly held in the folded position—out of the chair. She succeeded but didn't hold herself up too long before she let go with a puff.

"Then you were able to not only lift yourself, but to hold up your body and move it around like this." Again, she showed him what he was able to do after a couple of weeks into his health routine.

"It wasn't long before you got yourself out of bed and into that chair. Soon, you didn't need me or one of your brothers to help you do things like get dressed. You were becoming independent." She sounded excited.

"Now, you can move your legs while sitting down. I can hardly wait to see what you can do next."

"Evelyn. Did you really have to get yourself into that chair to show me how I have improved?" asked Hoss, smirking.

She smiled back. "I guess not. But I hope I succeeded in showing you that you shouldn't be discouraged. You are improving. It appears slow going but we haven't taken a day's rest from your health routine and I believe that has been the secret to your improvements. We need to keep going."

He wheeled his chair a few feet to where she was. He put his arms—that weeks ago had quickly returned to their original robust strength—around her waist and lifted her out of the chair. He set her on his lap and held her tight.

"What are you doing?" she asked with glee.

"I'm showing off my improvements. We'll be dancing soon."

By mid-July, Hoss would graduate from the chair to walking with the aid of a cane, but he didn't relinquish the chair for good—he would not leave the house without the chair in case he wanted to stay out longer but couldn't stand any more.

By August, after one more month of this boring health routine, he would stand up unassisted.

79

June 27, 1867

MY MOST PRECIOUS ANGIE,
I saw you hold Edwin today. He is
cute as a button. I watched you hold and
caress him. But moments later, you were
staring out at nothing and the joy was
over. Maybe next week you will have a
chance to hold him again.
At dinner, we found out that
Joe and Jeannie will be parents come
September. Jeannie is five months
pregnant already and they held back
telling us until you started to feel a little
better. Jeannie's mother gave them money
to start building their new home. She said
she would rather they have it now while
she is still alive to see them enjoy it. I
think that is very smart of her. I started
working on their plan. I would have loved
you to help me with the design.
I never thought I would be envious
of my brothers. I often assumed that they
were jealous of the life I was leading
because I outdid them in my education, I
can read music and have traveled beyond
Nevada.
But when we became husbands, we
were equals on those grounds. We had
married the women who completed us.

*The women who made life worth living
and provided us with more important
goals to achieve, like fatherhood. I—we,
deserve those things, Angie.*

*Love always. Your devoted
husband. Adam*

My dearest Angie,
*I must write down something that
I have been neglecting to address. The
months I spent waiting to confirm that you
had not gotten pregnant by those bastards
were dreadful. I am truly grateful. I know
in my heart that I could never blame a
child had it been born out of such pain,
but I am eternally relieved that I, and you,
and the rest of our families, will not have
to live with such a reminder either.*
*I love you very much, you know.
Please know and rest assured that I
would undoubtedly have loved any child
you bore. No matter what. I promise.*
Adam

My dearest Angie,
*For the first time in over six months,
I was able to spend the night in bed with
you and be there for you when you cried
out. I didn't hold or comfort you because
you just wanted to be assured that you
were not alone. It is progress though, isn't
it? We have moved from my sitting alone
with you during the day to now sleeping
beside you at night.*
*Oh Angie, I hope and pray that it is
the first of many steps we will be taking*

together. How I love you and hope for …
everything. Adam

My love Angie,
    I left you alone with Barbara
today as she was playing the piano. You
couldn't see me, but I watched you get
up to help her when she asked you about
something on the sheet of music. For a
brief moment, I saw you as you were last
summer. It was all too brief. You shut
down quickly. Why? Had you momentarily
not thought of them and just as quickly
when you did once more, you numbed
over again? Or were you afraid to enjoy
yourself? You deserve it, you know.
    Did you know that piece of music
is what Barbara has been humming for
the past two and a half decades? It is
Amazing Grace written by Franz Schubert
sometime before he died in 1828. When
she started playing it and realized what
it was, she wanted to share that so badly
with you because it was from the package
that your mother had sent you a lifetime
ago, but you were unresponsive, even to
her.
    I believe in you, I believe in music.
I believe in the music that is in you, just
sleeping at the moment, but ready to come
out when you say it is time. I love you.
Adam

My precious Angie,
    Today is our first-year wedding
anniversary. Not the way either of us
intended on spending it, I'm sure. I

*promise to honor, love and cherish you in
sickness and in health, for eternity and
beyond. I know that you cannot return
this vow now ... but one day maybe you
will. Adam*

~

Evelyn wheeled Hoss into the grand room and left him
to read his book as she tended to Edwin.

Barbara was tidying up the grand room, coming
in and out of the study as she returned books to
shelves.

Jeannie escorted Angie down the stairs and left
her at the sofa and said, "I'll get you a cup of tea and
be right back."

Angie was staring at her shoes but from the
corner of her eye she observed the giant of a man on
her far left. She knew something had happened to
him. She had overheard the family talking. She had
just never commented or expressed sorrow—not even
now when they were alone.

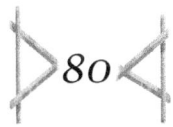

July 31, 1867

JEANNIE FELT AN OVERWHELMING SADNESS OVER Angie and Adam's situation. She did not know how they would ever get out of it. Angie had been the same non-responsive self for more than seven months and Jeannie wanted to help. She had admired Angie before all this happened and missed her sister terribly. So much so, that she decided to share her innermost secrets with her in the hopes that Angie would stir toward life instead of staying in this dark gloomy place.

One evening while the two women were alone in Angie's bedroom, Jeannie partially closed the door and then said, "What happened to you Angie reminded me very much of what happened to me as a child." Angie looked at her in disbelief and with anger in her eyes, daring her to explain herself.

"Oh, even though there are many differences, there is something that happened to the both of us. That is what I need to share with you. I am not trying to make what happened to you less than what it is. No, I wouldn't dare do that. I'm just trying to say that I too was helpless once. I wasn't sexually abused. I was physically abused and I don't know how long the abuse lasted or how often it occurred. I was defenseless and alone. I remember screaming and no one hearing me. No one came to my rescue."

"Tell me, do you remember how you got to this bed, Angie?" she asked.

Angie shook her head back and forth.

"I don't know how I came to be on the steps of the convent either," Jeannie said. "I do know that I didn't trust anyone after that time in my life for many years. I don't know why Ma and Pa put up with me. I was difficult, to say the least. I believe I screamed every night for years. I peed the bed until I was eleven years old. I had awful temper tantrums until I was twelve or thirteen when something didn't go my way. I didn't know how to express myself." Angie was starting to stir, remembering the story Ben had told them before Jeannie's arrival about the cigar burns on the child's back.

"I hated the Mathesons, I hated everybody. It is hard to believe that they loved me when I was so hateful. It took me a long time, too long really, to trust them. I ruined my childhood by not being able to leave the past in the past. I didn't talk to any of the school kids. I thought they whispered about me behind my back. I cared and I didn't. If they thought I was deserving of such evil or was a monster, I didn't deny it. But know this, none of that helped me get beyond my distrust or to love or to ever feel loved."

"Nothing worked until my Pa brought me with him to the stables. It's a huge building in Carson City where they bought and traded horses of all kinds. Being there, with the horses, was very helpful, almost medicinal for me. It brought me out of my shell, my umbrella of hate. I owe a lot to that man who called me 'Princess'. I miss him very much." She smiled a sad smile.

"And when I needed a new friend, Joe came into my life. I didn't know that I, the monster, would ever find someone like him. I didn't think I deserved him."

"Now, I know you have to go through what you must. I just hope you don't repeat my mistakes. Mind you I was a child and didn't understand the power of love. I just want you to know that I love you and hope you get better real soon. I miss the real Angie."

Angie thought her mind was as broken as she had observed Hoss' body to be—that she was as recovered as she would ever be. But the abuse that Jeannie, as a defenseless child, had endured struck a nerve with Angie. The younger woman's revelation was sinking in and making her think.

Joe had been outside the door and overheard the conversation. He had been looking for Jeannie to join him in the garden to see the bloom of a new flower. He was ready to knock on the door when he heard his wife's voice, quiet and pleading. He stopped his knock just in time and had fallen back against the wall to wait until Jeannie had finished sharing with Angie what she had decided to reveal. His admiration for his wife grew. What she had just divulged could not have been easy. She must truly love Angie. He was so proud of Jeannie's heartfelt sentiments. That was the most she had ever disclosed to anyone other than to himself.

Ben had been heading to his bedroom to fetch a book and had seen Joe in the hallway leaning against the wall. He stopped, listening to the conversation for a moment before moving on to his own room. Once inside, he looked upwards and thanked God for Jeannie. He too, like everyone else, had wondered why a child should go through such torture. He believed he had just found the answer.

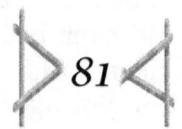

81

August 18, 1867

DEAREST ANGIE,
    *We moved into our new house today.
I took Joe's advice and burned down our
old house. I do not want to be reminded of
what occurred there and how I failed at my
responsibility to protect you from harm. You
seem to like this new house. I'm not sure
you noticed that I built it with extra room for
the piano. I hope you like it.*
    *I wonder how much more time will
go by before I can leave you alone while I
go over to Pa's for an hour or so. No matter.
Little steps, but still, progress.*
    *I know that you just go through the
motions of making meals, cleaning house
and doing laundry. Maybe one day you will
ask me questions and tell me about your
day. Maybe we will whisper tender words
when we lie side by side, our heads close
together on one pillow. Maybe one day we
will once more play music together or even
… laugh.*
    I love you more today. Adam

My love, Angie,
    *You are challenging me. I cannot tell
if you truly hate me or if you are frustrated
with my love for you. You seem angry with*

everything I do. Last evening, you came into the bedroom wearing the longest and ugliest nightgown I had ever seen. I followed you around the room with my eyes. You practically shouted at me "What are you staring at?"

I lied and replied, "Am I staring? I'm sorry. It won't happen again." And you huffed and puffed until you came to bed.

We never touch. As you don't cry out, I don't know if you wake up in the night anymore or if you need comforting. You roll away from me and face the wall. You insist I roll away from you and face the other direction because you cannot stand my breathing on you. Of course, I want to keep the peace and obey your request. And then you seem agitated with me even more!

I don't understand you. I long for your behavior to change. You are very negative and I'm not sure I like you. I love you, but there are things you do that I do not like. There is a difference. I hope you understand that. Always, Adam

My dear, surprising Angie,

I was in the barn this morning and heard your attempts at playing the piano. You must have been very frustrated when you pounded and slammed down on the poor keys.

Then moments later, I noticed you were outside. You had an attitude like you were having a temper tantrum. You kicked at some rocks and then took the ax and attacked the poor defenseless logs that were just lying around.

But I let you go at it. I prayed that you wouldn't chop off a toe though. I hoped that you needed to express your anger like I did in our first house and I think I was right.

You shocked me when you started calling those logs a bunch of dirty words. I never knew you knew those words. Then it dawned on me that they must have called you those despicable names. Let the shame out, don't own it, it is not yours. Call the logs anything you want. They are not you. I hope the logs represented them when you were chopping away. Hurt them. Hurt them bad! Hurt them for the both of us.

You lasted twenty minutes before you exhausted yourself. Now we have more kindling!

Please do not think that I am making fun of you. I am celebrating your show of emotions. I did not expect tenderness before anger myself either. Good for you. My goodness, how I love thee. Adam

My love, Angie,

Jeannie and Joe welcomed twins into the world today. They were a little early, but both are healthy. A boy, Peter and a girl, Kathryn. Barbara was there to help Jeannie, along with the doctor. Did you notice that when Barbara returned from their place, her face was all lit up like she had seen a miracle? Pa and I did. Always, Adam

My sweet, my angel, Angie,

Hoss and Evelyn are going to have a second child – a miraculous addition to

322

their household probably next year, March.
That's six months from now. I am truly
happy for my brothers and their families. I
am burdened with a growing jealousy that
I never knew could exist in me. I long for the
happiness I thought I deserved. We deserve.
I love you always. Adam

Sundays had become a day for Adam to mingle with other adults. He and Angie would get ready in the mornings and head out to church. Afterwards they would ride up to the ranch house where they would join in on the shared family meal. Angie never started a conversation and normally kept her involvement in one to a minimum. The family could see the progress she was making, slow as it was.

On one of those Sundays, a picnic was held in town after the church service. It would be the last before the arrival of the colder season.

Angie didn't agree to go, but she didn't disagree either. She was being her usual cloudy, uncommunicative self. Adam very much looked forward to the diversity of conversation the event offered and the relief from his mundane life and frustrating marriage.

Angie was sitting on a picnic blanket on the grass, observing several children playing tag, all the while circling around Hoss in the invalid chair he used when he became fatigued and walking with only a cane became impossible. No one could tell who was enjoying it more, Hoss or the children. Innocent enough, but their small game changed her life.

Joe happened to be near when he observed what she was looking at. He mentioned in passing, "Children have such freedom, don't they?" and walked to where Jeannie and the twins sat. He certainly didn't expect a reply from Angie.

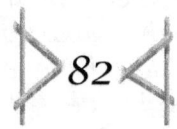

September 30, 1867

IN THE MIDDLE OF THE NIGHT, ANGIE WOKE AND sat straight up. She had not awakened Adam by her sudden movement and she quietly left the bed. She could feel her quickened pulse as she put her housecoat on and went downstairs to Adam's study. While there, she tried to calm herself down to relive the dream she had just had. She felt a need to remember every detail.

She was at a picnic. She noticed several children playing tag nearby, giggling and running. She noticed that they would include a boy, who was seated in a chair with wheels, in their game by circling around him while trying to tag the others. They were all laughing, screaming and enjoying themselves. When they had run away to play elsewhere, she approached the boy in the chair, placed her blanket on the ground and faced him.

She said to him, "You and I are very much alike. We are both inside a cage. You cannot go and play with the other children. You are stuck there in that chair."

The twelve-year old boy smiled and said, "I do not think I am in a cage! I am free. I love my life. Those other children always include me in their games. No one treats me like I don't belong. But, why do you say you are in a cage? You walked on your own two feet coming over here!"

Dreams being what they are, her subconscious could better explain how she felt like a caged bird. In her dream, the boy understood that.

> *He gave her this real grown-up, concerned look and all of a sudden the person in the invalid's chair was Hoss and he said encouragingly, "Just open the cage door, Angie. It is not locked. Do it for yourself. Open it now, only a little bit. Do not be afraid."*
>
> *"Can you feel the cool air coming in? Can you hear the birds singing? Open it wider and take a step out. Just a little one, Angie. You can do this. I have faith in you. The bad men are long gone. No one can hurt you. Are you out yet?" And as if the dream was real, Angie nodded a yes.*
>
> *She stepped out of the cage, her legs moving on the carpet as if she was truly stepping forward.*
>
> *Hoss stood, not even using his cane. Next to him stood Jeannie, her hand clasped in his large right hand. He reached out and clasped Angie's in his left.*
>
> *Jeannie said, "I was waiting for you to come out of the cage Angie. I am so glad you made it."*
>
> *Hand in hand, the three walked toward the field, lush with new grass. Angie felt the coolness of the air on her body and it felt liberating. She could feel the wetness from the dew on the new*

blades of grass under her bare feet and it felt wonderful. She felt the freedom that was out there, just one full step away. She embraced the independence. She wanted to run with open arms. She wanted to run!

Silently, tears began to fall down her less-troubled face. She had not cried in months. She had not felt many emotions in months. She felt them now.

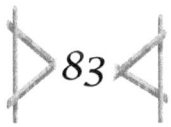

83

September 30, 1867

ANGIE CAME OUT OF HER DREAM STATE, THE TEARS
streaking her face and dripping onto her clothes. She
looked around at Adam's new study and saw the color
of the curtains for the first time. She saw the color of
the chair at the desk and the chair she was sitting in.
She had literally not registered color since the attack.
But she knew she saw them now and that it mattered.

She investigated her new house as if she was
only now entering it for the first time. The front door
was located in the middle of the anterior wall as in
her other house, but the grand room, fireplace and
staircase to the loft were now located in the heart of
the house. The study was adjacent to a guest bedroom
on the far left of the front entrance and the room for
laundry and washing was to the far right. The kitchen
was at the back on the same side of the washing area.
The space between the doors leading to the study and
guest bedroom provided ample room for the piano.
She ran her fingers over the keys without making a
sound.

Angie went to Adam's desk and sat behind it.
She opened the side drawer and saw his journal that
she had seen him write in every day since the assault.

She picked it up and began to read. Many times,
she had wondered what he had written to only find
moments later that she didn't care. But she was
reading it now. When a passage struck a nerve, she
would tag the page in one fashion or another. She

either dog-eared it or ripped a bit off the side of the page. She paid particular attention to the pages that had been wrinkled by Adam's tears and found herself re-reading those again and again, adding her own liquid sorrow to the fragile pages.

She learned so much about Adam through his journal. She would never have thought that he would have felt all those things. So many identical emotions had been felt by her too. She was marveled by the fact that she was reading her own thoughts that he had written on paper. He had felt them too.

He had proven his devotion and commitment repeatedly, lived it to the fullest extent of its meaning. He had shown his undying love every moment of every day through his messages and his actions. Several times she wanted to leave the journal to get up and go to him, but kept back for the need to read his next entry. She felt she needed to completely read the journal so she could finish with her transformation.

By morning, when she heard Adam stir, she put the book back with a promise to herself that she would pick it up again as soon as she could. Still in her robe, she prepared breakfast looking at her husband sip his coffee. She noticed for the first time the worry lines around his mouth and on his forehead. She was humbled that he stood by her all this time, through hell and now back. Had she spoken to him or looked up at him he would have seen the change in her. But she didn't speak and purposefully didn't look him in the eye so he wouldn't suspect she was aware she was different.

After breakfast, Adam kissed her on the forehead and went outside to tend to his chores. It was another beautiful warm autumn day. She had not bothered doing her morning tasks or even changing into her day clothes. Instead, she continued reading his journal and completed it by mid-morning, just as she started hearing the chopping of wood. She knew what she wanted to do then, what she must do. She stood near the entrance to the house, longingly looking at his wide shoulders and bare back, working up a sweat swinging the ax and called out, "Adam!"

He stopped chopping the wood, realizing that she had called out his name in that certain lilt in her voice that he had not heard since before that dark day. He turned with great hope that he had heard correctly. He saw her there, still in her nightwear and holding his journal in her left hand. She looked at him, her arms beginning to lift toward him and running to meet him.

Before she could run five yards, he was by her side. She held him around the neck and he held her around the waist. He could see the change in her, he could feel the life in her. She could see her reflection in his eyes, in his heart. They kissed with great hunger, satisfying the loneliness from the unjust mental separation. Still kissing, he lifted up his bride and carried her into the house to their bedroom. When he laid her on the bed, he motioned that he would go wash up a bit.

She said, "No, please, don't waste any time. Make love to me Adam. Now. I need to be near you. I need to be as close to you as humanly possible."

"Angie, it's been so long since ..." and he couldn't finish what he was trying to explain as their lips met again and they started undressing each other.

Suddenly, he pulled back, concerned that his furious lovemaking would remind Angie of the assault. Or at least not be as loving and careful as he could be.

"It's okay Adam. Just make love to me now. We can take our time again later. Please. It's really okay." She knew how completely he wanted to love her, for it was what she wanted too. But she could wait for that. What she couldn't wait for was his nearness.

His uninhibited freedom showed through in his tender touch. His caresses and loving kisses brought her back to near proximity of her old self. Never once did she compare Adam to her sexual assault. Everything she and Adam did was euphoric and no other thought could filter into her brain. After the gentle love they shared, she said to herself, out loud, "Welcome back, Angie!"

Adam was suddenly overwhelmed with emotion. He couldn't stop himself from sobbing. Angie became aware of his sobs and couldn't resist joining him. She lifted herself up on one elbow, looked at him, propped herself up further so her mouth was near his ear and whispered through sobs, "I'm so sorry it took me so long, Adam. I am so sorry."

"No, Angie. No. Do not be sorry. It was never your fault. These are happy tears. I didn't care how long it took you. I am just overjoyed with having you back. I love you so much. I didn't understand Pa when he said the journal was as much for me as it was for you. But I know now that if I didn't decide to love you every single day since that tragedy that I would not be able to honor my vows. Writing it down made it easier to live another day, too. Angie, we have God to thank for our love. I know you complete me, but I also know that your love for me and my loving you comes from God."

With tears dripping off her cheeks, she was nodding, not able to speak. He gently kissed away her tears and she his.

Adam continued now more calmly, "I may have blamed God at first for allowing what happened to you until I realized that this was the devil's doing. God became my strength. Sometimes He was the only thing keeping me sane. He and the hope that this would all pass one day."

She said, "But you went so long without knowing

if I would ever return to you, to us. How could you be so sure, Adam? Didn't you want to find another woman who was whole and could provide you with a good marriage, a good life? Someone who could love you back?"

"Angie, no. Don't ever think that. I love you, only you. And I considered the past ten months to be a sickness that we both needed to overcome, together. What we share in our most intimate moments is so strong for me that I couldn't see myself with someone other than you. I could never have stepped out, no matter how discreet. The love we make is a by-product of our marriage. It is like a bonus. I could never have sex with anyone but you. It would never fulfill my deepest desires. You fulfill all of my needs."

"Thank you, Adam. I came to realize that what happened to me was a gross indecency. I also realize that what I want most in life is our intimacy. This by-product of our love, as you say, for each other makes our marriage so complete that I couldn't go on without it. I needed it back," Angie said with all sincerity.

"You have it and me." They kissed in agreement, like a renewed covenant.

Their strong feelings finally subsided. She rested her head on his chest, and then suddenly propped herself up again and said, "Ah, sure. You can go wash up now."

Adam tilted his head back and laughed! She was certainly back. She had always liked his body to smell and feel fresh. He returned to bed moments later and she continued with her teasing nature. Again, he couldn't believe how quickly she had changed from the cloudy self she had been just the day before.

He soon became aroused again and took great pains in loving her with all the gentleness she deserved. His steady and determined penetration brought her to a climax like no other experienced before. His was seconds behind hers. He started to pull his weight off of her, but she held on tight.

"No Adam, please. I can't think of a place I would rather be than right here like this."

He kissed her and said, "I love you."

She kissed him back and said, "I love you too."

"I love you more."

With a huge grin, she replied "No, I love you more."

Adam and Angie rediscovered each other in the following days and lost themselves in the joy of it all, as all married couples should. They spent day and night in each other's arms, talking, laughing, sleeping, weeping, and making love.

She told him about her dream. She told him about those dreadful hours with those men. He told her about his despair even though she had read about it in his journal. They agreed to not reread it. Instead, they would remember some entry and discuss an aspect that had more meaning than others.

She asked for details of his feelings about Hoss' injury. He didn't hold anything back as he knew she would listen and hear every word.

She mentioned about the one entry of his deserving to becoming a father. She wept, "Remember the day Barbara lost her baby?"

"Yes, of course."

"Remember when we moved into the other house? How moody I was?"

"Yes, I remember thinking that there was something you needed to tell me. There still is, isn't there?" he asked gently.

"Yes. You see, just before he left, Doctor Grant told me that my test results had returned and they indicated that I would probably never become pregnant. I didn't know how to tell you." She sobbed. "You had just lost a sister and I worried about how to tell you that you would never become a father. And now I just read in your journal that you, we deserve to become parents. We do. We do. I'm sorry Adam. I'm so sorry."

Adam listened with his heart. At another time in his life, he may have lashed out in anger. Instead, he let her words sink in, unable to stop his own tears.

He put both hands up to his wife's cheeks, kissed her on the forehead, held her and said, "I am so sorry that you had to carry that with you all this time, alone. I am sorry I can't fix it. Angie, if you want us to adopt, we will. Whatever you want, my love, I will do. I am now just the happiest man alive knowing that you have returned and can love me back as much as I love you."

She could only nod in understanding of what he had just said. She whispered, "I would like to wait. We still have a lot of time to spend together, alone, before I want to make a decision that will change our lives."

84

October 1, 1867

THE FOLLOWING DAY, ANGIE AND ADAM BURNT the journal and she wrote to her parents with her wonderful news.

> *Dear mother and father,*
>
> *I am happy beyond words to tell you that I have come out of the hell I have been through. I want to thank you for coming to see me a few months ago and showing me how much you truly love me. I can imagine how difficult it was to leave me here with people you hardly know.*
>
> *I believe my father-in-law explained how much I am loved by him, his family and especially his son, my truly wonderful husband Adam. Adam is my hero. He will surely be yours too once you know all that he has done for me. Mostly, he never gave up. He loved me through my tragedy, my trauma, my moods, and my hate.*
>
> *I can love again. I am in love again!*
>
> *We are planning to come visit you in March when winter starts turning into spring. I, we, can hardly wait to see you again.*
>
> *Always and forever, Angie*

P.S. I appreciate you keeping my being barren a secret. I have now told Adam and soon we will inform his family.

85

October 6, 1867

ADAM AND ANGIE FORGOT ABOUT THE REST OF the world. They didn't have a need to leave their house until Sunday morning for the church service. By then, they were like any other happy couple. You couldn't tell they had ever been in a black hole. They were acting like newlyweds again. And, in essence, they were. They sat close together and held hands at church. Adam raised her hand to his lips on the buggy ride over to the ranch house. Their foreheads touching would suddenly come apart in a laugh after sharing an intimate comment.

Their love was stronger. They would never say out loud that this experience made their love for each other impregnable because that would almost be admitting that it had been a good thing—but it was just the honest truth. So many small things did not matter anymore. They would forever focus on the most important.

Joe was the first to notice the change in her. He had observed Angie lean into Adam at the church and how Adam had looked into her eyes and smiled. Just the simple fact that they were touching in public convinced Joe that they had reconnected.

Hoss and Ben had just entered the great room when the couple arrived at the ranch for the usual Sunday family meal. The other women were taking off their hats and cloaks and their laughter echoed down the hall from a shared moment.

Neither Hoss nor Ben saw what Joe had seen during church, but now, holding on to her husband's hand, she smiled, and spoke to the other men in her long forgotten abandoned and lighthearted manner.

Angie walked right into Ben's arms and said, "Thank you Pa, for your love and support. I truly appreciate everything you have done for Adam and me. I love you."

Ben became emotional as he could finally embrace her deeply in his ever opening arms. Hoss and Joe then witnessed Ben giving his oldest son a surprised, quizzical look. Adam smiled and winked at his father. Hoss and Joe smiled their biggest grins and patted Adam on the back, showing their love, support and relief. Everyone took joy in the knowledge of her recovery.

Angie hugged Hoss hard and told him he looked great in the shirt he was wearing. He exploded into laughter as he remembered that she had always joked around with respect to the checks and plaids of his garments not matching. She barely kept her composure when she finally registered his diminished weight caused by muscle loss from the crushing giant tree. She didn't focus on that sadness though. Maybe one day, but not now.

Her recovery was truly evident when she let Joe tease her. It was refreshing for her brothers-in-law to have the freedom of being carefree with their harmless bantering.

As Evelyn, Barbara and Jeannie entered the grand room, Angie approached her sisters with a smile and tears.

"Barbara, you have been my mother during these past ten months. I'm grateful for all that you have done for me," Angie said as she hugged her.

Barbara scarcely heard a word after mother. Tears welled up in her eyes and overflowed. She was speechless. The men formed a circle around the women and once released, Barbara leaned into Ben's arms.

Angie moved to embrace Evelyn. "Evelyn, I will never be able to recall all the things you have done for me. You care for me like I'm one of your own sisters and I will always appreciate you for that."

"Why Angie. It was not just my duty, it was a privilege and an honor. I am so glad to see you so well," replied Evelyn.

As they released each other, Evelyn's eyes were wet. Angie was surprised by Evelyn's apparent emotions. The woman who had been stoic when faced with cattle rustlers was moved to tears by appreciation.

Evelyn waved her left hand, pointed to her stomach and said, "I'm pregnant. I'm crying for no reason these days."

Everyone laughed.

Angie turned to face Jeannie. They fell into each other's arms, sobbing. "I cannot begin to tell you how truly blessed I am to know you. Your friendship has helped me in ways I could never count. Thank you, Jeannie. My sister."

Jeannie nodded. She cried for about an hour, not able to let go of Angie's hand. She was elated but overcome with emotion.

~

At the supper meal, Angie stood up. So did the men, of course.

She said, "No, please remain seated." They did, almost reluctantly. "I just want to propose a toast."

"Ah!" Everyone reached for their glass of water or wine, or cup of tea and lifted them up.

"To the man who was insurmountable in my

recovery." All glasses, cups and eyes turned toward Adam as she placed a trembling hand on Adam's shoulder. Angie continued, "Ben Cartwright." All eyes turned toward the unsuspecting Ben.

"For your devotion," said Angie, and Barbara's eyes met Ben's.

"Your loyalty," continued Angie, and Jeannie nudged Joe indicative of her agreement.

"Your patience," said Angie, and Evelyn reached out for Hoss' hand.

"And most of all, for teaching your sons these most precious virtues, thank you from the bottom of my heart. You must know by now that your sons love as deeply and completely as you do."

"Here, here!" everyone said in unison. And they toasted.

"Thank you, Angie. You have no idea how much that means to me. Now, while we are in a toasting mood," said a very elated Ben, "I would like to propose a toast to the man who carried us through this difficult period."

Everyone looked at each other thinking only that Ben was the man to fit that toast.

"Joseph, my Little Joe who is no longer the little boy he once was. These past few months have tested all of us. But, despite all the hurting and worrying, Joe stepped in during the branding of the calves, the cattle drive, and he spearheaded the logging contract. He was the last one to turn out the lamps and lock the doors at night and the first one up in the mornings. Joe, I have seen, we all have seen, how much you love us. You have never complained and always readily accepted to work on this very busy ranch. I am grateful that I bore a son like you. You are the glue that held us together. Your brothers were hurting, and you never once lost faith."

Ben continued, turning to his oldest son, "Adam, I applaud your devotion."

"Hoss," he said, "I am in awe of your courage."

"Barbara." Glasses moved in her direction. "I could not imagine the past year without you. You are one special woman."

"As for my daughters, if you don't know how I feel about you, I have failed. Evelyn, your strength is commendable. Angie, your determination is inspiring."

"Jeannie, ah Jeannie." He paused. He wiped a tear and carried on, "I'm sure you do not know this, but I overheard what you said to Angie about the abuse you suffered as a child." He hiccuped a sob and continued, "You are so brave. What you shared about your trauma is probably partly responsible for Angie's recovery."

Then he turned and looked at each face around the table. "My dear family." He closed his eyes, bowed his head, and prayed, "Thank you, Lord for all these gifts. Amen."

"Amen," replied the seven.

86

October 26, 1867

ANGIE STARTED TO BE AT EASE WITH HER NEW found freedom. She appreciated all things, big and small—like the new dishes that Adam had purchased. She cherished all the music sheets that she and Barbara shared. She tolerated the stray cat that set up a home in their barn—not something she would have endured prior to the attack. She noticed these things about herself and accepted them as part of her new life.

Both she and Adam were very excited about their plans to travel east and visit with her parents.

She thought there would never be anything negative that would occur in her life again—until the day she burned dinner. She cried about it. Adam chuckled. She pouted. Five minutes later, she burst into laughter at her behavior. Something bad had happened, something normal.

But one morning, she vomited. She hadn't eaten anything out of the ordinary. Why had she gotten ill? Then the next morning, she vomited again. Her chest, especially in the evening after supper, hurt. *No, no, no*, she thought. Not when she and Adam had finally found each other again. The thought of illness, perhaps a debilitating one, made her hopes for the future come crashing down around her. She feared she was seriously sick. Oh, but it couldn't be. She had just claimed her life back.

Should she tell Adam? The last thing she wanted

to do was alarm her husband by telling him about these worrisome things.

Instead, Angie asked Jeannie to accompany her to town to shop for a new dress. It wasn't entirely a lie, she did need a new dress. Only when she pulled the buggy in front of the doctor's office did she tell Jeannie about her health concerns.

"I brought you along, Jeannie, in case I'm too distraught to drive home," confessed Angie.

The doctor was just as concerned with all her symptoms. He did some tests and confirmed, "Angie, you are pregnant."

She shook her head back and forth.

"Yes. I'm just as surprised as you are. We doctors can be wrong. You are going to have a baby!"

87

August 8, 2019

AUNT YVETTE OFFERED HER HOME ON THE Ponderosa as a comfortable meeting place for the eleven cousins. They gathered at the ranch house over the morning hours and soon learned that their great-aunt would be joining them at noon.

When she walked into the grand room, they each had their laptops open and running in search for any information on an Annette Devon in the early 1800s.

"How goes the battle?" she asked.

They each put their computers aside, rising as a group and greeting her one by one with a hug.

"Empty," said Camille, resitting with her computer on her lap.

"Me too," replied Stephanie and Jacqueline, as they sat back down at the table close to the fireplace.

"Yeah, nothing here either," said Joel, looking down at the laptop beside him on the sofa.

"If she had lived to adulthood, her family had not registered her birth, or marriage or passing," said a discouraged Natalie, pacing before the hearth.

"You're not giving up, are you?" asked Aunt Yvette as she walked towards the kitchen knowingly.

"No way." "Never." Several replied.

The cousins revisited their search limits and expanded the search. The new parameters paid off and they rejoiced when Natalie found a document proving the uncle Henry's existence on a school roster when he was seven years old. He had been registered in a small town near Sacramento called Elliston. The scanned copy of the worn document was difficult to decipher, but they were able to read that he was the son of a Liam and Donna Devon, originally from Utah. A further search of the same registry showed that their oldest son was named Blake.

"Lunch," called out Aunt Yvette.

They slowly closed laptops, brought coffee mugs to the kitchen, washed hands and gathered around the dining room table for salad and sandwiches.

They hardly missed a beat in their discussion of the mysterious Blake.

"This is so exciting. In just one morning, we found out the name of Annette's father. I hope we find more information on Blake. I hope there weren't more siblings!" said Philip.

They let their imaginations run wild and speculated what had happened to him. Being the eldest, he should have inherited the farm. So, what stopped that from happening?

"Maybe he turned into a bad apple and was wanted by the law," speculated Eriq.

"Maybe he ran away with an unsuitable woman whom he loved," said Dominique, the romantic.

"Maybe he had to be placed somewhere because he wasn't of his right mind," Jacqueline threw in.

"The parents could have disinherited him for all three of those reasons, especially during the 1800s," said Natalie.

"No. He couldn't have been a wanted man. We didn't find any newspaper articles naming him. Or even wanted posters," said Stephanie.

"He definitely was not placed in some kind of home or asylum. His name would have shown up on archived records," said Céleste. "It had to be a reason that caused a disinheritance. It had to be unforgivable. Otherwise, don't you think that his parents would want to have him back in their lives once he became a father? At least, just to meet their grandchild?"

"You're thinking like a Cartwright. Not every family forgives just so the family can stay together," said a pragmatic Gabriel.

Aunt Yvette listened to her young relatives talk, her eyes jumping back and forth like she was watching a ball at a Wimbledon tennis match. Finally, she threw up her hands and said, "Stop. I'm lost. I need to start at the beginning."

She stood, putting her hands on her hips. She began to pace, turning around with each significant fact.

"4G Grandpa Ben got caught in an avalanche."

"He lost a package that was inside his satchel around the horse's neck."

"You excavated the avalanche's aftermath from the slide of that same mountain on July 9."

"You found the contents of the package, remnants of Ben's satchel and rifle sheath, and four horseshoes."

She stopped and looked at the group.

They all nodded.

"You then got the bracelet cleaned and were able to read the inscription *Annette Devon, beloved niece.*" More nods.

"You had the leather analyzed even though you knew about the inscription?" Aunt Yvette asked.

"We got the analysis of the leather fragments two weeks after dropping off the remnants, so no—we didn't know at the time that we had excavated the right mountain," clarified Natalie. "We found the remnants and during the time they were being analyzed, we learned what the inscription on the bracelet said."

Just then the oldest, full-time resident of the ranch, Emmanuel walked in. They watched him walk to the center of the grand room.

He said, "This is all I could find. The Cartwrights never had need to change their brand. It is one of the oldest around these parts and no one else had the right to make anything similar to it," he said, handing over the metal rod with the hand-crafted iron mark.

They all looked at the Cartwright branding iron, passing it from one set of hands to another. Finally, Dominique placed it in the container of black ink that she had brought just for this purpose.

Céleste placed a piece of thick paper on top of a flat board and Dominique pressed the inked brand into the paper. Crowding in, the cousins could clearly see the mark—a circle around the drawing of a fir tree. The most prominent tree on Cartwright land.

Natalie placed the piece of paper that Gerry from the leather shop had given her next to this one. She turned Gerry's paper until it best matched up with the brand.

They were already certain that they had found the engraved item that had been lost by Ben—the bracelet that was in the satchel. The Devon name on it proved that. Matching the mark of the satchel to the Cartwright brand just added to their proof.

The cousins settled back into their places and Aunt Yvette began her questioning and pacing, "So, then two of you went in search of archived records and found the letter from Ben's lawyer, Fred Mason to Devon's lawyer, Arthur Richardson, in Sacramento. Have I got all the names right?" she asked.

They nodded yes in unison.

"So, mystery solved?"

"Not at all. We found out that Henry ended up with everything and yet he never forgot his brother. We know that Blake and Henry stayed in contact at least long enough for Henry to know that Blake had a daughter. But why did he have a change of heart late in life and named Annette as one of his heirs?" Jacqueline explained.

"Maybe Blake died young and his widow and daughter went to live with her relatives. You might never solve it," said Aunt Yvette.

"Ah, that's discouraging. We were so pumped a little while ago, but now we are stuck," said Camille with a hopeful lilt in her voice.

~

"I found something!" Gabriel said. "Look! A marriage registration for Henry's brother Blake. He married a woman named Crystal in Pomona, California. Blake was nineteen and Crystal was sixteen when they married."

"Where did Crystal come from? Even her name is mysterious! Crystal—I wonder if folks thought that was an odd name," said Dominique.

Camille flipped her browser to a new google page. "Starting in the nineteenth century, some parents named girl babies Crystal. It is a coinage derived from the transparent quartz gemstone, usually colorless, that can be cut to reflect brilliant light. The name comes from Ancient Greek for ice."

"I found a citation on Annette!" Céleste read and summarized, "Annette Devon attended school until 1824 when she turned fifteen years of age."

Eriq asked, "I wonder what happened to Annette that made her end up approximately 450 miles north-east from where she grew up?"

"Hey, does anyone know if Annette could be shortened to something?" asked Dominique.

Without hesitating, Aunt Yvette replied, "I think it can be shortened to Nettie."

Stephanie and Michael had been tasked with

searching the same words as everyone else, but to add parenthesis marks before and after the terms. In his haste, Michael missed the opening bracket and typed Nettie Devon with only a closed bracket. He jumped up, holding his laptop high in the air.

"I've got something. OMG! This is it! We have solved the mystery!" He stood, all excited.

"What? What do you have?" they all asked.

August 8, 2019

"THIS IS THE PIÈCE DE RESISTANCE, AUNT YVETTE." Everyone sighed. Michael looked around and said, "Sorry. I couldn't resist the drama and I need to practice my French. But this is so exciting. This was written in the newspaper of the town of Noco: *Vincent Burke ...*"

"Noco? Never heard of it," Céleste said.

"Wasn't Vincent Burke 4G Grandma Barbara's dad?" asked Jacqueline.

"Yeah, let me read on. *Vincent Burke, his wife, Nettie (BORN ANNETTE DEVON)* in brackets *and three of their children were killed by a group of bandits last Friday, May 8, 1840, after the bank was robbed.*"

Not a word was said for half a minute or so.

"Nettie was Barbara's mother!" screamed Aunt Yvette, her hands flying to her cheeks. She sat down in a chair, amazed.

The cousins hollered and high-fived each other.

~

Joel put his laptop aside and walked to the coffee table where he retrieved the small bracelet. He said, "Anyone else want to come with me and bury this at Annette Devon's daughter's grave site?"

"I'd love to do the honors, if you will permit me," said a serious Aunt Yvette, awed by the coming together of the family mystery.

"Of course. How appropriate."

"Imagine, the bedtime stories all the Cartwright descendants have heard all these years are all true," said Dominique, shaking her head.

"Just think. Barbara's great-uncle was on the path to finding Nettie and by default, Barbara. But—remember—if 4G Grandpa Ben had not been caught in the avalanche, then he wouldn't have been saved by Barbara. Either way, Mr. Devon wouldn't have been any closer in finding her," said Eriq.

Jacqueline asked, "If Annette or Nettie's death was reported in the paper, how come her uncle didn't find out about it?"

Aunt Yvette and the cousins continued to walk, deep in thought.

"I think I know the answer to that," said Aunt Yvette. "Newspapers were not shared from town to town. Unless the article was of national interest like politics or a disaster like an earthquake, stories were focused on local issues."

"It might not have been national news for the country, but it would have been major news for Barbara. Her uncle would have found her and she would have had a much different life. One of privilege, not mountain survival."

"But then she wouldn't have found Grandpa Ben and her life wouldn't have been changed. They wouldn't have fallen in love and set the example that his sons followed ... which led to ... well, us."

They stopped at the grave of Barbara, pulling into a circle and holding hands. Eriq dug a hole a foot deep near the gravestone, put his shovel aside, and joined his cousins. Aunt Yvette, holding on to the arm of Joel, lowered herself to gently drop the bracelet into the hole. Eriq stepped forward and filled the hole with the soft pile of disturbed soil.

Aunt Yvette stood up and joined the circle, clasping Joel and Eriq's hands. In unison, the group bowed their heads for a moment of quiet, remembering those who had gone before.

The Family Tree of the Eleven Cousins

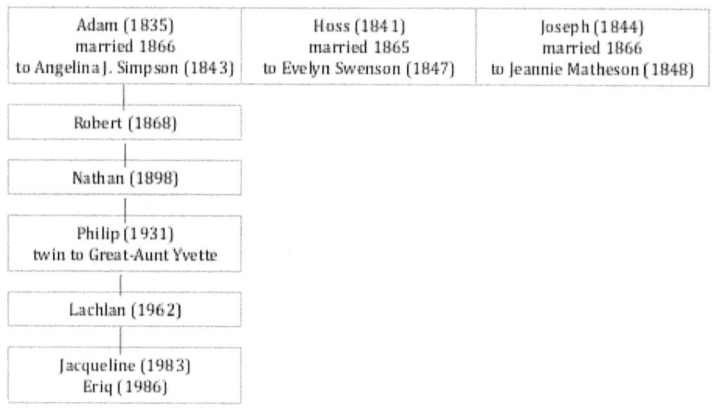

Ben Cartwright (1814)
last married in 1863
to Barbara Burke (1825)

Adam (1835)	Hoss (1841)	Joseph (1844)
married 1866	married 1865	married 1866
to Angelina J. Simpson (1843)	to Evelyn Swenson (1847)	to Jeannie Matheson (1848)

Robert (1868)

Nathan (1898)

Philip (1931)
twin to Great-Aunt Yvette

Lachlan (1962)

Jacqueline (1983)
Eriq (1986)

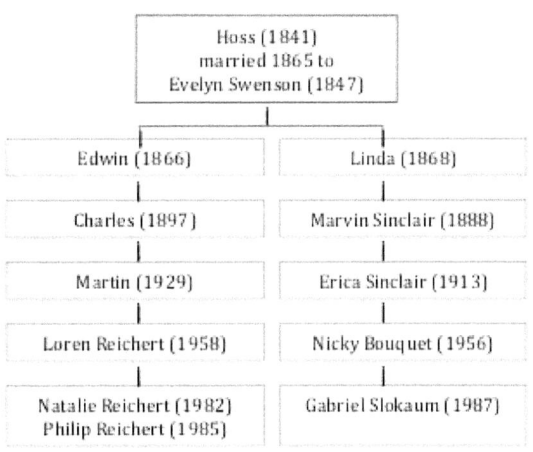

Hoss (1841)
married 1865 to
Evelyn Swenson (1847)

Edwin (1866)   Linda (1868)

Charles (1897)   Marvin Sinclair (1888)

Martin (1929)   Erica Sinclair (1913)

Loren Reichert (1958)   Nicky Bouquet (1956)

Natalie Reichert (1982)
Philip Reichert (1985)   Gabriel Slokaum (1987)

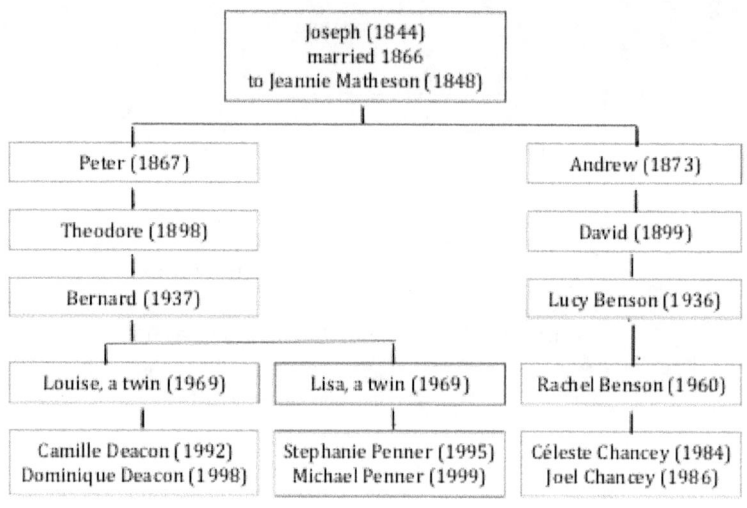

Why I wrote The Cartwright Men Marry

I binge-watched Bonanza in late December 2018. The virtues and values of the characters on the show struck a chord. I soon imagined what kind of husbands those men would have been. I could see my own late husband (a Biblical scholar and man who loved the Lord) and my father (an ordained Deacon) in those men. Their devotion to their wives and children were their priority.

My imagination invaded my dreams and I envisioned what kind of women would be strong enough to be able to match the conviction of men like that. I quickly wrote about each character and the circumstances of the women who entered into the men's lives. Then I expanded on events and presented my manuscript to my dad. He gave me a great review and I was encouraged to pursue further.

Through my publisher, I learned that the last fourteen episodes of the first season and the first seventeen episodes of the second season of the show were in the Public Domain. That meant that everything said on those thirty-one episodes were no longer protected by Copyright laws. I could safely use in my book the men's character names and any other detail I saw and heard. What I could not use were many background details, such as the name of the house cook at the Ponderosa or the fact that Ben had been married and widowed three times.

What I tried to keep in the foreground throughout the book is the righteousness of the Cartwrights. They always endeavored to not forsake their wholeness for anything they might regret. Their characters on the television series were believable. I tried to copy that realistic feeling into my book.

Questions for Book Clubs

- Before Barbara and Ben met, she lived in a unique and challenging situation. Having read about her home, could you have survived under those conditions? Why or why not?

- Ben had been widowed and felt that there was no need to consider love at his age. Do you think there is a time limit on romance and love? Why or why not?

- When Evelyn hit her head and discovered that she was not as strong as she thought she was, did you feel in unison with her and cheer her on? Why or why not?

- Was the depiction of Angie's recovery realistic? Is it possible for someone to come out of such an experience as well as she did? Have you seen something like this in real life?

- Ben believed that Jeannie sharing the tragedy of her youth was instrumental in Angie's recovery. Do you agree? Why or why not?

- Adam said that the Cartwright men don't "skimp" on their vows. Do you know someone who loves his wife the way the Cartwright men love theirs?

- When Hoss had a loss, he came to terms with the changes in his life only when it was pointed out to him. Do you think people usually accept their situation, or do they, like Hoss, need to have it pointed out?

- Today's Cartwright cousins took time off to work together. Would you be able to work with your family, even distant relatives, for such a goal as solving a mystery?

- Not all families have a solvable mystery to help them tie their past to their present. Have you ventured online to discover your ancestry?

- All four women in the book have unique perspectives on the role of women. When did women's roles change in the old west? Would their choices today be normal or would even some of these extraordinary women be unique today?

- What is it about Western novels that continue to appeal to readers?

- What did folks worry about in 1865 that we don't concern ourselves with today, and what do we worry about that they didn't?

- If you were making a movie of this book, who would you cast in all eight roles?

Acknowledgments

I am forever grateful for my parents who continue to recount stories of their youth.

I thank my family and friends who have read the drafts of this manuscript and whose input encouraged me to brave on.

I will forever be thankful for my editor Jeanne Martinson, Publisher and Senior Editor of Wood Dragon Books, whose suggestions, questions, and recommendations have made this book the best it can be.

I thank God, every day, for everything else.

About the Author

Monique's parents led very interesting childhoods and recount endless stories of their youth. Both parents come from very large families themselves where storytelling was a great pastime. Their background is predominantly French (from France).

Monique's beloved husband Kurt passed away in 2014, the day before his 62nd birthday. Monique's extended Penner family, who share stories of their beginnings in Russia and Ukraine, add flare to her tales. She loves to travel and learn about the places she visits. This is where many new ideas for creative writing arise.

When Monique isn't thinking up love and adventure in the Nevada historical west, she loves to play Bridge—if she could get paid to play cards, she would do it all day long. She has a unique collection of more than seven hundred Joker and Wild cards from around the world and is always on the lookout for new ones when she travels.